Love's Ransom

Lisa Samson

HARVEST HOUSE PUBLISHERS
Eugene, Oregon 97402

Cover by Terry Dugan Design, Minneapolis, Minnesota.

LOVE'S RANSOM
Copyright ©1997 by L.E. Samson
Published by Harvest House Publishers
Eugene, Oregon 97402

Library of Congress Cataloging-in-Publication Data

Samson, Lisa, 1964–
    Love's Ransom / Lisa Samson
        p. cm. — (Abbey series)
    ISBN 1–56507–529–3
    1. Great Britain—History—Henry III, 1216–1272—Fiction. 2. Civilization, Medieval—13th
      century—Fiction. I. Title. II. Series: Samson, Lisa, 1964 – Abbey Series.
    PS3569.A46673L6 1997
    813'.54 — dc20   96-41549
                                                                        CIP

97   98   99   00   01   02   /BC/   10   9   8   7   6   5   4   3   2   1

For Jennifer,
friend of my heart.

Acknowledgments

Once again, my primary gratitude is given to Bill Jensen for his time and editorial talent. I am blessed to have you for a friend.

Many thanks to James Byron Huggins for his friendship and vision.

To Betty Fletcher, Margie Brown, and Carolyn McCready, I say thank you for all you've done on behalf of this book. For all the help in the area of herbal healing, I extend a big thank-you to my Internet buddy Michelle "Starr RavenHeart" Bowers. I would also like to thank Dr. Homer Blaas of Liberty University for loaning me research materials from his personal library. To those who read the first draft—Lori Chesser, Carey Cothren, Iain A. Fraser, and Jennifer Hagerty—thanks for the encouragement! Thank you to my mom for not getting tired of hearing my plots over the phone.

Also to the readers who have written me to express their enjoyment, I would like to say thank you. Your letters mean more than I could ever say, and I value them highly. Keep those cards and letters coming!

Will, Tyler, and Jakey: I do love ya' so!

"Thanks be to God who giveth us the victory, through Jesus Christ our Lord."

Author's Note

I'm especially excited in bringing this book to you. In contrast to my other novels, here we are more often down in the kitchens of a great medieval castle with the servants and less upstairs with the lords and the ladies. My main character, Jane Lightfoot, is a humble cook. And I've so enjoyed getting to know her and her fellow servants. I trust you will, too.

While *Conquered Heart* swept over the course of years and exciting political intrigue as well as the building of Edward the Confessor's abbey, *Love's Ransom* explores the hearts of two very special people who have a love not only for the Westminster Abbey but also for God, and takes place over a relatively short period of time. The year 1229 was not an especially exciting one in the English landscape of time, but I'm of the romantic belief that everyday life can often be as stirring and intriguing as the movements of a nation. At least in a work of fiction. *Love's Ransom* is all about forgiveness, redemption, and second chances.

The tournament which takes place in this book was loosely designed around one which occurred at a later time (held by Edward I in 1278) and is based on what I consider the greatest fictional account of a tournament ever written—that found in *Ivanhoe*. To get a wonderful flavor of the more detailed workings and relationships of a medieval tournament, I would encourage you to read *Ivanhoe* by Sir Walter Scott. The armor and equipment used in *Love's Ransom* is by no means the only way a tournament was held during this time. They were as unique as their sponsors and participants.

You will notice the use of medicinal herbs throughout this book. I have referred to them only in the most general terms for the most general ailments. Please do not take what is written here as any kind of advice for treatment from me or Harvest House Publishers, Inc. The reference I used most heavily for this aspect of *Love's Ransom* is *Culpeper's Complete Herbal* compiled in the seventeenth century by Nicholas Culpeper, a very famous physician, husband, and father of seven children. Although he never became a wealthy man, he was always pleased to give free advice to all the poor who came to him seeking help. It is his charitable spirit that I hoped to impart to Jane Lightfoot.

Jane's counterpart is a physician, Doctor Patrick MacBeth. Much of medieval medicine was steeped in superstition, astrology, planet alignment, seasons, and other variables we disregard in medical treatment today. Although they used medicines made from various plants, they also employed such "magic" methods as these: a garnet worn round the neck to alleviate melancholia, or spring water drunk from the skull of a murdered man to cure the falling sickness. And those treatments adhering to a more "spiritual" approach made not much more sense. For example, the key to a church door was a cure for rabies, a Bible placed on the forehead relieved insomnia, and splinters from the cross or martyrs' bones could cure all manner of sickness. That such thinking was taken seriously by educated men at any time in history is hard to comprehend by modern man, and for that reason I've limited Doctor MacBeth's methods to medicines, bloodlettings, and other practices that we in the twentieth century can take seriously. In other words, I tried my best to keep him from looking like what we call a "quack."

May God bless you as you read what is written on the following pages, and may you enjoy what you find!

❧ PROLOGUE ❧

1214 A.D.

Spring is the time when kings go off to war. But spring it was not. Chilly nights were now nothing more than a nostalgic memory in the minds of the villagers who resided in the region of Lambeth. Jane never could sleep when the summer winds blew warm in the night. Her breathing would become shallow, stifled, and her back wet with perspiration.

Tonight it was just the same.

Lying on her pallet, she imagined the clouds outside the cottage, bearing heated faces with swollen, rosy cheeks, exhaling their torrid breath over southern England's parched fields. Earlier, she and Mother had sought their best to cool themselves, sitting on the banks of the Thames, watching as the sailing barges soaked up the colors of the sunset.

Their hearts were merry despite the heat, and they talked of many things in the evenings when they sat close together. Sometimes Jane would recline upon the grassy banks, her head in her mother's lap. She would stare upward at the bony U of Emma Lightfoot's unimposing jawline as it moved up and down in rhythm with her speech. It was a graceful jaw sitting upon a graceful neck. Her soft earlobes glowed from the rays of the sun, and when she looked down upon her daughter's face as they conversed, Jane felt that she was the sole recipient of the world's vast storehouse of love.

"Are you happy with Allen?" Emma asked of Jane regarding her daughter's new betrothed.

"As happy as any woman is, Mother, at this time of the relationship."

"You will grow to love him, even as I grew to love your father." She sounded confident of this as she continued to look out over the river.

"I will try. I want to be a good wife. And I want most of all to be a good mother."

They sat in silence. Emma thought how innocent Jane still was. But she had every reason to believe that Jane would be a faithful, industrious wife. It was how she had raised her, how Emma had lived her own life.

"Mother?"

"Yes, child."

"Will it hurt?"

Emma knew exactly what Jane was referring to and, looking down, she locked the gaze of her loving brown eyes into her daughter's. "Yes. But the pain does not last forever."

Several hours later, Jane found herself back at that very spot, her bare legs swallowed to mid-calf by the cool, dark waters. The midsummer stars cast a soft light, the silver beams upon her skin as refreshing as the Thames.

Perhaps if I take a quick bath in the river, I'll cool off enough to sleep.

Jane had done this many times before. She looked quickly around in a circle to make sure no one was there, and in one swift motion her gown was off and she was submerged up to her shoulders in the water.

But she was not alone. There was a man. A traveler.

He had been watching from behind a group of trees several yards away. Knowing he was invading her privacy, knowing he should turn his head, he could not tear his eyes from the maid in the river.

Lovely she was to gaze upon. And a sudden, intense desire singed his already-lacking conscience. Overwhelming. All the voices of reason and morality which bade him stop were deafened by the seismic throbbing of his heart.

"Walter," he whispered to his companion, "fetch my wineskin and a goblet, lay out my pallet, fetch the girl, bring her to me, and then take a leisurely stroll toward home. I shall meet up with you later."

"Yes, my lord." The servant was taken by surprise, but he did not show it. Such behavior was unlike his master. Nevertheless, he attended to his lord's bidding, slipping the skin of wine out of the saddlebag and unrolling the pallet on the ground.

"Here," the stranger said, removing his outer tunic, "put this on her. I'd like her to come to me wearing it."

Walter nodded his head in obedience and walked toward the river with great reservation in his heart. *This is not right.* Jane's back was facing him as she stared up at the stars. He found her undergown and submerged it in the water before calling to her in a loud whisper. She started at the sound of his voice, on impulse making sure she was decently submerged. "What, sir, are you doing here?"

"Pardon me, if you please, miss. A fox just ran away with your garment. My master and I saw him pass by our camp there in the woods."

Jane, horrified to know they had been there the whole time, was not concerned about the fox. "Could you not have made your presence known when I arrived? 'Tis unseemly that you should watch me bathe!"

"You are correct, miss. However, my lord isn't an unchivalrous man. He bade me bring you his tunic and offer you a cup of wine in his presence before you go back to your home."

Jane was wary, but she *was* in a bit of a spot and couldn't very well refuse the tunic. Just beyond the tree line lay her parents' cottage. She knew she should return before she was missed. "Please leave it on the bank. Turn your back, and I'll slip it on. Then, if you'd like, you may take me to meet your lord so that I might thank him for his kindness."

A minute later, clad in a garment finer than any she had even touched, she walked, trembling, to the dark, silent camp of the journeying lord. Walter seemingly disintegrated into the humid backdrop of the foliage.

"Are you there, sir?" she whispered, leaning forward, unable to see much of anything.

"Come closer. Straight forward. I am in front of you."

Jane advanced, hesitating slightly before each step.

"Worry not, fair maid. I would do you no harm."

His voice was calm and golden. Jane's fear wandered quietly away, although the voice of her mother purled in her brain breathing, *"Be wary, Jane."*

Finally his outline materialized, and the slight glint of a silver cup winked in the low light as he held it toward her. "Here, share a cup of wine with me and tell me your name, child. For indeed, you are most fair, and I would learn by what name such beauty is known."

"Jane," she whispered, taking a sip of the fine vintage. It was like nothing she had ever tasted before. Sweet, red, and not bitter like the ales and meads she had grown up drinking. She took another sip, enjoying it, a smile on her face. The smell of him was pleasing as well.

"You like it?" he asked, sensing rather than seeing her smile, for within the trees it was impossible to distinguish her features.

"Very much, sir."

"Would you like some more?"

She held her cup forward. "Please."

❧ ❧ ❧

"Bless me, father, for I have sinned."

Jane wept as she confessed to the village priest the shattering event by the riverside. "I am a sinner, defiled and wicked. How can God forgive such a deed?"

Behind his screen, Father Phillip, having recognized her voice immediately, was kind. He had always liked Jane, watching her as she grew to womanhood, appreciating her joy, her hard work, and her obedience to her parents. Granting absolution, he told her the tale of a woman named Bathsheba.

❧ ❧ ❧

Last autumn it had fallen off the tree. It sat by the hut throughout the winter, beneath the snows, withstanding the rains of springtime. And she had found it, deeming it a small treasure. Ugly without, nourishing within. How the squirrels missed it all this time was a mystery.

Jane Lightfoot cradled the walnut between index finger and thumb. She turned it over repeatedly, examining the puckered shell, running the thumbnail of her other hand into the shallow crevices, wondering if the meat inside bore the exact patterns in its flesh.

"What were you thinking?" her father yelled from across the small front room of their cottage. "Who's the father?"

Jane crushed the walnut to her sweaty palm, feeling her body heat warm the surface immediately, and whispered, "I don't know."

"You don't know?"

"Father..."

"Not another word to me! You traded in that privilege when you began a life of whoring! What would your mother have thought? Thank God she isn't alive to hear this, Jane. For the first time since she died, I'm glad. Glad, Jane! Do you realize what you've done? What's going to happen now?"

"I don't know."

"I don't know! I don't know! Is that the only thing you can say?" His eyes narrowed, speaking of sudden decision. "Get out, Jane. Get out of here now!"

"But, Father . . . I've confessed—"

"You heard me! You've spurned the love we've given you these past 16 years. When I think of all your mother tried to teach you. . . . I will not be responsible for you any longer." Jane sat transfixed in her seat, her worst fears breathing foul air upon her tormented soul. "You heard me. Leave!" Edward Lightfoot stormed outside, wiping tears of fury from his eyes with the back of his forearm.

Jane gulped down a sob, threw the walnut on the table with great force, watched it bounce on the floor, then began to gather her belongings. *Where will you go, Jane?*

"I don't know . . ." she whispered over and over to each question her mind emitted. "I don't know."

Somehow her other gown and undergown made it into the sack. She cut a small piece of bread off the loaf that she had brought back from the village ovens that morning, and did the same with a hunk of white cheese. *How will you feed yourself, Jane? How will you take care of a baby?*

"I don't know . . . I don't know!"

A desperate hysteria threatened to bubble up in her throat, but she shoved it down, remaining dry-eyed. She looked around the tidy two-room cottage she and Father had shared alone since the death of her mother two months previous.

The very table she had been sitting at bore the load of a serious conversation a few weeks before Mother died. Painful memories of her loving mother, holding her hand, telling her how to be a wife and a woman of good standing.

Emma would have understood—not from experience, but somehow she would have understood.

Jane knew this.

What of Allen?

14

He had always been a good friend, but she knew this was too much for any young man to accept.

It was too much to bear. Jane found the walnut near the hearth, screwed her eyes shut against the tears which threatened to flow, and hurried for the door. With her knapsack on her arm, she fled into the autumn noontide and down the narrow path which fell between the now-harvested leeks, parsley, and cabbages of the household garden. She had harvested them alone that year—a task she and Emma had shared ever since she could remember. Which direction should she travel?

I don't know. I don't know.

Her father stood in the center of the road which ran to the village. Tears slipped down his large, sunburned face. She expected him to turn away from her, his only good-bye the broad back whose corded muscles toiled in the fields during every daylight hour. But he ran toward her instead and gathered her into his burly, mahogany arms.

"You're all I have left, my Jane," his voice rasped as they crumpled down on their knees together on the dusty road. "We'll get through this, Jane. Somehow we'll make it through together."

"Oh, Father, I'm sorry," she sobbed, her tears flowing as freely now as her father's. "I'm so sorry I did this to you. I never wanted to hurt anyone."

Edward helped his daughter back into the cottage and put away her belongings himself. When Allen came by later that day, Jane's father broke the startling news. Jane's betrothed cried, but no offer to marry her right away accompanied his tears. There wasn't a person in the village who wouldn't have thought him a fool for marrying her in the condition she now found herself.

For as long as possible, Jane's father sought to hide her pregnancy from the inhabitants of their village, but it was realized when Jane was six months along. She bore her punishment with as much dignity as she could call to her aid.

Stripped to the waist in the public square, the lash came down again and again. Dry-eyed, she bore the burning pain, knowing for certain that if Father loved her she could persevere her way through anything. Women shook their heads with eyes of scorn and despising, feeling infinitely superior to the poor, bound, promiscuous thing before them. Men jeered and ogled her breasts. Children stared and even laughed at her plight. It was a time of nervous emotion for all who gathered for the public display. For deep in their hearts they had liked Jane. But now they had a part to play.

Father, strong and previously well-esteemed, shed ten tears for each time the whip descended, each inch of flesh lacerated by the cruel lash.

Three months later on a rainy March morning, Nicholas Lightfoot was born.

ONE

Fifteen Years Later

O nly a few more buckets to go, Mother, and the task is done!"

He was a strapping lad of 15 with a gaggle of admirers among the young castle wenches. An easy flair for life was his possession with his dark-brown hair and luminous eyes the color of hazelnuts. And his hands were strong, the well-developed muscles on the backs of them moving fluidly beneath his olive skin as they crooked around the thick rope and pulled the wooden bucket up from the well. A little water sloshed over the side and onto his dark-green woolen tunic as he poured it into a large clay jar. He removed the coarse, sweaty garment and threw it on the ground by the well, where it became an exhausted heap of broadly woven fiber.

"Hasten, Nicholas! 'Twill be our folly if the water is not put on the boil right away!" His mother, of the same coloring and pretty-featured, looked on from the door of the great kitchen of Marchemont Castle and called between cupped hands in a voice so loud as to be shocking.

Muttering something about a workhorse, Nicholas ferried the load into the octagonal stone kitchen, while another kitchen urchin who had been waiting nearby threw the bucket back down into the well, listened for the splash, and proceeded to rotate the large crank.

Nicholas tipped the contents of the jar into the black caldron suspended above an intense fire in a large central pit surrounded by a shallow wall of stone block. A side of oxen spun slowly on a heavy spit, turned by a naked scullion about eight years old. His wiry musculature gleamed with sweat from the intense heat, and his skin appeared paper-thin as it glowed in the crimson light. Ten geese were being plucked, readied for another spit. Pike caught fresh in the Thames only hours before were being scaled; eels were being skinned; and onion, leek, garlic, fennel, and all manner of herbs grown in the castle garden were being chopped at one of the three long, scarred wooden tables.

And this was just for supper's first course.

But the Lord of Marchemont enjoyed good food and wished to share his love affair of the palate with guests, with the many soldiers garrisoned at the castle, and with the household itself.

The din was overwhelming. The smell was just shy of intoxicating as the flavor of onion and garlic clung tenaciously to the roasting beef and fowl. Although working in the kitchen had its advantages: working under shelter, first call on the leftovers, treats every now and again, it could also be the most maddening. Over the years, Jane had slapped many a young hand away from all sorts of mouth-watering delicacies.

Other castle servants darted about as well. Laundresses gathered water from the well inside the kitchen. At a sturdy table against the wall, three bakers were busily creating sumptuous breads, pies, and tarts, respectively. Another scullion washed wooden trenchers and spoons in a stone sink near the door. And Jane Lightfoot plunged her wiry frame outside to the side steps of the castle keep. Her destination: the wardrobe. Her mission: to procure the precious bags of spices necessary to make the special preserve that Alexander de la Marche, the Earl of Lambeth and master of Marchemont Castle, favored so greatly.

She wiped an olive-skinned arm across her perspiring brow, threw her long, thin brown braid back over her shoulder, and proceeded up the steps.

"Mother!"

She turned, her small nose wrinkling at the bridge. "What is it, Nicholas?"

"May I go to the stables for just a moment? I promise I'll return ere long." His expression was pitiful. He looked so endearing, his sweaty hair curling around his smoke-reddened eyes and plastered onto his high forehead.

"All right. But put your tunic back on. I mean it, Nicholas."

"Bless you, Mother!" He turned and whipped across the bailey, the tunic as well as his mother instantly forgotten.

Jane, still a young woman at 31, merely shook her head and continued back up to the wardrobe. "Let's see," she whispered to herself as she counted on her fingers. "Eleven things I need. Now what are they? Half pound each of mustard seed, anise, coriander, cloves, cinnamon, ginger, saffron, nutmeg, grain of Paradise, caraways . . . and wine . . . I mustn't forget the wine!"

Already the nuts, carrots, turnips, pumpkins, and pears had been chopped, and the raisins were mashed and ready to be thrown into the pot. She turned around and called back into the kitchen. "Joseph! John! Come hither and help me carry the spices! Each of you bring a basket!"

The door to the wardrobe—a storage room for all the castle luxuries, a fantasy room of wealth and privilege—was opened by the castle steward himself. Walter Skeets, 60 years old and a man well-loved yet highly respected, awarded Jane with a yellowed, thoroughly cheerful smile. He was a large, corpulent man with splendid pale-blue eyes and astonishingly white hair. Everything about him was wide. Wide smile, wide-set eyes, wide hands, wide body, and wide paddle-like feet which seemed especially amusing in the pointed-toed slippers that folk had taken to wearing. He had a wide heart, too—capable of caring for the needs of even the lowliest servant, as well as loyally serving his noble master. Jane never found it strange that Skeets hadn't taken a wife. Not only was he married to his job, but after 35 years in the position, he was still in love with it, too.

"I knew that had to be you, Mistress Jane! It's just about the right time for it."

Jane chuckled. "I am that predictable, am I, Mister Skeets?"

"You are. And I thank God for it. For today nothing has gone as planned, and in the midst of chaos you, my dear madam, have not disappointed this old man."

"Before you judge my felicitous timing, wait until you see how much spice I need today, Skeets!"

"Let's see, it's the first Tuesday of the month of August, which can only mean it's time for your special preserves."

"You fare well at not disappointing yourself, sir."

"I already have them set aside."

Jane shook her head and clucked her tongue. "Promise me you'll live forever, Skeets!"

"Would that I could, child. Would that I could. Here you go then. Joseph, John, bring the baskets hither and I shall bestow upon you a most aromatic burden."

"Thank you, sir," Joseph bowed. But mostly he was thankful to Jane, for he knew that simply because he helped to carry down the spice, he would be rewarded with a large spoonful of the tasty preserves on a piece of warm bread. John did the same, and soon the two lads were on their way down to the kitchen, their youthful chatter filtering back into the wardrobe.

"Gregory was most upset when I took back upon myself the regulation of the spices," Skeets remarked of the new clerk of the kitchen. "But he didn't seem to understand that Lord Alexander has always been most generous when it comes to such."

Jane agreed. "Aye, he loves his food with a lot of taste, sir. One rule we have down in the kitchens is 'Never be stingy with the spice!'"

"That's right. How do you think Gregory is faring down there?"

"As you say, he's in need of a little learning. But we'll teach him."

"No doubt there! Well, we both know that for all practical purposes, Jane, that it is you who runs the kitchen and not Gregory."

Jane's smile was playfully smug. "I manage."

"I don't know what we'd do without you!"

"You'd be eating under-spiced food and never partaking of a good compote!"

"Absolutely right. We'll let him think he's doing his job and let you continue to do yours!"

"If he lets us go that far. There's sure to be a confrontation or two before Gregory and I settle into a satisfactory routine."

"I've no doubt of that. So how do you fare these days, Jane?" The friendly steward laid a fatherly hand upon her shoulder. "Are you happy with all your staff?"

"Oh yes, the staff is fine. I couldn't find better people myself. There's the occasional one who needs a little time to adjust to the flurry of activity we find ourselves in daily, but nothing a little help from the others, sometimes less than friendly, doesn't take care of."

"I suppose it's a matter of 'work or be trampled down' in your kitchens, eh, Jane?"

"I've never been able to abide a sluggard, sir."

"That is why you are so appreciated. You've given me your best since the day you arrived 14 years ago."

"And you've done the same for me, Mister Skeets. Your kindness to Nicholas and me has never gone unnoticed or without thanks. You've been the closest thing to family we've had here through the years."

He turned red above his neckline. "So you keep telling me, Jane! I guess my hope is in vain that you'll learn to take my pitiful gestures of kindness for granted and so keep me from these repeated times of embarrassment."

"Never, my friend!"

They laughed together, and she gathered the skirts of her gown in preparation for descending the steps. "I'll save aside a little pot of preserves just for you, Skeets. Our secret."

He patted Jane on the shoulder, watched her descent down the stairs, and was already engulfed in his ledgers by the time she reentered the kitchen.

❖ TWO ❖

Nicholas vaulted from the dim regions of the kitchens into the bright August heat. The sky was immaculate—a cloudless, unblemished blue. Almost everyone had been complaining that this summer was the hottest they remembered in many years, but Nicholas enjoyed it immensely. He was a summer creature, always dreading the arrival of winter and the cold that never seemed to dwindle inside or outside the thick stone walls of Marchemont. To Nicholas, such cold was a mindless thing, exhibiting no ability to exercise discretion for its own sake or anyone else's. Why, he figured, if winter eased up a bit in January, it would store up enough resources to keep everyone miserable well into March.

He shook his head quickly as he walked across the spacious courtyard, forcefully shoving thoughts of winter aside lest they spoil this moment of lustrous warmth. Many buildings huddled next to the great stone palisades: chapel, smithy, piggery, storehouse. A walled garden in front of the keep boasted of several fruit trees, beehives, the herb garden, and a dovecote which provided plump birds for the earl's table. Nicholas walked right by them all. He saw only one structure, snuggled up tightly to the keep, constructed of wood and roofed with thatch—the stables were a welcome sight.

"What do you want, lad?" the stablemaster, leading a stomping stallion, called out good-naturedly. "Get back where you belong, you flea-bitten kitchen rat! And you might want to put your clothes back on as well, spare us all from having to look at that ugly fairy-bite on your chest!"

Nicholas's fingers automatically touched the red, bird-shaped birthmark on his chest, and he laughed. "I like my fairy-bite. It suits me well. You only speak so boldly, Richard, because you can hide behind that magnificent creature for defense."

A broad smile lit up the swarthy face of the black-haired, middle-aged man. "He's a beauty, isn't he? The earl just brought 'im in yesterday from London."

"A proud Arabian."

"Aye. What think you?"

"As I said, he's a magnificent creature. Would that I could ride him. Would that I could ride *any* horse." Nicholas rubbed the horse's nose, calming down the agitated creature immediately.

"You've a way with these beasts, Nicholas. I've always said you're wasted over there in the kitchens with your ma."

"Ah, well I know it. But even as much as I love horses, I love her better, and certainly owe her much more."

"Maybe someday you can have a talk with her, tell her how you feel. You can't abide in the kitchens forever, lad."

"Believe me, Richard, the kitchens are the last place I wish to spend the rest of my life."

The attention of both Nicholas and Richard was suddenly drawn by an imperious shout from the steps of the keep. "You there! Richard! Bring hither that beast straightaway."

"Yes, m'lord!"

"And bring that boy with you!"

How Nicholas wished he had listened to his mother and donned his tunic when he had the chance! Now he was to stand before Lord Alexander in only his hosen and shoes. He hurried over with Richard, head bowed deferentially, yet seeing the humor in the situation. By this time Lord Alexander was at the bottom of the steps. Walter Skeets was just coming down the stairs, hoping to offer his lord one last matter of business before he went off to inspect the new windmill being erected several miles away. It was the talk of the countryside.

"You, lad, what is your name?" the earl asked almost harshly, but not unkindly.

"Nicholas Lightfoot, sir."

"The cook's boy," Skeets offered by way of explanation from behind his grace, making drastic motions with his hands to Nicholas about his lack of a tunic.

"And where is your tunic?" the earl asked. Skeets rolled his large eyes in exasperation.

Nicholas dropped to his knees. "Forgive me, m'lord. 'Twas overly hot in the kitchens, and I took it off. I came over to look at the horses, and in my excitement I forgot to—"

The earl held up a hand. "Silence. It is all right. And what think you of Bedivere?"

"A worthy name for such a beautiful horse, m'lord."

"How would you like a turn on such a beast?"

"M'lord is most cruel to taunt a mere scullion with such impossible fancies." Nicholas rose to his feet, head held high now that the worst was over.

Lord Alexander swung himself up onto Bedivere and gathered the reins from Richard. "Stranger things have happened, lad. By the way," he began to inch the horse forward, "lovely fairy-bite you sport there!" Richard laughed out loud. Skeets couldn't help but turn red with amusement.

"Thank you, m'lord," Nicholas said in all seriousness.

"So you are proud of it?"

"Not proud, sir. But in the life I live my birthmark is one of the few things that I can truly call my own!"

The earl's left eyebrow raised. "Indeed?"

"Indeed, sir."

"Good." He galloped off, leaving Richard and Nicholas to stare after him, watching in awe the powerful force of the great gray horse, Bedivere. The noble pair loped across the courtyard, through the gate house, and out into the open field.

"Your mother will have your hide for this, Nicholas," Skeets reported matter-of-factly and turned to go back inside.

"It was worth it." Nicholas was watching the horse. Richard sighed appreciatively at such magnificent breeding and turned back to the stables, saying over his shoulder, "Have that talk with Mistress Jane, lad. And soon. You'd do well working for me. Yes, you would."

Nicholas merely raised a hand in farewell and walked slowly back toward the kitchen.

"Nicholas!" A sweet voice called softly from around the side of the small stone chapel, built by the countess herself ten years before.

The cook's boy hurried around the side of the pretty stone church before anyone could see him. "Agnes! You'll find yourself in all manner of trouble if you're caught out here. No matter, the deed is done. Kiss me quickly and let me savor the taste of you until tomorrow."

Agnes raised her pretty round face to his, and Nicholas kissed her quickly on her pink lips. He ran a hand over her blond curls, laughed, kissed her once more, then hurried across the courtyard and back inside the kitchen to help his mother.

Jane stood with her hands on her hips. "Just a few moments, eh?"

"Mother, forgive me." Nicholas was handed a bowl of cinnamon which he presently dumped in the caldron. "Lord Alexander asked to speak with me!"

Jane was alarmed. "He did? Why? Oh, Nicholas, and you there without a tunic! I told you to put it back on!"

"Yes, Mother, yes. I know. He just wanted to know who I was, asked my opinion about the new Arabian, made fun of my fairy-bite, and off he went on one of the most beautiful horses I have ever seen."

Jane sighed at his shining eyes. "You're growing into quite a young man, Nicholas. I've known that for some time. This kitchen is no longer the place for you. What is it you'd like to do with your life?"

"Oh, Mother, you need my help. And as long as you need me, I'll be here for you, you know that. We've always said we'd make it through somehow, and always together."

"We can still be together, Nicholas, in the evenings, at meals. You wish to go work for Richard, don't you?"

"Of course I do, but if you need—"

"I can always find another scullion, my son. But Richard will be hard-pressed to find a lad who loves horses more, and who communicates with them better. Go—" she shrugged softly, "go find him and see if you might take on a job with him and his boys. I'll talk to Skeets about it. I'm sure he won't mind."

Nicholas's youthful enthusiasm got the better of him, and, without so much as a thank-you or a 'By your leave,' he was out the door and halfway across the courtyard. Jane looked on from the doorway as he ran further and further away. She saw his tunic by the well and, picking it up, called, "Nicholas! Nicholas!"

He skidded to a halt and turned around to see her waving his tunic over her head. They met at half the distance, and he took the garment. "Well, Mother, it just goes to show the both of us that I'll always need you!"

She kissed him quickly on the cheek and waved him on, knowing all the while she did so that Nicholas was wrong.

THREE

*W*hen the setting sun shines on the Thames of a summer
eve, it makes the waters a field of gold.

Spoken in the voice of her mother, the velvet words ruffled
softly through Jane's mind as they always did during her nightly
ritual. Recalling their precious times together, tucked along the
banks of the Thames each evening through good times and bad,
plucked a sad, lonely melody on the strings of her heart. It was
only now that she allowed herself to fully experience the flag-
ging solitude that had settled in to stay years before.

Sitting atop the castle wall which overlooked the mighty
river from a distance, Jane sighed, refusing to think about the
now-finished preserves, the scoured tables, the banked kitchen
fires. This was her own time—a time to think about nothing
and everything, those she loved, those she didn't, the past, the
future, but rarely the present.

The sun dipped low in a golden sky, innumerable shards of
light coming down to rest upon the rhythmical river. Lustrous
waters. A shining flood. *Fields of gold.* Jane fondly remembered
the words, happy and young once again. Adored. Free from care
and responsibility. Loved simply because she was Jane. Some
evenings she chose to cry, others to laugh.

Today had been a good day.

Nicholas found her several minutes later, her shoulders shaking in quiet laughter.

He lowered himself next to her, his movements lithe and economical, the sweet smell of freshly strewn hay surrounding his person with a pleasant, aromatic halo. She reached up and removed several pieces of straw from his wavy brown hair.

"What do you find so funny this night, Mother?"

"Oh, lad, I was just thinking about Father. His jokes, his deep, jolly laughter." They looked out at the Thames, which was separated from them by 200 or so yards of rustling meadow. The evening breeze blew about their faces, cleansing them of the day's tasks, saving future worries for the morrow. Nicholas wrapped his lanky arm around Jane's shoulders as she continued to speak, always aware of the fact that Nicholas should know as much as he could about his family. "My father could make my mother laugh at almost anything. 'Tis why she married him she told me one day when we watched him harrowing the oat field and blessing the oxen more loudly and colorfully than he had done the year before! Ah, my son, 'tis a wonderful thing to hear as a child the laughter of your parents as you're drifting off to sleep. One night I heard a playful smack on her backside as she banked the fire. He said, 'Who needs a padded chair when I've got you, Maggie!'"

Nicholas laughed with his mother. "I take it your mother was well-rounded?"

"Just a wee bit of extra padding from the waist down. Father looked after her well, fed us well, cared for our needs. He was a priceless gem, a jewel of manhood. I wish you could have known him, my son. He loved you greatly and was planning on taking care of you as well before he died so suddenly."

"Is food poisoning painful?"

"Yes. Poisoning must be a terrible way to die, I'll warrant. I wouldn't wish it on my fiercest enemy."

"Not that you have any. I think everyone loves you, Mother."

"Except maybe Gregory," she laughed.

"Even he will come to in time. He isn't the first kitchen clerk you've had to get adjusted to. Remember how much you couldn't abide Hugh?"

Jane nodded enthusiastically. She had a special fondness for the fiery-haired Hugh whom Gregory replaced. "I thought I would kill him at first, didn't I?"

"And you turned out to be the best of friends."

"Yes. 'Twas a sad day when he left Marchemont. 'Tis always sad when a valued friend moves on. Perhaps that is why I'm having so much trouble adjusting to Gregory."

They sat in silence for a while longer, the sun divided halfway by the horizon. Jane picked up the tempo of the conversation and strove for happier conversation. "I take it Richard found a place for you easily enough!"

"Yes, Mother."

"Ridding the stable of manure?"

"Of course! You surely didn't think he'd have me grooming the horses on my first day?"

"Naturally not! My poor Nicholas. And to think you were finished with scrubbing floors in my kitchens years ago. Now you'll have to work your way up all over again!"

"It's worth it, Mother."

"I know. Nothing worth having ever comes easy, my son. I'm glad you'll not have to learn that lesson the hard way. Just take life as it comes, with a bit of a smile, and a lot of muscle, and you'll do fine."

"I've learned from a true master. Besides, it could be much worse, Mother. At least manure is a highly valued commodity!" He tightened his arm around her shoulder and gave her a warm squeeze. "What do you say we go in? Tomorrow's probably going to be busy for both of us."

"You're right, my sweet. How did you ever come to be such a practical young man?"

31

He helped her onto the pathway atop the walls which the guards patrolled. "As if you didn't know!"

What was once a small storeroom off the kitchen was their abode. Jane lit an oil lamp as they methodically hung their outer garments on pegs driven into the mortar of the stone wall. Minutes later they were tucked into the bed, which was only a straw-stuffed mattress covered with a light summer blanket—the room's only furnishing besides a small chest she had conveyed from her home. A week after their arrival, Skeets had arranged for Jane and Nicholas to stay here. Taking pity on the young child and his mother, he rescued them from sleeping on the rush-strewn, foul, greasy floor of the great hall. Originally they had made their bed among sacks of flour and other provisions. But now they could basically call the room their own. It was a luxury uncommon for a castle servant.

Nicholas's breath was already shallow and steady as Jane extinguished the lamp. She prayed as she did each night for Nicholas, for herself. And her prayers were uttered to inner conjurings of golden fields, glittering with hope that she might someday be loved. She had many friends among her fellow servants, but the womanly portion of her heart was lonely indeed.

Nicholas turned over on his side just then. Jane reached out, lightly touched the fairy-bite on his chest, and smiled, knowing that through this lad she had been supremely blessed.

❧ ❧ ❧

The castle came to life, slowly blooming in concert with the sun which proceeded in a mellow fashion to lighten the morning skies. Nicholas and Jane dressed hastily, drew water from the kitchen well, and gave their faces and hands a thorough scrubbing. He ran to the stables but returned only a few minutes later.

Jane's hands went readily to her hips in mock consternation. "So they've become tired of you already!"

"No, Mother! One of the grooms' wives," he whispered conspiratorially, "needs something to ... well ... get her back to normal."

"What do you mean, Nicholas?"

"You know, she's not able to ... go ..." his hand moved in a circular motion.

"Oh! She needs a laxative!"

Nicholas ducked his head under his hands, at the same time crying in a loud whisper, "Mother!" Each member of the kitchen staff swiveled in his direction and gave a great, unanimous laugh.

"A spoonful of honey after each meal. That should clean her out."

Nicholas grimaced and went back out the door.

"Fine lad you've got there, Janey." One of the bakers sat down next to her where she resumed the chopping of carrots and cabbage for the servants' breakfast of oatmeal pottage with vegetables. He turned out some freshly mixed dough on the table and began to knead.

Chop, chop, chop. Jane's knife moved quickly.

Shove ... puff ... turn. Shove ... puff ... turn. Stephen kneaded the dough.

"Aye, Stephen, it seems like only yesterday he was born, and now he's taller than I am."

"Don't I know the feeling! Surely I thought I'd be taller than at least one of my two boys, but no ... they've already beat me at that, and most handily. Not only that, every suggestion I make is met with derision and superiority. Children get smarter and smarter, don't they?"

"Certainly do. Did you see Edith's little one when she brought him 'round the other day?"

"Edith?"

"The smithy's daughter ... married a country lad about a year and a half ago. The redhead."

"Oh yes, yes. Always liked that one. So she's living the country life. Did he come by a nice spread of land?"

Jane nodded. "Happily for her, yes. Lord Alexander is most kind when it comes to heriot."

"I heard about a manor over near Sussex where the lord claims almost all the animals and anything metal when the man dies! I heard tell a widow was left with nothing but her home and a couple of chickens. Her ox was taken, as well as her ewe."

"What happened to her, Stephen?"

Gregory, the new kitchen clerk, breezed through just then. "A little more work and a little less talk, thank you!"

They looked after his retreating form, waited until he shut the door to the clerk's closet, and continued on.

"Dunno what happened to her. I just say 'God bless Lord Alexander!' Not only are we lucky to be in his service, all who live on his lands are blessed to have a lord of the manor who isn't so harsh."

Another servant joined in on the conversation—a woman, busy preparing pastry for some pasties. "You wouldn't know it to hear them speak! Why, I was just at my son's last week, and don't you know his wife's father was complaining twice-fast about having to come to guard duty. Serfs!"

"Aye! They don't know how good they have it, Mattie," Stephen agreed. "At least they're Englishmen. I assume the harvest will be coming in shortly. 'Tis a busy time out in the fields soon."

Jane rubbed flat hands together, pieces of cabbage falling to rest in the large pile which had accumulated in the center of the table. "Busy for us as well. Lord Alexander usually seems to take to Marchemont in the fall. There's to be a feast soon."

"Aye?"

All the servants within earshot listened in to the conversation.

"And who's to be coming?" Mattie asked, rolling out her fifth round of pastry by this time. Her brown hair was lightly dusted with flour, concealing the bit of gray that had begun to show last year.

"I don't know. I suppose the usual assortment of abbots, bishops, earls, barons, doctors, and so forth."

Stephen became excited. "How many are we to prepare for?"

"Skeets said roughly 600, not counting servants."

"My, my," Mattie clucked, cutting vent holes in the pastry. "It's thrice the work, but I do so love preparing a feast. We'll have to start getting in some extra help."

Jane nodded in agreement. "Let's just leave that up to Mister Skeets. He's the best at dealing with such matters."

"Aye, it will take a special man to step into those shoes someday. Let's hope it comes none too soon." Stephen arose from the table and took a wooden paddle off the wall. "Well, I'd better get the first batch out of the ovens!"

"You were up early!" Jane commented, piling the cabbage onto a round wooden platter.

"Aren't we all?" Mattie quipped, spooning a savory lamb filling into the center of each circle and folding the pastry over.

And the work continued on, the servants stopping for a quick bit of Stephen's bread and Jane's pottage before setting back to their many tasks which ensured that at precisely eleven o'clock the lord's dinner would be served in the great hall of the keep.

❧ FOUR ❧

Nicholas raced into the kitchen a second time that day. Skeets hurried in after him, looking almost as youthful as Nicholas, eyes brimming with excitement. "Tell her, Skeets! Tell her!"

"What?" Jane's brown eyes brightened, and she hung the great wooden paddle she had been using to stir the broth in the caldron back on the wall.

Skeets, by habit, inspected the kitchen in a glance. "Your son has most interesting news."

"Mother, you'll never guess. It's a miracle!"

"A miracle? I don't believe I've ever witnessed one of those!"

"It's true, Jane. I assure you," Skeets attested to the highly unusual circumstances that had just erupted. "Immediately following the meal, Lord Alexander summoned me to his side and gave me a most unusual order. Apparently after his conversation yesterday with your son, he has decided to elevate his position in the household."

"What did you say to him, Nicholas?"

He shrugged. "Nothing particularly memorable, Mother. We talked about horses and my state of undress, which led to his remark about the fairy-bite."

"What fate awaits my son?" Jane couldn't help but feel ruffled that never once had the matter been discussed with her.

If Nicholas was to become an upstairs servant . . . well, she knew him better than to believe he would be happy cooped up inside all day polishing silver plate and fetching things for the noble family.

"He is to be apprenticed to me, Jane."

"What!" Her mouth dropped open in pleasant surprise. "Why, that's wonderful, Nicholas! I can hardly believe it." She hugged him. "Does the earl mean to make Nicholas his steward someday? May it be far far in the future, by the way, dear Skeets!"

His smile was warm. "That is exactly what he means to take place. From tomorrow onward, Nicholas will learn my job."

"But that isn't all, Skeets!" Nicholas pulled away from her embrace, his excitement refusing to be contained. "Tell her about the abbey!"

"Yes, yes. Lord Alexander wants Nicholas to begin learning from the brothers at the abbey. He even mentioned university someday."

"Maybe Paris, Mother!"

"It will be imperative for him to learn how to read, write, and cipher if he is to be the earl's steward. It isn't an easy job, but I've every confidence in Nicholas's capabilities, and he does have a good teacher!"

Jane had been standing with her mouth open. "My son will be getting an education. A true education!" Jane could hardly believe the words, truly spoken, were coming out of her mouth. Nicholas! Learning to read and write! The boy was right. "It is truly a miracle, my son." She turned to Skeets. "But why Nicholas all of a sudden?"

"Why not me?" Nicholas objected.

"I'm not trying to offend you, son. It just seems rather strange. A simple conversation with a half-naked boy in the bailey, and suddenly you're to be elevated to such a high position? What think you, Skeets? And did you have anything to do with this *sudden* idea of his lordship?"

"No, no, no. I promise you I never said a word about who will follow me as steward. It wouldn't be proper. Besides, if you are around the nobility enough, you learn it's best not to question why they carry out the whims that they do. Lord Alexander did say much about the boy's obvious intelligence and his confident spirit—"

"I told him I liked my fairy-bite!"

Jane was shocked. "Oh, Nicholas! The impertinence!"

Skeets continued, cheerfully ignoring Jane's reprimand. "I do believe it's something he has been thinking about for a long time, but hadn't done anything yet."

"Couldn't he find another more capable young man?"

"Mother! What are you saying?"

"I'm saying you've only been a simple kitchen lad and nothing more. You'll need much training. It's all so strange, but," she decided with finality that it's best not to question too deeply such abundant blessings, "I'm happy for you, Nicholas. You'll make a fine steward someday."

She held out her arms and hugged him again tightly. "And as for you, Skeets, even if it was by seeming accident, you've got yourself the finest lad at Marchemont."

"It is as you say, Jane. Completely right you are." He leaned in and said with a conspiratorial whisper, "And that includes that no-good son of his lordship's sister."

She and Nicholas pulled out of the embrace. "What's Percy done now?"

"It's what he *hasn't* done! That woman is too protective. Much too protective! It isn't as if he cannot hold his own in battle!"

"Well, being a master swordsman doesn't necessarily make you worthy of a title," Jane said, dismissing the subject. "How about a cup of ale to celebrate?"

Skeets looked shocked. "Ale? My good woman, come up to the wardrobe, and we'll all partake of a glass of the earl's better wine."

"Won't he be angry?" Nicholas asked wide-eyed.

The steward put his arm around Nicholas's shoulder. "What you are about to learn, Nicholas, is why it is so good to be the steward!"

Jane laughed and followed the two men out the door of the kitchen and up into the keep.

꘠꘠꘠ ꘠꘠꘠ ꘠꘠꘠

The western face of the abbey was lit up by the setting sun, a warm glow across its face. Jane sat across the river from the abbey and stared in wonder. She loved the old church across the water. Too seldom she found herself within its formidable walls, but she watched it from afar, making up fanciful stories of events which might have taken place within its walls. Love. Betrayal. A meeting of eyes for the first time at Mass. Many people thought of a church as a place for only God. But Jane thought of it as a place for people. Where they could come and worship, gathering together, separate units conjoining into a whole. More than just worship happened at churches. People chattered with one another, met new acquaintances and business partners.

Several times she had been to the abbey alone, sharing the mammoth structure with a few others who sought the same quiet solitude she herself was in search of. And at these times it was clearly not a social gathering, but a time where she might light a candle, pray, and feel the seeming weight of God's glory descend upon the top of her head.

He created her.

It was a comfort. Yet more often she found herself in the small chapel at Marchemont. And although she never felt that same feeling of holy majesty the abbey bestowed, she still felt His presence. His understanding presence moved around her and within her heart, mind, and soul.

He knew all about her.

His love was of the utmost comfort. Loving her anyway—
it was almost incomprehensible that the God of the abbey met
her at Marchemont. On different terms, it seemed. But Jane assumed that God wore many faces, as did His children. Some
He kept hidden, only to be revealed at the precise moment
when they were needed the most. Others were easy to find: His
mercy, His love.

God's sorrow.

She knew He felt such. Was He not sorry He had made
man? Jane would remember that Jesus wept in the garden of
agony, already shedding tears over the sins she would one day
commit. God's sorrow.

It was why she tried so hard. To be a good mother, a good
servant, a dedicated Christian. She was reasonably sure she
would someday go to heaven, and she only wanted the face of
her Lord to light up when she was at last ushered into His very
presence.

It had been a week since Nicholas had begun his appren-
ticeship. He had gone to the abbey twice already, returning both
times with a smug satisfaction at his newfound state. Jane
doubled up on the prayer for him during this time, knowing the
folly of pride would lead him down a very dark, precipitous path.

In fact, she was praying that very prayer when a footfall on
the path which led around the top of Marchemont's walls distracted her. She turned to see who had disturbed her solitude,
taking in the guard who had come to serve at Marchemont only
three weeks before. "Hello, Geoffrey."

"Hello, Jane," the muscular 18-year-old replied shyly, rubbing a nervous hand over his cap. "Looking at the river again
tonight?"

"I always do."

"Yes. Well, off I go. Patrolling, you know."

Jane laughed. "Yes, I know."

He walked off, cursing himself for saying such stupid things.
Jane smiled wistfully at his boyish, innocent crush. It would

take a blind woman not to notice the infatuation in his sweet gray eyes, or the obvious discomfort he felt in her presence. And he was almost young enough to be her son! Jane laughed now that he was out of earshot, inwardly pleased that at least *someone* found her attractive. But then, she hadn't really made herself readily available to anyone or shown any interest whatsoever in a romantic liaison of any nature. Sinful coupling was easy enough to find, but those days were behind her for good. At least she prayed daily to that end. Jane knew temptation was a powerful thing, frantic, and, once yielded to, voracious.

The entire world believed her to be a widow, that Nicholas was born the son of a huntsman on an estate far away. That huntsman supposedly died before their son was born. And Jane had lived with her father until the old man's passing. Jane often felt guilty for the lie, but she had seen no other way once Father had passed on and she was on her own. One day the truth would surface from the darkened waters, but until then she tried to say as little as she could.

The water shone more bronzy that evening than gold, and Jane watched in fascination as the sun dipped closer to the horizon and the faint sound of the abbey's tolling bells caressed her ears. Nicholas would be waiting for her in their room, she realized, sliding off her perch to make her way around the top of the walls and down the steps which led into the bailey. The now-purple sky above bid her press on, lest Nicholas wonder what happened to her.

He was sitting at the kitchen table eating. As usual.

Jane joined him at the large table. "Some honey on that bread?"

"No thank you, Mother. Just needed a little something extra tonight. Don't feel like anything sweet, though. Why not join me and have a slice yourself?"

"None for me. I'm exhausted. I've been waking up extra early, what with the feast coming shortly."

Nicholas knew what she meant. "Skeets has been running me like a mad horse."

"Do you like it, Nicholas?"

"Well, yes. Yes, I guess I do. I wish I could spend more time with the horses, but it is a move up and an opportunity that shall never come my way again, I'm sure."

"You're quite right. You probably just need to get adjusted to the new position. It was nice having you down here this afternoon while you were helping Skeets take inventory of the provisions."

Nicholas only smiled and bit off another hunk of bread. "Old Stephen makes the finest loaf around," he declared.

"Yes, he does. Perhaps I'll join you after all. But I'll definitely take honey on mine!" Jane loved her sweets.

"By the way, Skeets was complaining he was having trouble falling asleep. Do you have anything you can give him?"

"Of course, I know just the thing!" Jane took a quick bite of bread and got to her feet. She took down a jar in which she had placed a tincture of meadowsweet a month or so before. "Tell him to mix a spoonful of this with a bit of wine. He'll sleep like you do, which, you may not appreciate this now, son, is a sleep of the gods!"

"That's pretty deep," Nicholas said wryly.

"Go on with you, Nicholas! Finish your bit of bread and take this to Skeets. I assume he wanted it tonight?"

"Aye. In his words, 'One more night like last night, and you'll be steward sooner than you thought!'"

"Then you'd best hurry. We'd hate to have Skeets's demise on our heads."

FIVE

Lady Alison perched on the edge of her bed, pleading with her physician. "But Doctor MacBeth, it is simply not working! Perhaps we should try another bloodletting?" she suggested eagerly.

Patrick MacBeth—tall, handsome after a unique fashion, with a head of thick, wavy red hair—straightened his gray tunic with a sigh and hooked his thumbs in his thick leather belt. Yet the warm, obligatory smile never left his face. All who knew the Irishman found him slightly enigmatic, personally private. But his warm, easy ways caused them to reconsider that he seemed to be a man with something to hide. "Lady Alison, I assure you, I find nothing wrong with you other than the cough. If any bad humors were in your body, they should well be gone by now. Why not give yourself a few days to rest? Walk a bit. Breathe the glorious air of summer. You know there's nothing you like more than a walk in the woods!" His soft Irish accent washed over her, causing goose bumps to glide across her flesh.

"Why won't you listen to me?" she pouted, her full, red lips a stark contrast to her pale skin, hair, and eyes. She looked much younger than her 51 years, a bit of girlishness still displaying itself in her demeanor. "I'm not feeling as I should. I alone should know when things aren't right, shouldn't I, doctor? Come closer and give me a bit of comfort, won't you?"

Patrick drew a bit closer and took her outstretched hand with inner reluctance. The sunbeam that stretched through the small window caused the embroidery of his round cap to twinkle in a merry way, which contrasted directly with the way he felt. He briefly squeezed the Lady Alison's slim fingers, then placed her hand back in her lap. "Please, Alison," he pleaded, carefully making his tones warm, yet professional, "take my advice, just this once, and see how much good the fresh air and exercise will be for you."

Her head turned and she looked out the window, oblivious to the beauty of the English countryside. "Oh all right, Patrick, I will. But you must promise me that tomorrow you will join me."

He grimaced inwardly. "If it means you will do as I ask, I'll gladly comply." His smile, deepening the crow's-feet at the corners of his pale-green eyes, never faded.

She clapped her hands together. "Wonderful! I do believe I feel better already. I can't wait until tomorrow," she said excitedly, a rosy flush coming over the once-pallid skin which stretched in translucence across her bony features. She had been a beauty in her youth, but her propensity for little food had sharpened her face. However, her bone structure was still good, and it was easy to see what a beautiful bride she must have made over 25 years before.

"Other patients await, so I'll be going. I'll come round tomorrow afternoon."

"Why don't you join us for dinner, and we'll walk afterward?"

"Thank you. That would suit me well. I haven't talked to your brother in quite some time. Fascinating man. Till tomorrow then, Lady Alison." He shut the door to her solar behind him with a sigh of relief.

Patrick MacBeth, as physician to the abbot of Westminster Abbey, the Earl of Lambeth, and many other nobles and dignitaries who made their homes in and around London, was a highly successful man. Fortunately, Lady Alison was one of only two patients so voraciously demanding. And over basically nothing. But she cheerfully paid for every visit, he admitted, and in that regard alone she was worth ten other patients to his purse.

Down the steps to the second floor of the keep, his wide, purposeful feet carried him swiftly. Lord Alexander was holding court in his great hall, colorful silk banners hanging above the dais which supported his massive chair. "The only comfortable seat in the house!" the servants complained. Several serfs from his demesne had been caught poaching fish in his forest and were now receiving their just rewards. Four more men were waiting for their petitions to be heard. They sought permission to convert some of the forest waste into arable land by cutting down the trees and grubbing up the brushwood. Already they had great plans for the assart. "Surely Lord Alexander will grant our request rather then let the land just sit idle, won't he?" they said to each other as Patrick passed by. "It's just that much more money for him in the end!"

The earl raised a bored hand in greeting as Patrick passed through, but continued listening patiently to his subjects. Goodness, but he hated these days when he opened up his hall to hear petitions and cast judgments. He would rather be almost anywhere else!

"The fish jumped right into my hands, my lord!" the head poacher and designated spokesman said in all seriousness. "I swear by the heavens, it is the truth."

Alexander arched his brows and sat up. This was a new excuse. He had to give the man credit for his creativity, however ridiculous. Maybe he could have some fun with this one.

Patrick saw the glint in the nobleman's eye and hurried out of the room so that his laughter would not be heard. Pity the man who matched wits with the Earl of Lambeth!

The bright sunlight accosted his green eyes and pale, freckled skin as he emerged from the keep, already mentally preparing for his next appointment. But the sound of an angry voice stole him thoroughly from his thoughts. Employing his hand as a visor, he scanned the bailey for the source of the shouts and found it easily in front of the kitchen.

"You are a most foul fellow!" Jane was shouting in her loudest of voices, ire raised higher than she normally dared allow it ascend, as she inspected some meat a butcher from London had brought round in his cart. "This stinks! How *dare* you try and pass off this infested flesh to anyone, let alone the Earl of Lambeth!"

"But, Madam, I had no idea it was rotten." The man held his hands out.

"You're a liar! It's as plain as the nose on your face, which either refuses to smell the stink or is incapable of it! Did you honestly think I would buy this from you, no matter how cheaply you're selling it, and risk making the entire castle sick? Now be gone! And take your festering load with you. Next time you come you had best bring your finest or you won't be coming within these walls again. I'll see to that, and you can believe my word is good!"

Grabbing the reins to his donkey, the man bowed quickly and hurried off lest more be done to him than a simple tongue-lashing. Yet he couldn't help but smile at the fire in the woman's eyes. *She is a fine one*, he thought. *Much too fiery for the likes of me, though.*

Gregory, a skinny, birdlike man, walked over officiously. "What was the problem, Jane?"

"Just a butcher trying to pass off rotten meat. What nerve!"

"How much was he asking for it?"

Jane's mouth opened in horror. "Does it matter? Bad meat is bad meat!"

"Not if you cook it long enough, it isn't."

Jane remembered her father. "Not in *my* kitchens."

"They're not *your* kitchens, Jane. They're *my* kitchens. I thought you understood that. I'll go bring the fellow back."

"You do that, Gregory, and you'll have to bring back another cook as well. I will not have such infested meat come into the kitchen. You could get sick just looking at stuff such as he was trying to sell!"

"That decision is not yours to make."

"No?"

"No. I am the clerk of the kitchen." His long chin jutted forward.

"Fine. We'll take it up with Skeets." She turned, her old gown swinging around her, and began to walk toward the keep.

Gregory caught up quickly. "Wait. I order you to stop, Jane. I'll not allow you to bring Skeets in on this. Everyone knows you have a special place in the man's heart, if not his bed."

Patrick, just about to move on, decided at that moment to keep listening. *This should be good*, he thought.

"What? How dare you, Gregory. How *dare* you! No one says such things, and if you spread such lies, I can promise you you'll have to find another position elsewhere. I will not stand for such insinuations against my character!"

"As if you've never sinned!" he snorted.

Jane was immediately caught off guard. "What?"

Oh dear, thought Patrick, still listening in, *pity the poor man now!*

"Oh, come now, Jane. You're too attractive a woman to be widowed all these years. It's a wonder the earl allows you here in such a state, unmarried, without a husband to farm his land and bring him more money."

Jane's eyes flashed. "Maybe it is strange. But it's not for you to question my reasons for not seeking the company of a man. In fact, it's entirely none of your business. However, since I'm in a good mood today and more than a little excited from the argument with the butcher, I'm prepared to make a deal with you, Gregory. I won't mention anything about this discussion or your willingness to buy spoiled wares to Skeets. In return for your continued employment, I expect free rein in the kitchen.

You'll simply have to make yourself look busy, and I'll assume all the responsibilities."

"Why do you think that would be an agreeable arrangement? I'm not a man who wants to skulk around here and there, pretending to be something I'm not."

Jane sighed and drew him away from the waiting vendors. "I'm sorry that I misjudged you then. Gregory, we have years ahead of us, years in which we must work alongside one another day after day. Don't you want them to go as smoothly as possible?"

"Of course. A smooth kitchen is a productive one."

"My thoughts exactly. Take my advice, Gregory. I've been employed in these kitchens for a long time. I know the routine; I know the servants well, their habits, where they excel, where they don't. Just take a little time to learn our ways. We will all appreciate your willingness to see how we work before you start making suggestions that we've already tried and have found to be unfit. And you'll find as well that they'll warm up to you, and quite quickly. We are a highly forgiving group, being much too busy not to be otherwise. I will take on all the major responsibilities just for a little while. Watch us, then step in after a time and do what you were hired to do."

"What will I do in the meantime? Watching is fine, Jane, but I need to keep busy. My mother kept all of us busy from sunup to sundown. I need hard work like I need air."

"I understand that all too well. To begin with, your closet is in need of reorganization."

"True."

"And once that is done, perhaps Skeets will give you more responsibility, leave you in charge of the spices. But observe us and see how we are frugal in the areas that matter to the earl and extravagant where he demands such. Spices. Fine meat."

"Won't your workload be considerably heavier?"

Jane looked at him wryly, crossing her arms across her bosom.

"All right, all right. I suppose I haven't been much help at all since I've come. So I'll agree to your proposition. But I would like to explain that the baron I last worked for was very stingy."

"Well, the earl is not. And you must admit that it will be much more enjoyable to work for someone who is generous and likes good food."

"You're right there. All right, I'll do as you suggest. But I'll still have to lead the procession into dinner each day, what with your being a woman and all."

"Naturally." Suddenly Jane became warm and smiled once again. "Gregory, it's been a pleasure negotiating with you!"

"Likewise." Gregory nodded officiously, a sense of relief washing over him. He had truly felt lost in the great kitchen since he had come to Marchemont.

Jane walked to a cart of produce. "What have we here?" And the haggling and dickering started afresh.

Shaking his head with a smile, Patrick laughed at her spunk, crossed the bailey, and went through the gate house. There was nothing like a drama. Besides, she was a magnificent creature, he realized. How long had it been since he had stood motionless for several minutes just to watch a woman? Her hands moved with graceful strength, and if he could have seen her face more closely, he knew he would have thought it beautiful. And that voice! That loud voice! He would have laughed out loud if it wouldn't have made them aware of his nosy presence. She was utterly unique and completely charming. But of course, she was just a servant, so he easily set her aside and began to think once again about his next call. This man, a monk from France, was seriously ill. It was to be a much different call from the one he had just finished up. Still, he was going to the abbey to see him, and that was always a cause for gladness. The abbot, Richard of Barking, was a close personal friend of the doctor.

Several minutes later he was by the Thames, embarking on one of the earl's three barges. The ride took much too long for a man of action such as Doctor MacBeth. And he began to remember, his green eyes glazing over at the recollection of his past. The violence. The blood. The pleading cries of the dying.

The bargeman had to shake him from his trancelike state when the vessel touched the other side of the river.

❧ ❧ ❧

"First the laundresses were taking more than their fair share of time at the well this morning. Poor John and Joseph were running to and fro, like two mice caught between four cats, so that we could get the soup done in time. Then James, who was turning the spit—or should I say who was *not* turning the spit— started daydreaming. Almost ruined a joint of beef. Which leads me to the worst part of the day when a butcher from London showed up with the foulest meat I've ever seen. 'Twas going to be the death of me, I became so angered!"

Nicholas laughed in the darkness of the room and shifted his position on the bed. "Well, if I know you, Mother, he made out much worse than you did!"

"Naturally. I run a smooth kitchen, son. And you will learn to do the same at your new position, someday running Marchemont and Lord Alexander's other estates with efficiency. Well, anyway, it turned out to be a fine day despite its beginnings. A cart from over to the west of the manor came by with some lovely turnips. They'll come to good use at the feast, I assure you."

"Skeets told me today that the number is up to 700 now. And it has turned into a tournament, Mother. Imagine... knights jousting on the lists. I've never seen a tournament before."

Jane had no interest in knights and tournaments. "We'll be busy enough, certainly. So tell me about your day, my son. How was your time at the abbey?"

Nicholas's voice sounded skeptical. "To be honest, Mother, it isn't easy going from a life of manual labor to sitting and learning about words and numbers. 'Tis quite frustrating. However, inside of me I feel this drive to succeed. It's more a matter of destiny and an obedience to the inevitable than anything else. I'm doing a poor job at describing what I mean. Brother Boniface would be most displeased."

"No, no, Nicholas, I know exactly what you mean. It must be nice to see the abbey so regularly, though. I've always loved the place."

"Then why don't you come with me one morning?"

"I don't see how I can get away!"

"Shall I talk to Skeets about giving you a morning off? You've not taken any time for yourself in months."

"Yes, but the tournament—"

"No matter. You know you'll get everything done. Just a couple of hours, Mother? We can walk around the church and hear high Mass at eleven o'clock."

The matter was decided at the thought of Mass. "All right, Nicholas. But I'll talk to Skeets myself. If you don't mind, I can still take care of my own affairs."

Nicholas laughed and kissed his mother good night on the cheek. "I didn't doubt that even for a minute, Mother."

SIX

Two days later Jane tugged open the lid of a trunk. The battered wooden box, bound by leather straps, held her possessions in their sparse entirety. She had saved up for several years to buy a new gown. An extra garment. Frivolously so. A special gown to wear only occasionally, but to gloat over frequently. It lay folded neatly on top of the few articles she and Nicholas could call their own, and she pulled it out by the shoulders. A satisfied smile crept to her lips as she inspected it with delighted eyes. Four months now she had owned this gown, and this was the first time she was going to wear it somewhere other than in the confines of her room.

It was to be a special day with Nicholas.

Laying out the gown and then the light-gray undergown upon the bed, she dashed into the kitchen to the well and brought back a bucket of water to wash with. The night before she had washed her hair and, once dressed, she would wind up the long, warm-brown braid by the nape of her neck, holding it in place with a loosely woven crispinette.

The cold water was invigorating as she scrubbed her skin. Minutes later she was wearing the buttery-soft undergown, feeling refreshed and at peace from the scrubbing and a good night's sleep. Again she inspected the gown itself. Running her fingertips over the fabric, she didn't at all regret having gone to the expense. Sleeveless with open sides, the gown's mustard color complemented perfectly her dark hair and eyes, and gave her a soft, glowing appearance, turning her into all that was beautiful in a woman. She was utterly feminine, comforting, fair, and fragrant with the sweetness of the dried wildflowers she had placed in the trunk. She didn't realize such a transformation had occurred as she slipped on the soft leather shoes, worn only once before. The simple belt she tied around her small waist completed the ensemble. Her only regret when purchasing the outfit was that she didn't have enough money to buy an embroidered belt. It had always been a secret wish of hers to learn the art of fine embroidery. But she had neither the time nor, she felt, the aptitude.

Nicholas entered the room. "Are you ready?"

"Yes, my handsome son." She turned in a circle.

"You look lovely, Mother."

"Without a train I certainly don't appear to be a lady of quality, but then I don't quite look like a kitchen cook, either!"

"You're beautiful, train or not! And I'm proud to be your escort."

Jane smiled up into his eyes. "It's always been us, hasn't it, Nicholas?"

He returned the expression and took her arm. "Let's get down to the barge."

She walked through the bailey to the gate house, head held high, proud of her peasant finery. Men's heads turned, and for the first time in many years, Jane noticed. Nicholas did as well, glaring in their direction in a most overprotective manner. She was his mother, after all.

The short cruise across the river was a pure pleasure, delighting all the senses. A light breeze blew across them, scented with the first promise of a changing season. The smell of the late-summer flowers was a treat Jane could almost taste as the aroma mixed with the warm zephyr. Autumn would arrive next month, and with it a relief from the August heat. It had been an especially warm summer, and all the castle servants were eagerly looking forward to a change in climate. But for now, it was still hot, and Jane's woolen clothes wore on her heavily. Yet she would not let it dampen her spirits as she sat quietly on her seat enjoying the short morning passage.

Nicholas sat opposite her, his hair blown into wisps by the breeze, his eyes shining golden in the sunlight.

Daydreaming overtook her consciousness as she remembered herself at Nicholas's age. Headstrong, naturally. Betrothed to Allen. Now, years later, she couldn't picture herself living the life her mother had lived. Emma had relied on her husband for everything. Jane was self-sufficient. And she liked it that way. It had made her strong ... sometimes a little hardened. But she knew the trusting young girl was still to be found somewhere beneath all that courage and conscientiousness. The right man had simply never come along to draw her back out.

"We're here, Mother," Nicholas announced as the barge touched the dock on the opposite side, right up to the steps leading to the palace at Westminster and the abbey close by.

The brisk staccato of workmen's hammers dented the air around them, and busy people hurried by carrying planks and wheeling barrows filled with stones, tools, or other supplies. King Henry, the third Henry to sit upon England's throne, was busy remodeling the once-glorious, now decrepit palace.

"Have you seen King Henry yourself?" Jane whispered as she came to the top of the steps and onto the grass. Being such a simple woman, she was naturally overcome by all the activity commissioned by the king himself.

"Not from any closer distance than when he last visited Lord Alexander."

"Such a young man to sit on so great a throne."

"But think of it, Mother, he's been king since he was nine years old. He has a wealth of experience though he's only 22. And just look what he's doing to the palace!"

"Too bad he isn't refurbishing the abbey with such vigor."

Nicholas shrugged. "Who knows what the future may hold? Let's go into the church."

The west entrance of the great church stood before them. Built over 150 years before by King Edward, the last true Saxon king of England, it had once been the most glorious, majestic church in all England. But Edward had died only days after its consecration. And the Monastery of St. Peter's at Westminster had failed to assume the grand and glorious role that the now-sainted king had hoped it would achieve. Fewer than 20 monks were now cloistered in the monastery. And though it was still the place for the majority of coronations and most royal burials, the buildings were in a sad state of disrepair. The Cistercian and Carthusian monasteries had mightily eclipsed the Black Monks in importance, and King Henry himself was devoted to the Dominicans.

Jane stepped softly inside. The once brightly painted walls which depicted saints and scenes from Scripture were peeling and forlorn. All seemed dull and sad and greatly in need of someone's tender care. "I wonder what it looked like when it was first finished."

Nicholas gazed up at the triforium and the rounded arches that lined the upper passages. "It must have been beautiful."

"Let's honor the king who built this place, Nicholas. We should offer up a simple prayer by his tomb. Where is he buried? I can't quite remember."

"Up here." Nicholas led her up a side aisle of the nave to the lantern, the spot of the church where the transept and the choir intersected. Saint Edward the Confessor was buried behind the high altar in a shrine built during the reign of Henry II, in 1163, two years after he was canonized.

"Such a lovely tomb," Jane commented upon viewing the stone tomb. "I wonder what kind of a man he was?"

"I don't know. Brother Boniface hasn't yet brought me to that time period in history. We're still on the Greeks."

Jane continued to stare at the tomb, intrigued that the man responsible for this church, now a saint, rested, ultimately, in much the same state as those around him. And despite the fact he died as all men do, he was set apart. She wanted to know more.

A footstep behind her caused her to turn.

"I couldn't help but overhear what you were saying," the tall, redheaded man said kindly. "I've long admired the abbey myself, and, of course, Saint Edward."

"Do you know much about him?"

"A little."

"What kind of man was he?" Jane asked again.

"He was a very pious man, yet interested in the arts and all things beautiful. It was natural that he should build a church. He grew up in exile in Normandy and learned the importance of such from his uncle, the Duke of Normandy."

"Was he a good king?"

Patrick MacBeth shrugged a little, knowing he had seen this woman before, but unable to recall under what circumstances. She was undoubtedly familiar. "Some say yes, others say no. 'Tis not for me to judge, really. But I suppose all men might look back at what they've done over the course of a lifetime and wish to make changes. England was full of internal struggles at the time."

"As it is now." Jane turned back to continue looking at the tomb. "I've always wondered what it would be like to leave such a legacy behind. And yet, the thought that perhaps these places end up glorifying the builder rather than the God they are supposed to magnify always crosses my mind."

Patrick lifted his brows in surprise at her thoughtful statement. "Yes, that seems to be the case looking back over a century later. But God knew King Edward's heart in a way only He could."

"It is as you say. Thank goodness He does see the inside of man, especially me, for I've done many stupid things, but not out of a heart of hate and rebellion. I just wasn't thinking."

Nicholas had left the pair and was talking to a monk farther down the nave. Jane presumed it was Brother Boniface, his tutor.

"I understand completely."

"Do you?" She turned to face him fully, and Patrick was struck by her unusual beauty. Though her eyes still bore into his, her face haunted him like a specter that had followed him all his life. The wide mouth, the slightly slanted eyes, the straight nose. Her pointed chin he found highly endearing.

"We all live with regrets. We all have a past to deal with. It's part of living, and in the end God's mercy and lovingkindness is displayed through His working in our lives. We can make changes for the better through His strength. Don't you agree?"

"Yes. I know what you say is true. But to feel that in my heart is truly another matter."

The bell began to toll for Mass. "My name is Patrick MacBeth."

"I'm Jane Lightfoot, and that was my son, Nicholas, you were talking to. He studies here at the abbey with Brother Boniface. So I thank you, good sir, for taking the time to talk with me." She turned to go, but was detained by a large, gentle hand on her arm. Jane looked down at the square-tipped fingers, the large knuckles, the light skin, and strawberry-blond hairs which shimmered softly in the dim light.

"They say miracles have happened here at this tomb, Mistress Jane." His words were soft, tension spilt between them as his eyes trapped her in their gaze. Her mouth parted slightly as she slowly breathed in, caught in a moment unlike any she had ever experienced before. "Do you believe in miracles, Jane?"

"Yes," she breathed and quickly left his side, her entire body tingling from his touch. She muttered almost silently into the solemn air, "I do now."

60

Patrick stared after her retreating form, her gauzy veil fluttering behind her. He crossed himself without thinking and left the church through the north entrance, filled with the remembrance of Jane's dark-brown eyes and her slender arm beneath his hand. No doubt she was a merchant's wife or the widow of some burgher. She certainly wasn't common.

But she certainly was beautiful.

ugust continued its predetermined course toward September. Ten more staff had been temporarily hired on in the kitchen, and only Skeets knew how many extra hands were scattered about the castle attending to the tasks he set before them.

Exhausted, each evening Jane dropped into bed beside an already-sleeping Nicholas. Such business was welcome. It kept her from thinking too much about the handsome stranger in the abbey. Over and over again she conjured up the remembrance of his hand and his voice—not a deep voice but a kind voice, one that sounded as if he liked to sing. Some people have faces which always look ready to burst into song. Blustery, deep-toned faces—heavily jowled, red-nosed . . . birdlike faces with pointy noses and weak chins, ready to twitter a ditty . . . and clear-countenanced, wide faces that, though silent, make one recall sliding notes and breezy staccato.

Patrick's face was ready for song. But Jane could not determine what manner of tune would issue from him. He was happy on the surface and maybe a few layers down. Way below, however, she thought she heard a melody of sadness issue forth . . . perhaps regret.

The tournament was now only eight days away, which didn't stop the earl from organizing a smaller supper for several important men to take place that next afternoon.

Skeets detained her in the kitchens. "Jane, I hate to do this to you, but I simply cannot spare the time or men to go into London for the lampreys that the earl has requested. Do you have someone who can do it?"

"I do, Skeets. But to be quite honest with you, I'd rather do it myself. The last time I had someone pick out my eels they were sickly-looking creatures. Not fit for Lord Alexander's consumption. If I leave before light tomorrow morning, I'll be back in plenty of time to make sure everything is prepared as scheduled for supper."

"Do you think you can make it back no later than eight o'-clock?"

"Certainly. Were there any last-minute invitations issued?"

"None that I know of, but I'm making sure there are enough trenchers, spoons, and cups for at least ten extra. And the linens... I mustn't let Gregory forget extra linens!"

"But the earl is only inviting five people, Skeets."

Skeets's expression was as expected. "I hope you're not using those figures to prepare the food by, Jane."

She laughed. "Of course not, dear man. 'Twas merely a jest."

And so the next morning Jane found herself on the barge once again, bag of coin hanging from her waist, a basket containing clean cloths and an earthenware crock on her arm. This time the water was a flat, inky black, shorn clean of any significant rays of moonlight. The crescent moon hung suspended barely above the western horizon. She was too sleepy to think about anything other than the specific mission awaiting her. Even the many tasks that the next few days held failed to push themselves up through her conscious thought. There had been no time in the past week even to sit upon the wall and gaze over the river. But she had promised herself last night that she would make time this afternoon, even if it was only for ten minutes.

Soon London appeared before them, and Jane disembarked from the barge at St. Andrew's Hill to begin the walk to Cheapside, London's main market street. At six in the morning it was just starting to gain momentum. Jane knew that soon after the first ray of the sun shone above the horizon, the marketplace would become a bustling center of human and animal activity.

She knew this place well, coming here at least once a month to single out a special piece of meat or produce on her lord's whim and Skeets's request. The eel monger's stall was as yet uninhabited, so Jane wandered a bit.

"Ho there, Jane!" called the cheese merchant with a wave.

"Henry." Jane nodded serenely in acknowledgment, almost sailing amid the market like a queen. As the head cook of Marchemont Castle, she was well-esteemed.

"Have a nice round from Cheddar, here. You know your earl likes a fine Cheddar!"

"That's right." Jane thumped the cheese. "And you've done much better by me before, Henry. When you get something in of a little better quality, send it over."

"You're much too discriminating, Jane." He shook his head, sad to have lost the sale.

"I'm discriminating because the earl can afford to be."

She cruised off toward the pen where live cattle and oxen were kept. The sun was starting to rise now as Jane looked over the animals whose pen was next to the butcher's stall. They stood eyeing her, their blinks slow and suspicious. *Well, they ought to eye me thus!* Jane joked to herself.

"Good morning, Jane."

She turned on her heel and leaned back against the fencing at the sound of the voice. "Patrick, what are you doing at market? And so early!"

"I had to take care of one of my patients through the night."

"I *knew* your name sounded familiar. You're the physician to the Earl of Lambeth, aren't you?" She was suddenly embarrassed at being seen in her homely green gown and brown undergown.

"Yes. And you're one of his servants?" The esteemed physician felt his heart plunge in disappointment. Still, he kept a smile on his face. He remembered now: She was the fiery woman shouting angrily at the butcher and then the kitchen clerk.

"I'm the head cook," Jane's head went up proudly, "and I do a fair job of it!"

Patrick couldn't help but laugh at her decisiveness. "I wouldn't expect anything else, especially after the way you bullied that butcher the other day!"

She raised her eyebrows in surprise. "You were there?"

"Yes, and I must say you handled yourself quite admirably. I wouldn't want to go up against you in a battle of wills!"

Jane took it as a compliment. "Thank you. But why should an esteemed man like yourself be talking to me here at such an hour?"

"I saw you as I was passing through on my way home from the bedside of a particularly needy patient. I thought I would tell you that I've heard your son, Nicholas, is doing well in his studies."

"How did you find this out?"

"The abbot himself told me. He is a patient of mine. Apparently Nicholas is an important pupil. The earl himself checks on his progress regularly."

"Truly?"

"Yes. Why does that surprise you?"

"Forgive me, sir. But as we are of such different stations, you couldn't possibly understand how odd I find the earl's sudden interest in Nicholas. Has he spoken of it to you?"

"Just a bit. The other day. He seemed excited that he had found Skeets's replacement with someone who had grown up at Marchemont."

Jane shrugged. "I guess there's something to be said for that. Nicholas does know almost every square foot of Marchemont. It really is his home."

"And as his home," Patrick continued the thought, "he will surely tend to it in a far more loving and caring way than an outsider."

"It certainly is good for Nicholas to have the influence of another man in his life."

"What of his father?"

"His father is dead," Jane lied, trying to take comfort in that she might not really be lying. The man *could* be dead for all she knew.

"So you are a widow?"

"Yes."

"I see. And you never married again?"

"No. I didn't see the need. I enjoy my work at the castle, Doctor MacBeth. Having a man around would just complicate things."

"Well then, I see I'd best be on my way, Jane Lightfoot. By the way, that's an interesting name. Is it Saxon?"

"Yes. Not a drop of Norman blood flows through me." Jane heard the fishmonger setting out his boards behind her. "Well, sir, I thank you for the kind report and for the informative talk we had in the abbey two weeks ago. Will you be coming to Marchemont soon?"

"Naturally. Lady Alison keeps me busy."

Jane put her hand up to her mouth and laughed. "Ah yes, Lady Alison!"

"And I shall be there for supper tonight as well."

"Will you? Tell me, Doctor MacBeth, what is your favorite dish?"

"Rabbit stew."

Her eyebrows raised. "Cooked in a nice ale?"

"Absolutely."

"Consider it done! I want you to be greatly looking forward to the meal!"

"I already was. Supper at Marchemont is a coveted invitation. You've garnered quite a reputation, although no one knows your name."

"Thank you, sir. And though I won't see you at Marchemont, I trust you shall enjoy your time with us."

"I'm certain I will." His eyes smiled into hers, and again that current ran between them. "You're a beautiful woman, Jane." He didn't know why he said it. It was stupid. She was a cook. But he did it anyway.

She dropped her eyes in embarrassment, the feeling taking her off guard. Two seconds later she was with the fishmonger sorting through the fresh lampreys. And on the barge ride home her basket held not only the seafaring creatures but two good-sized hares as well.

❧ EIGHT ❧

Everyone prepared?" asked William, the marshall of the hall, a small, officious-looking man, with a nose the size of a cucumber and red as a radish. Answerable to Skeets and in charge of the meal's proceedings, he gathered the serving men and women outside the entrance to the hall, tugging on his best tunic and straightening his belt. "Linens? Utensils?" He raised his head and stuck out his jaw as short men tend to do when their insides are in a dither.

The servants nodded solemnly, excitement nevertheless milling beneath the first layer of their skin. Many had performed this task thousands of times, but each day at this time their hearts sped up in anticipation as they waited to do their job with flair and elegance. It was a high lord's table they were to dress, and they never forgot that fact.

The procession began to the blare of pipes. It was a spectacle of organizational beauty and attested to Skeets's powerful sense of order and preplanning. With a snap, cloths were drawn over the table which rested on the dais, then spoons and cups were laid out for the diners. Down the left side of the room intricately carved cupboards displayed gold and silver plate, bowls, and all manner of decorative objects. These were rarely used, their chief objective to exhibit the great wealth of Alexander de la Marche.

While the flurry of the preparations continued in the hall, the din growing more loud with each second that passed, the food was borne across the courtyard, up the steps of the keep, and into the hall. Around the fire screens they marched and continued down the center of the massive room. Above their heads the great timbered beams of the ceiling went unnoticed, for all eyes were on the food.

The procession approached first the earl's table. Delight and anticipation surfaced upon the diners' features as the first course, which consisted of larded boar's head, swan, mutton, and pork, was laid before them on wooden trenchers.

The gentlemen of the household, including Skeets and some of Marchemont's knights, were served next, at a table off to the side and nearest the dais. The earl's garrison were then served, and well they deserved such a repast after a morning of heavy training for battle readiness, should England call for such. At the lower tables the other servants were given their meal. Dogs eagerly sat on their haunches nearby, tongues wagging as they awaited the scraps that would be thrown down onto the rush-strewn floor. Their barking, such an accustomed sound in the great hall of a lord, went unnoticed by the hungry group.

Knives were drawn from belts and all fell to, consuming the delectable food for which Jane, Stephen, and the rest of the kitchen staff had spent all morning in preparation.

In several months the earl would move his court to one of his other castles. For by then the moat would need to be de-fouled, and the castle cleaned by the skeleton staff that would remain behind. But always he would return to Marchemont by spring. It was his favorite residence. More times than not, he would leave only long enough for the castle to be freshened, and would carry the extra expense of having food transported from farther away as the local supply from his own lands nearby was depleted. Besides, being near London was helpful when it came to supplying food for his household. Marchemont was

Alexander's home, and he loved it well. He was never away from the formidable gray walls for very long.

Lord Alexander, the smile of a gracious host upon his face, turned to the man beside him to answer the question placed before him. "Yes, your excellency, my Lady Marie will be returning from Normandy shortly."

"A most pious woman, your wife," the archbishop of Canterbury acknowledged with a brusque nod. "And she still diligently serves the poor." His questions never ended on an upward inflection.

Alexander nodded. "Yes, she believes it to be her life's calling."

It had to be, he thought with remorse, for they had never been blessed with children. A child. How Alexander de la Marche longed for children. Not just an heir, but daughters as well. Yet even now, it was too late for that, he thought, as he picked up a piece of stewed mutton between his fingers and bit down. Lady Marie was well past the age of childbearing.

"What is keeping her occupied in Normandy?" the archbishop asked as if he already knew the answer.

"She is visiting a convent. The abbess is a childhood friend of hers. She invited her to visit the monastery. I'm sure she was seeking Marie's patronage. From what I understand, it is in need of extensive repairs."

The abbot of Westminster Abbey, Richard of Barking, joined in on the conversation, rubbing his hand over his bald head. "Ah yes, we all must do what we can to bring in the needed funds. I fear I am in the midst of the very same battle."

"Not an unusual predicament!" the archbishop pronounced, remembering all too well what it was like to be an abbot, but not sounding altogether sympathetic. However, that was merely his tone of voice and his manner of speaking. His heart cared deeply for such matters.

"How progresses the construction on the new Lady Chapel?" Lord Alexander inquired.

71

Richard shrugged. "As well as can be expected, your grace. 'Tis my hope that it is merely the start of bigger happenings for St. Peter's. The monastery is literally crumbling round our heads. Stand too long in one spot, and you'll spend the next five minutes dusting yourself off."

"And with the palace being refurbished nearby, it must be tempting not to pull some of the workmen away from the king's project," Lord Alexander surmised.

"If you only knew," Richard of Barking replied as he rolled his eyes at the ceiling.

The archbishop leaned forward to get a look at the abbot. "The king enjoys building projects more than anything. You must pique his interest in the abbey, Richard."

"Easier to talk about than achieve," the abbot grumbled.

Now Patrick, physician to both Richard and the earl, leaned forward. "Isn't it true that he goes on pilgrimages to various shrines? Perhaps you could somehow interest him in Saint Edward. It would combine both loves of his soul together in one neat, convenient parcel called the Westminster Abbey."

"A saint *and* building!" Richard cried.

"Indulgence without the guilt," the archbishop said sarcastically.

Lord Alexander nodded in agreement. "Precisely. And that is the beauty of the thought. If he could be persuaded that Saint Edward deserves a proper shrine and he is just the man to build it, perhaps your troubles will be solved, Richard."

The abbot threw a gaze of admiration in Patrick's direction. "Leave it to a medical man to come up with the answer!"

Lord Alexander and the archbishop agreed. But the abbot continued, "The question is how to get King Henry interested in building a shrine to Edward and a worthy church to house it in."

"Paint the circumstances so dire that he will act upon it through sheer guilt," the archbishop suggested.

"Well," the abbot said, believing the king *should* feel a little remorse for being so remiss in his responsibility to the abbey, "circumstances are *most* dire. I hate to be another jackdaw queuing up before the king, cackling about the less-than-perfect state in which I find myself. But as I said, the Monastery of St. Peter's at Westminster is literally crumbling down around us."

The archbishop's words were dry. "If you don't fight for it, Richard, no one else will."

"I was noticing the condition of the murals just the other day," Patrick remarked, remembering Jane's face with a clarity the paintings in the church once enjoyed. "It would be a wonderful thing to bring them back to life again."

"Pah! The murals are the least of it! The roof is badly in need of repair, and many of the windows have no glass in them at all. Would that I were an architect—I could detail it more highly for you," the abbot said, enjoying his own grumblings despite the reasons for them. It wasn't any wonder that he and the archbishop were such good friends.

Lord Alexander's green eyes rounded for a brief moment. "The king is coming in a week's time for the tournament. You all will be present, so why not bring the matter before him then?"

"An ambush?" Richard's eyebrows raised appreciatively.

"Exactly. At the very least, Richard, you can ask his expert advice on the Lady Chapel. Once he's involved in that project, no matter how small the extent, he may want to take it further."

"Excellent idea, Alexander. I'll do just that."

The conversation was interrupted by the second course, which consisted of pheasant, jelly, hedgehog, and much to Patrick MacBeth's delight, the most succulent rabbit stew he had ever tasted. It amused him when he realized that he was in the presence of three of the greatest men in England, and all he could think about was Jane Lightfoot.

Sweet Jane.

Industrious Jane.

The stew let him know she had been thinking about him. And that pleased him greatly. Disconcertingly so. The last thing his tortured mind needed was another distraction. He felt as he consumed her cooking that he knew her better. Her food was like her—sweet at times, spicy at others. Filling. Completely satisfying.

But she's a cook, Patrick. You must remember that. She's only a castle cook.

❧ ❧ ❧

Like a molten pendant, a pulsating sun hung just above the horizon, a splendid orb capable of simultaneously provoking feelings of hope, as well as insignificance. But Jane, aching of bone and bleary of eye, felt neither, wanting only to clear her mind of lampreys, ducks, cabbages, cloves, and berries. Nor did she wish to think about kettles, and tongs, and spits, and caldrons. She was sore all over, and her bloodshot eyes were grateful to be free of the smoke-infused kitchen.

Barges sailed slowly up and down the Thames, fluid-black silhouettes against the golden waters. The small, dark outlines of the bargemen were a striking contrast against the large, shimmering scene of which they were part—a scene where they provided movement, focus. The air was clear, promising a soon-coming autumn, and Jane felt as if she was inhaling the pure, dark azure of the eastern sky directly into her lungs. It was cleansing and as rejuvenating as a plunge in a spring-fed pool.

Reaching up, she pulled off her linen hat, undid her braid, and let her long hair fall free. She sighed with relief when the constricting headgear was removed. Geoffrey, the young guard, looked on in boyish admiration and ventured closer to speak with her. His hands broke out in a sweat, but he bravely proceeded on course.

74

"Hello, Jane," he greeted her nervously, his short, bright-blond hair, thick yet fine, catching the wind. "You cooked the dinner."

"Why yes, of course I did." Geoffrey inwardly winced at his sore excuse for conversation. But Jane was kind. "And did you enjoy it, Geoffrey?"

"Oh yes, there's no one who can make a finer joint of beef. Must be the spices you use." *Of course it's the spices, you idiot,* he thought. Nevertheless, he was pleased she had remembered his name.

"Yes. Spicing meat just right takes years of practice and experimentation. I'm glad you enjoyed it."

She turned back to the water.

"Well, good-bye then," Geoffrey said nervously. But Jane, already lost in thought, failed to respond. There was much to ponder and remember just then, much joy in which to bask, much regret in which to wallow. And on an evening when she had purposed only to enjoy the beauty of the sunset, she found herself locked in the past, in the embrace of a stranger. So absorbing were her thoughts that when Patrick MacBeth sought some fresh air from the almost-suffocating air of the hall, she took no notice.

"What are you gazing at, Jane?"

"Fields of gold," was all she softly said as she continued to stare at the river and remember what might have been.

With a puzzled shake of his head, Patrick MacBeth left her to her solitary musings. Lady Alison watched the brief exchange from the window of her solar.

❧ ❧ ❧

Unfortunately for Jane, the day didn't end there. After putting away the leftover food into the kitchen cellar, she sat down for a cup of homemade honey mead. The sole light in the immense kitchen emanated from the cooking pit in the center and the two wall fireplaces where the fires were banked for the night. The red glow was comforting. The silence calming. And having the normally bustling room to herself made Jane feel a little bit special. She sipped the mead, which she had made herself, and rolled the sweet mixture across her tongue. It was always the same after such days: The residue of excitement lasted long into the quiet hours and kept her body going well after she wished it would stop. The mead helped her to sleep. Already Nicholas was slumbering in their room, his young heart cloven over Agnes's recent decision that he had grown too high and mighty for the likes of a simple kitchen wench such as herself.

Jane's heart hurt for her son, yet at the same time she was keenly aware that Agnes had been looking for more than kisses in the dark from Nicholas. She sighed at the thought of being 15, and in the dimness of the kitchen she remembered Nicholas's conception. Involuntarily, she reached behind her shoulders and felt the scars which were given to her by the sheriff's lash in the public square of the village, for her fornication. Jane's father had given up three prized sheep in private to assure her life would be spared. He had taken her home, laid her on his own bed, and cleansed the wounds as she bit down on a stick to keep from screaming. Father's fingers had pieced together her back as gently as they could, and his ferocious, tenacious love did the same for her heart. For she couldn't help but feel betrayed by the jeers of those she had known all her life.

The memory of the mysterious man who bedded her by the midnight banks of the Thames made her angry. He had been a grown man, a gentleman, and he seduced her with fine wine and gentle words. Though she never said this to anyone else, she thought of him now as a rapist. He had taken advantage of her youth. In the darkness she had never even seen his face. And when he had gone, all she had left of him was a gold bracelet and the memory of a kiss that tasted of wine. He also left her with Nicholas. The one delight of her life. His conception was not something she was proud of . . . but she likened it to the story of Joseph—a grievous sin occurred, yet God's mercy prevailed and good somehow resulted.

And so she tried to emulate Joseph, making good out of less-than-perfect circumstances. Her life wasn't perfect. She was lonely, sometimes afraid of what was to come, but she recognized that God had always taken care of her, and that if she was unhappy, it wasn't because of her everyday circumstances.

Her similarity to Joseph extended itself to her sense of industry and responsibility. She had risen quickly at Marchemont because she worked hard and did her job, whatever task she was given, better than anyone else. From the day she started— fetching water, cutting up vegetables, stirring the contents of the great caldrons—she desired to oversee the entire kitchen. After only a year she became one of the under cooks, and after only five years of employment the head cook passed away. Skeets's decision was easily made. There was only one who was worthy of the position: Jane Lightfoot.

And so her goal was achieved. She ran an efficient kitchen, and she did so not for the apparent reason of rising to a greater position. She did it for a much more simple one: As long as she was in charge, she and her son would always have something to eat.

"Jane Lightfoot," a voice whispered in the darkness, catching her off guard. "Mistress Jane!"

"What is it?"

The red of the fire eerily lit up the pretty, soft, young features of Agnes. "'Tis my sister—she needs your help."

"You must tell me what is wrong so I know what to bring."

"She's to have a baby, Mistress Jane."

"And what of the village midwife?"

Agnes bit her lip. "The father abandoned her months ago when he found out Joan was carrying. No one knows but Mother and I. We sought to protect her from ..."

"I see," Jane said through pursed lips, failing to move.

"So you won't help her?" Agnes looked frightened.

"I didn't say that."

"Then hurry, Mistress Jane, please. Already the pains are strong and deep."

There was no one to help me! Jane wanted to cry out, and the scarlet memories of Nicholas's birth into her father's waiting hands threatened to overshadow all else.

"*Please!*" Agnes's voice cut through. "There's no one else."

Jane stood to her feet. "All right, but in exchange you must tell me what happened between you and Nicholas. And you must tell no one what has happened this night."

" 'Tis a fair bargain—one I gladly accept."

Jane grabbed a knapsack, put in a decoction of rue, dill, and flower petals for the pain, a decoction of sage to deliver the afterbirth, and some fresh rags. "Are there enough blankets in the house?"

"Yes, ma'am. Joan may be foolhardy, but she's tried to prepare for the babe as best she can."

Under a star-strewn sky they hurried out of the kitchen and across the bailey. "Where do you live?"

"In the woods not far from Lambeth Palace."

"Why do you work here and not for the archbishop?"

"Mother works at the palace, and Joan used to. I have my reasons for staying away."

"Your own reasons, or reasons you'd like to share?"

"My own."

Jane certainly understood that. *Better silent than a liar like me*, she thought. They walked across the fields, the long meadow grass snagging against their gowns, the dew wetting their hems. "So tell me, Agnes. Why did you break my Nicholas's heart?"

Agnes sighed, pulling a blond curl behind her ear. "I didn't wish to, ma'am, honestly. But...he's changed. He used to be so caring and fun, but now he's only distracted."

"Perhaps he needs you more now. Why forsake him during this time of change?"

"It isn't just that. He's different. Higher. Oh, ma'am, Nicholas has always been seen as a little different than the rest of us. You know that."

"How so?"

"I don't know. It's his bearing. His pride. He's like no other boy at Marchemont. At first that was a great attraction to me, but now . . . it just leaves me feeling inadequate and wanting. Not that Nicholas has ever said anything. But he seeks me out little these days, and when we are together his mind is far from me. I was only seeking to preserve what little dignity I have, ma'am, and not hang on like a leech until he got sick of me on his own and cast me aside."

Jane said nothing as the journey progressed. Agnes grew more uncomfortable, but didn't know what to say. Finally, the field gave way to trees. And about a quarter of a mile in, Jane saw a light through the midnight.

"Is that your hut?"

"Yes."

Without knocking, Jane entered the rudimentary abode, and the relief on the women's faces at her appearance was all the reward she needed for giving up a much-needed good night's sleep. "I'm Jane Lightfoot," she quickly introduced herself. "I've come to help you." She reached into her sack and pulled out the medicines. "Agnes, make yourself useful and bring me a cup of ale. Now, Joan, I'm going to give you a decoction to dull the pain. The ale should help you relax a bit."

The poor girl was frightened, but was doing her best to be brave. She nodded in agreement, but cried out in pain seconds later. Agnes held the cup as Jane poured in a few drops of the rue decoction. After the contraction abated, she thrust the cup forward. "Here, drink every drop. And I promise you that once this night is through and you hold your own baby in your arms, all of this will be forgotten and all the heartaches you've borne because of this will be worth it."

Joan gritted her teeth against the rising contraction and handed the cup back to Jane. "That's easy for you to say."

"It certainly is, dear child."

Jane perspired almost as much as Joan did that night. Her heart and soul had been wrung tightly as she sought to deliver a healthy baby. She saw herself in Joan's face; she saw Nicholas beneath the mound of Joan's tummy. And a connection was made. She would do all she could to help these two so they wouldn't have to make it all on their own, like she did.

By five o'clock the next morning there were four females in the small hut. Joan was proud—so proud of this new little person, born in terrible circumstances, and because of this, that much more precious. "Thank you, ma'am," she said, her words slurred by exhaustion, as Jane gathered her things. "You were right. She was worth it all."

"You're welcome. Now, you take care of that baby. What will you name her?"

Joan looked at her mother and then her sister. "I'm naming her after you. She'll be called Jane. There's not many babies who are named after an angel!"

Jane smiled warmly, opened the door, and faded into the dawn.

❧ NINE ❧

ane paused just a minute by the river to gaze at the sunrise. It refreshed her surprisingly and, once back at the castle, she set to work with a vigor. After all, a new life had come into the world, had even brought a little hope to Agnes and her family. Life could be good. And it usually was if you let it be.

She took just a minute to eat a piece of brown bread that Stephen had taken out of the oven only a few minutes before.

"You look tired, Jane," he said kindly.

"Not more than usual after such a dinner."

"And it all starts up again immediately," Mattie said, walking by with a bag of flour delivered from the mill only an hour before, her steps heavy, her legs bowed. "Have you seen the storehouse next door? Skeets has outdone himself this time."

"I'm sure he has." Jane gathered several scullions and kitchen maids around her who began to pluck the pheasants she was pulling out of the boiling caldron.

"Yes, we'll be keeping the ovens going all day and all night from now on," Stephen informed her. "A quiet night kitchen will be no more until this tournament is ended."

"Are they still planning on a four-day stay?" Mattie asked, having dropped the sack. She knew the answer but was futilely hoping the length of the festivities would be shortened.

81

"Oh yes." Jane began plucking as well, the pile of feathers in the middle of the table growing bigger and bigger, looking more and more like the mattress they would eventually become. The younger servants listened eagerly to the conversation of their elders. "Skeets says they're still planning to have a tournament. Imagine it: The pavilions, the knights, all the ladies in their finery! It should be quite a spectacle." Now that it was getting closer, Jane was finding herself increasingly intrigued with the entire affair.

Mattie nodded, sitting down beside Jane to catch her breath. She was not a small woman. "Aye, I do love the colors of the tournament. I believe it is my favorite part after looking at all of you all day in your grays, greens, and browns!"

They all laughed. But they agreed with her. Bright color was a luxury.

Gregory came in from the clerk's closet where the more expensive supplies were kept, trying to look officious, asking just the right questions in case Skeets should quiz him as to the progress of the kitchen.

"So what is the official count up to now?" Stephen asked Gregory.

Gregory looked into several of the pots Jane had bubbling over the flame. "It seems word has spread throughout the land. More lords have decided to come, and now that a tournament is part of the festivities there are knights aplenty. Skeets is calling for over 1200 now, not counting the servants. How many oxen have been butchered, Jane?"

"Twelve hundred people?" All of those sitting at the table dropped open their mouths.

"Oh dear," Mattie groaned to her feet and waddled slowly to the ovens, "we won't sleep for the next three days!"

"I fear you are right, Mattie," Jane agreed. Then she turned to Gregory to answer his original question for his ears only. "Come to the well with me whilst I draw a bit of water, and I'll give you a rough estimate of the supplies we'll need now that the amount of guests has increased. Then you can pass the information on to Skeets."

Actually, since the confrontation of two weeks previous, Jane and Gregory had been getting along quite well. He left her to do his job as well as hers, and all went smoothly. He was learning quickly, and Jane knew it wouldn't be long until he truly ran the kitchens. "We'll need another 30 oxen, 500 chickens, 150 calves, 400 pigs, not to mention 200 deer, and as many fish as you pull out of the Thames! Any wild birds, pheasants, partridges, woodcocks will come in handy as well. And eggs, Gregory—we'll need at least 5000 more eggs. We'll be making custards in plenitude."

Gregory rubbed the back of his neck. "I'd better go talk to Skeets right away. By the way, Jane, will you be making leche lumbarde?"

"A feast isn't a feast without it! And I'll be sure to save you a bit. But just a bit, mind you!"

"You have my blessings, woman." He hurried away to find Skeets. Jane raced back inside the kitchen to continue the supervision. Multiple wagon loads of foodstuffs were arriving daily, and she needed to find places for the extra supplies. Thank goodness, Skeets had a temporary shed constructed.

"Slow down, Mother!" Nicholas told her an hour later as she flew across the courtyard to find an extra hand to draw water. "You've been preparing for this at length. I'm sure things are quite under control."

"Oh, Nicholas!" Jane breathed heavily, wiping the perspiration out of her eyes with the hem of her apron. "You've no idea! Well, maybe you do, working alongside Skeets and all of that. Which leads me to ask you why you are here roaming the bailey in the middle of the day. Where are you going? Where's Skeets?"

"Skeets has gone to London to the live meat market to get those oxen you needed and all the extra lambs, pigs, and calves he can find. I'm on my way to the stables. We'll never be able to furnish all of this meat from our own reserves."

"Why didn't you accompany him to London?"

"Mother, I'm actually going to learn how to ride today!"

"What? What does that have to do with learning to be a—"

"I don't know. But last night after dinner, Lord Alexander called me and Skeets to him, and he told Skeets that he would be teaching me how to ride today."

"Lord Alexander is teaching you himself?"

"Yes."

"That's strange. Why do you think he's doing that?"

"I don't know the answer to that question, Mother. But I do know if I don't get to the stables right now, I'll be late."

"Well, you must hurry. You certainly don't want the earl to arrive before you do. We'll talk about this later."

"All right." He quickly kissed his mother on the cheek and ran toward the stables. Jane watched him proudly, her arms crossed over her bosom. Skeets had had a new tunic made for him, new hosen, new shoes, and a new cap. He looked so grown-up in the soft, dark-blue garment and hat. Maybe someday she would be lucky enough to talk to the earl himself and ask the reason for his sudden interest in a lowly kitchen boy. But for now, she wouldn't dare risk taking this opportunity away from Nicholas. He seemed so happy, so at home in his new circumstances.

He's outgrowing you, Jane.

She shrugged the thought away and hurried on to finish the task at hand.

❧ ❧ ❧

The earl walked down the steps of the keep as the horses were brought around from the stables. Nicholas waited for him at the bottom. "Well, Nicholas," he called pleasantly, putting on his gloves, "are we ready?"

"Yes, m'lord."

"Good. Do you prefer learning the hard way or the easy way?"

"Well, I don't know if it is as much a matter of preference as it is a matter of which lessons stick more heartily. If it is a case of which way I learn the fastest and most thoroughly, it is definitely the hard way."

Lord Alexander laughed. "I like you, boy. Truly I do. All right. Richard!" he yelled to the stable master. "Bring around Jasper for Nicholas here."

Richard's eyes grew round. "Jasper? Oh, m'lord, I don't mean to be disrespectful, but wouldn't old Daffodil here be a better choice for a beginner?"

"Yes. But not this beginner. I believe that Nicholas is a lad who is capable of doing whatever he sets his mind to doing."

"Thank you, m'lord," Nicholas bowed formally.

"And how are you faring with old Skeets?" Lord Alexander made conversation as they waited for Richard to take Daffodil back and bring Jasper.

"Just fine, sir. He is a most patient teacher."

"Come now, you're not giving yourself much credit. You must be learning these things easily enough. You seem like an overly bright sort to me."

"I'm not sure about that, your lordship. But 'tis true that I do enjoy learning new things."

"Such as learning to read?"

"Most truly, that is wonderful. To be honest, 'tis hard for me to sit still having always been a servant who labors in one form or another. But that doesn't detract from my feelings of gratitude to you, m'lord. I must thank you again for extending to me such an advancement."

The earl waved a hand. "Nonsense. I'm relieved that someone from the castle will fill Skeets's shoes someday. Here comes Richard!"

Holding onto the reins, Richard walked two horses up to the steps. "Here they are." His reservations were clearly evidenced on his face.

Alexander mounted his horse with a ringing laugh. "Don't fret, Richard. I'll answer to his mother personally should anything go wrong."

"Spoken like a true nobleman," Richard muttered under his breath regarding the assurances of the lord of them all.

Just then a shout was heard from the door of the keep. "Uncle! Wait! I should like to accompany you!" It was Percival Hastings, Lord Alexander's nephew and the son of Lady Alison.

He was a sight! Shot through with much gold thread, his fancy tunic with its dagged hemline glittered in the sunlight. His boots were painted in a variety of colors, bright red being predominant, and his hat's embroidery was worked by a highly skillful hand. Most probably Lady Alison's. He was fancy through and through.

His features could be thought of as comely if he wasn't so ridiculous, Nicholas mused as the young man raced down the stone steps. He had a nose that looked as if he pushed it up with his index finger all too often as a child and one day it decided to stay that way. His cheeks were flushed from too much wine. And his teeth seemed to be in overabundance for his small mouth. Lord Alexander had been trying to find a redeeming quality in his nephew for years—after all, this was his heir. But so far he had failed at the task. Percy was possessed of no industry, and certainly no economy. Lord Alexander winced inwardly that the estates he had worked so hard to maintain could fall into the hands of 21-year-old Percy.

"I was just saying to Mother that a good ride would do me well. Richard, get back here!" he called imperiously to the stable master.

The earl held up a hand. "Be that as it may, Percy, you'll have to find other company for sport today."

86

"What?" His pale mouth dropped open.

"M'lord?" Richard asked but was ignored.

"You heard me. I'm teaching Nicholas to ride today. I want as little distraction as possible."

Percy pointed his gloved hand at Nicholas. "Him? The cook's boy? Ha, ha! Oh, uncle, you are quite a funny man!"

"I'm not joking, Percy. Remember your place."

"I do. I'm your heir."

"That may be so, but I'm hardly near death. Ride if you must, but leave us be."

Nicholas used all the control he owned to keep from smiling.

"Well, uncle, if that is what you wish, I have no choice but to comply." His expression was disagreeable. But Lord Alexander had already turned to Nicholas, who was sitting stiffly atop Jasper. "Are you ready?"

"Yes, m'lord." His eyes were round, but his chin was set in determination. He felt no fear, only a sense of elation.

"All right then. Let us be off."

Nicholas fell off Jasper at least four times before they had even ridden through the gate house. Percy laughed loudly from the steps of the keep.

❧ TEN ❧

Skeets's eyes glistened with genial mischief as he pulled an earthenware crock from the back of one of the carts that had followed him in a grand procession from Cheapside, over London Bridge, and down to Marchemont.

"Oysters!" Jane, pulling back the burlap covering, cried with delight. "Oh, Skeets, did his lordship ask for them or—"

"You and I have been working awfully hard lately, Jane."

Jane clapped her hands. "I could kiss you, Skeets! Do you want them now?"

He looked at the sun. "There are still two hours before supper time. I say we should take advantage of the time and have our own little feast."

"Is there enough for Stephen and Mattie? You know that they love these little creatures, especially Mattie."

"Yes. But no one else. Or we'll all be eating only one oyster apiece!"

Jane was excited and had already begun to plan. Every once in a while Skeets surprised her like this, but he hadn't done so in a long time. "I'll tell Stephen to pull out a loaf of braided bread, and I'm sure Mattie has an extra chicken pasty around. I love the combination of chicken and oysters."

He handed her the jar. "As do I. I'll return in half an hour. Will that be ample time?"

LISA SAMSON

"Of course. But send Nicholas down with some cloves and ginger." Jane smiled appreciatively, patting the earthenware fondly, like the back of an old friend. "These little lads cook up quickly enough."

She placed the crock on the table and shouted to Stephen, waving him over. "Get Mattie and a loaf of your best," she whispered. "Skeets brought us some oysters."

Stephen threw up his hands. "Praise be to God! Is this a closed gathering?"

"Absolutely. Unless you only want one oyster apiece!"

Jane hastily hung a small pot on one of the great iron arms and swung it over the fire to begin heating. She then proceeded to pull honey, almonds, and onions from the shelves. Nicholas arrived a minute later with the cloves and ginger that Skeets sent down. Soon the ingredients along with a little water were bubbling away, the sweet flavors intermarrying with the spicy ones. When Skeets's shadow dimmed the doorpost 20 minutes later, Jane dropped the oysters into the rich liquid.

Skeets sat down at the table as one of the scullions set four spoons and four bowls in place. "Ahh, now *this* is what I call eating." He sniffed in the aroma as Jane ladled the precious stew into his bowl. The lesser servants cast hungry eyes upon the table, but knew better than to complain out loud about being excluded.

Stephen laid a thick slab of bread spread with lard beside each bowl, Mattie cut up a large pasty, and the four old friends began to heartily consume the delicacy. Jane, having been at Marchemont 14 years, was the newcomer of the group. Among the four of them almost a century of faithful service had been given to the Earl of Lambeth.

"Delicious as usual, Jane," Skeets said.

"As always," declared Mattie.

"Naturally," nodded Stephen.

Jane lifted the heavily-laden spoon and closed her eyes as she breathed in the aromatic steam through her nose. "I think this dish smells even more heavenly than it tastes."

Stephen chuckled. "Good. I'll let you smell my stew if you let me eat yours!"

"Not for a minute, Stephen, not for one minute."

"A man can always hope," he sighed dramatically, and they continued eating, chatting with the lively, warm camaraderie that a good meal begets. All too soon the savory stew and delicate bread were consumed, and the kitchen again picked up its frantic pace in preparation for supper.

❧ ❧ ❧

Percy sniffed. The set of his jaw and his pouting lips gave evidence of his feelings.

"What is troubling you, my darling angel?" Lady Alison asked, rubbing a protective hand over his lovely, curly brown hair.

"It's Uncle Alexander. He's up to something, I just swear it!"

"Whatever do you mean, lamb?"

"He refused to allow me to accompany him on his ride this morning."

"What?"

"He said he was teaching Nicholas to ride," Percy sniffed again, "and that I would be too much of a distraction."

"Who's Nicholas?"

"The cook's boy."

"Why would my brother be teaching the cook's boy how to ride?"

"Haven't you heard?"

"Heard what?"

"He's got Skeets training him to take over the stewardship someday. He's even being taught by the brothers over at the abbey."

Lady Alison's pale eyes hardened, the crow's-feet deepening at the corners, nevertheless her voice remained sweet and kind. "Worry not, my darling. I will take care of everything as far as Alexander is concerned. I don't wish for you to be at all concerned about anything other than becoming the finest swordsman in England. How else will you protect your future earldom? Pity the man who will come against you someday, Percy. Now, you go down and get Monsieur de Chauliac. It's almost time for your lessons. I want Alexander to know that his actions have not affected you in the least. You're truly becoming a fine swordsman, my darling. Finer than even your uncle. Prove yourself worthy as his heir, my lamb, as I know you are capable of doing."

Percy leaned over and kissed his mother lingeringly on the cheek. "I love you, Mother."

"Of course you do, my pet. Now go look out the window. Are they still in the meadow?"

Percy walked across the solar and looked out the window. "Yes."

"Good. Now do what I've told you, and all will be well."

"If I don't, will Tatty-Nan visit me in the night?" he joked, and his spontaneous smile caused his mother's heart to leap.

The local mothers had been scaring their children for years with tales of the old crone, Tatty-Nan, who lived in the woods.

"Tatty-Nan is the least of your worries, my love."

Percy scuffled out of the room, and Alison sat on her bed, tapping her fingertips on her folded arms. She still saw her son as the frightened little boy who wouldn't let go of his ancient father's corpse. In the eyes of his mother, Percy would always be 11 years old.

Another dinnertime had been executed with perfection, and supper was already cooking. All had eaten, and the scullions were busy scouring the pots. Jane slipped out of the kitchen to sit in the quietness of the chapel. The velvet dimness was soothing and immediately conciliatory. But no sooner did she close her eyes for a moment of peace than was her quiet solitude disrupted. It was Charles, the armorer.

"Your wife again?" Jane raised her eyebrows. It was always his wife.

"My whole family. We're heaving and have hot sweats and cold chills." He held his hat in his sensitive hands, twisting it like a rag, his corded muscles flexing with each nervous movement.

"Did you eat anything foul?"

"Well, my wife held back some of the pork patties you made several days back. We thought they would be fine to eat, as we couldn't make it to dinner today."

Jane stood up in dismay. "Oh, Charles! That was a foolish thing to do! It's summer!"

The great man was duly chastised. "Can you help us, Jane?"

"I'll try. I'm out of the herbs we'll need. Tell them to persevere for another hour and I'll help them."

Jane hurried back to the kitchen and grabbed a clean sack. "What a time to run out of kidneywort," she grumbled. But nevertheless, she would never want Charles's family to bear such sickness without help coming from somewhere. Tromping out of the kitchens, across the bailey, and through the gate house, Jane dashed toward the woods to the patch of kidneywort, under an ancient ash, that had not failed to supply her needs yet. Sure enough, the plants were as before, healthy and ready for her to pluck off their leaves. She hummed a bit as she knelt down and removed the smooth leaves, looking on the little diversion as a chance for solitude. Jane didn't know why she didn't take more walks. At times she felt as close to God in the midst of His creation as she did in Lady Marie's chapel.

The bushes close by began to rustle, and, much to Jane's horror, Tatty-Nan appeared. Jane immediately rose to her feet, examining the woman she had seen only once from afar but had heard of many times.

Tatty-Nan was encased in a dirty white gown, and her yellowed, wavy hair grew almost to the back of her knees. Her last bath was most probably something she couldn't quite remember. She might have been pretty as a young woman, but now her face was a series of deep lines, her features deliberately crabbed and distorted by the industry of time. No one knew how old the tiny crone really was. No one was willing to seek her out to ask. For although she knew herbs, she wasn't seen as wise, but as one who could not cope with the human existence.

Jane disguised her fear behind a forthright mask of derision. "What do you want?"

The voice emanating between the toothless, blackened gums and the white, puckered lips was disconcertingly youthful. "I should ask the same of you, Jane Lightfoot."

"How do you know my name?"

"Tatty-Nan knows more than you would wish her to know."

"What do you mean?"

"Never mind. Past sins are best left to rot within." She laughed a trilling, bell-like titter which ended up in a wheezy gasp. "What are you doing in my woods?"

"I've been here many times before. You should know that. And you should know why I've come."

"Fetching kidneywort again, eh? Something going around the castle? Or did you merely serve a bad meal?"

Jane chose not to answer and continued gathering the needed herb. But Tatty-Nan was not to be put off so easily. "You know you're special, Jane."

Jane said nothing.

"Oh yes, very special. I've seen you here often over the years, but it wasn't until now that the spirits have compelled me to talk to you."

"Spirits?"

"Yes, they're all around us, leading us, guiding our very foot-steps."

"Then it's true what is said about you? You really are a sorceress."

"I prefer to think of myself as a high priestess, but if you must use such common terms, then a sorceress would describe me well."

"Why have your spirits chosen for you to converse with me now, after all this time?"

"You are a strong woman, Jane Lightfoot, but even now I sense that you are searching for more, that change is soon coming. The spirits are generous, Jane. They will help you make the passage."

"Hah! Each day every human stands at a crossroad searching for more, old woman. Your prophecies are nothing more than generalities."

"But do you deny that what I say is true? Do you not stand upon the landscape you call life and search out the distant horizon for relief?"

Jane refused to answer, and Tatty-Nan tittered again. "You have been chosen by the spirits, and to deny them would be most dangerous. You are possessed of the 'gift,' child."

"I don't know what you're talking about!"

"Of course you do! You *heal*, girl! Do you think these leaves and roots and bark work on their own? No! It is the hand that wields them which bears the gift of healing. It is the benevolence of the spirits, the sun, the moon, which give your hands the power over others' bodies."

Jane rose to her feet and put her sack over her shoulder. "You're wrong. They heal because God meant them to! I must go."

An almost tangible presence surrounded the old woman that thrust deep fingers of fear into Jane's heart. An evil breeze.

She prayed that no one bore witness to this unsought meeting in the forest.

But someone did see.

ELEVEN

From the edge of the forest, Lord Alexander de la Marche looked on at the exchange between the two women. Nicholas was too busy trying to keep his reins straight. Neither woman detected the hidden observer only yards away.

The earl took note but said nothing to his future steward. Jane Lightfoot wasn't a cohort of the foolish old woman. She couldn't be. He took a long look at Nicholas, shook the present thoughts out of his head, and they continued on their way.

✥ ✥ ✥

"It was a wonderful day, Mother!"

Nicholas sat down at the table the next day while Jane peeled some turnips for the morning's pottage. He let out a sudden cry as his muscles revolted against the strain.

Jane looked quickly up, and he gave her a sheepish grin. "I never knew riding a horse would make me so sore." He looked boyishly apologetic at such a large reaction to a small infirmity.

"I've heard that the first time you go riding, you pay for it handsomely the next few days."

"It's true. Mother, I feel as if each of my muscles has a mouth which is letting forth a most harrowing scream. I feel so . . . lop-sided!"

"I'll rub in some ointment tonight before you go to bed, son. But was it worth the pain?"

"Oh yes. It was considerably worth it."

Jane had been quiet since the haunting confrontation with Tatty-Nan. The other servants merely thought the business of the preparations for the upcoming tournament days were beginning to exact their toll from Jane's normally exuberant spirit. But Nicholas knew differently, and so he sought to cheer her as only he was capable of doing.

"And not only did Jasper and I get to know each other better, Lord Alexander and I did, too. We got along well with one another."

"You were most respectful?"

"Certainly. You've taught me well, Mother."

"So, naturally, you will be riding with him tomorrow."

"Oh no. Tomorrow I go to the abbey—you know that. Besides, I don't know if these legs could hoist this body up onto a horse's back."

"I forgot."

"But the day after I shall accompany him again. He says I did remarkably well for someone who had never ridden a horse before. I told him that Jasper knew me already, and it was only natural for the horse to attend to my wishes."

"Nicholas, you didn't!"

He looked puzzled. "Well, why shouldn't I have said such?"

"It's impertinence, Nicholas. Plainly, it's just that!"

He laughed. And it was a manlier, easier laugh than it had been two weeks before. "Don't worry, please, Mother. Lord Alexander finds me amusing. And I'd hate to spoil his fun."

Jane's expression was grave; her eyes cautioned him. "Nicholas, remember this well. They're not like you or me. You may be amusing today and despised tomorrow."

His eyes flashed. "That's not true of the earl! I can't believe you would say such a thing, Mother."

"I can say it because it is true. We're servants, my son. Chattel. You're smart enough to realize that. Don't play the jester at the expense of being someday viewed a fool."

"I don't play the fool, Mother—to you, the earl, or anyone else. I know the difference between amusing and pathetic. Apparently you don't know me like you thought you did. If I didn't know better, I'd think you were jealous!"

Jane's temper was roused, and she stood to her feet. "You're not to speak to me like that, Nicholas. Ever! I'm your mother and before God, you will respect me as a good son should!"

Nicholas stood up as well and raised his chin defiantly. "Stop treating me like a child. I'm well over 15 years old, becoming educated, and will be the steward to one of the noblest men in all of England. If you want me to respect you more, maybe you should give me the same courtesy."

Before Jane could stop herself, she reached out, the flat of her hand contacting harshly with his cheek. "Get in the room!"

He glared at her, his brown eyes piercing her through. His chin rose slightly and his fists clenched against the sides of his thighs. In defiance, he hobbled painfully out the door and into the night courtyard.

The few servants that remained in the kitchen quickly returned to their tasks, unsuccessfully trying to pretend they had heard not a word. Jane rose to follow him. But watching the back of her son's head as the darkness covered it, she knew it was not the time to address what had just happened.

She sat back down, staring into the fire, seeking to keep all thought from her tired mind, and feeling completely and utterly alone.

Heavyhearted.

❧ ❧ ❧

The bell of the castle chapel bonged, calling to morning Mass those inhabitants who chose to go. Jane quickly untied her apron, ran into her room, and donned a veil.

99

Naturally, she couldn't understand a word of the Latin spoken by the de la Marches' priest, but she felt closer to God in the small stone church with its arched windows and doorway, its tapestry hanging on the wall behind the altar. She felt as if she knew every stitch of the work, having stared at it for countless hours over the years. But she never tired of the depiction of Jacob's ladder and the lovely angels ascending and descending the golden rungs.

Nicholas was changing. She was losing him.

And it's about time, Jane! At 15 he's a man. He's right—he deserves a little more respect from you. Her self-chiding did little to give her comfort. Nicholas was all she really had—the only person who held her heart in his hands. Always she had been glad that she was not vulnerable to anyone. But now that Nicholas was leaving her behind, as she knew he someday would, that invulnerable armor she had placed so carefully around her was slowly changing from a protective device to one which suffocated, constricted, imprisoned.

Loneliness. It would be sure to follow on the heels of Nicholas's emotional departure. Sadness and utter longing were a few steps behind that.

The future was a bleak tapestry of gray hues, no angels, no prophets, and certainly no fields of gold. Nothing but slick rock and unscalable glass mountains whose peaks shadowed all the lands about them.

Communion was distributed, and Jane partook gratefully. She sought to trust in the mercy of the Almighty. Yes...He would see her through her troubles. He always had. But she wanted more than the ability to just manage. She wanted life, love, and the chance to give herself to another, to be happy. As the host was placed on her tongue, a revelation came to Jane.

She had never asked God for these things.

❧ ❧ ❧

Patrick slid onto a bench at a local inn near his house in Westminster. The Two Bargemen was his regular place when he had no invitations to supper. It was late and he was inwardly agitated, his usually calm self choosing to depart under a great deal of stress. To be sure, it had been a harrowing couple of days. Lady Alison had been especially needy, claiming the preparations for next week's tournament were completely depleting her of the little energy she possessed. The doctor couldn't quite imagine what Lady Alison would have to do with any of that, but he just smiled and continued to press on her the need for fresh air and exercise.

"The tournament promises to be quite a spectacle. The most promising young knights in the kingdom are coming," she said expectantly. "I've decided I will sit in the gallery and watch, if you will promise to sit with me. I don't wish to collapse without you nearby."

Patrick decided to agree to her proposition, intrigued at viewing the joust and the most fascinating of the events: the grand melee. Next week all the guests would begin to arrive. Those unable to fit into the keep would set up their pavilions and tents in the courtyard. Those who could not fit in the bailey would make camp outside Marchemont's walls in the meadow nearby. Personally, he always thought that was the better location, but "the closer to the keep, the higher the honor" seemed to stand true.

How long it had been since he had attended a tournament! He could hear the sounds of crashing armor, men's shouts, the roar of the crowd. His eyes locked onto the blaze of the fire, and he felt almost hypnotized by the memories. France, Spain, Germany. The jousts, while outlawed for quite some time in England, had continued with vigor across the channel.

The innkeeper set down a bowl of rabbit stew in front of him, jerking him from visions of the past.

"How are you this evening, doctor?"

Quickly coming to full realization, Patrick motioned for the man to have a seat. "I've been better, Albert. But I've been much worse, and I've found that unloading my relatively few troubles leaves me with nothing left to brew over, so I'll just keep my trials to myself!"

"Pity the man who can't pity himself, I always say!" Albert laughed and sat down, laying his great forearms on the table in front of him. "I suppose you've heard about the tournament over at Marchemont?"

"Yes, I've been invited to attend the feast as well. Will you be going to watch the jousts?"

"Nah!" He waved the idea away with a large hand. "The missus and I are simple people. But my son is going to go over with a small band of his friends and have a look. Let's hope he don't come back with impossible hopes of being a knight himself!"

"Stranger things have happened." Patrick, who knew that statement firsthand, put his spoon into the stew and took a taste. It certainly wasn't Jane's, but it was doing right by him on this rainy late summer night.

"Best stew you've ever eaten, I'll warrant." Albert's eyes sparkled with pride.

"You've outdone yourself tonight, Albert. That's most certain!"

"Well, doctor, we'll always treat you well here. You can count on that."

"As I well know. Why do you think I'm here so often? It isn't to see your lovely face, Albert!"

Albert laughed a breezy chuckle. "Don't say another word!" He arose from the bench. "I'll get you another cup of ale." The innkeeper hurried away, bellowing to his frazzled wife to "pour up another one for the good doctor." Patrick took another bite of the stew and thought again of Jane. Not that he needed much prompting these days.

Fields of gold.

The words haunted him. She was searching for something. Capable, a good mother, yet the river called to her. Was she asking it to carry her away? A puzzling mixture the woman was. Simple life, complex character. Yes, she was searching, running forward toward a dream. And he was running away from a nightmare.

Perhaps one day they would meet in the middle. He couldn't see how it would be possible. But a spark of hope drifted up from his heart to ignite his reluctant brain. And with a slight smile he realized that already Jane Lightfoot was having a profound effect on his soul. He hadn't felt hope for years, and he had forgotten what an utterly lovely thing it was.

TWELVE

Three days had lapsed since Jane had last watched a
sunset. Her private time was long overdue, and the
castle cook sought the solitude of Marchemont's walls. September had arrived, much to everyone's relief. The tournament
was only days away, and the closer it drew, the more the activity
around the castle intensified.

But now the cool breeze of eventide washed over her tired
limbs, through her sweat-dampened hair, across her closed eyelids. A loving caress of nature, a gift from the God who watched
over her.

Glorious.

Someone sat down next to her, the rays of the evening sun
lighting up his red hair to a burnished copper.

"Doctor MacBeth, what a pleasant surprise." Jane struggled
to sit up straight, but he detained her with a gentle hand. "Please,
keep still. You look so relaxed, it makes me feel better just sitting next to you. I was paying a call to Lady Alison. She is in
rare form again this evening."

They laughed together.

"But," Patrick continued, "I shouldn't complain, for I'd be
half as wealthy as I am now without the monies I receive from
Lady Alison Hastings and her like!"

"You're so wonderful with people, doctor. That much is easy to tell."

"And how do you know that?"

"By my own reaction to you. I tend to be on the distrusting side."

"You?" His eyebrows arched, remembering the butcher.

"I see that not-altogether-attractive attribute is more evident than I wish it to be."

Patrick patted her hand. "You are a woman of caution. Think of it that way. It sounds much nicer."

"Yes . . . it does. A woman of caution. Who would have ever thought I'd turn out to be thus?"

"What do you mean?"

"Just that my parents wanted to change my name to Impetuous by the time I was three!"

"I can hardly imagine it. You seem so steady, Jane, so grounded."

"Such qualities are bred, doctor, not born."

"Bred by what?"

"That's my secret. But just know that it wasn't an easy road that I traveled to get where I am today. Let's talk about something else, though, shall we? I wanted to thank you again, doctor, for inquiring after Nicholas at the abbey. It means a great deal to me that someone has taken an interest in his education there other than the earl."

Patrick decided to let the previous topic fade as Jane wished. "And why is that?"

"Well, chiefly because Alexander de la Marche will not be giving me progress reports!"

She turned back to look over the sun-strewed river. Patrick did the same.

"Fields of gold," he whispered. "What did you mean that day, Jane?"

"You'll find me just another silly woman if I tell you, so I believe I'll keep silent."

106

"I can't believe you've ever been called silly."

"You didn't know me when I was 14!"

"Come, Jane, answer my question."

She sighed, a rare occurrence for her, and remembered how painful it really was to be invulnerable. "All right, Doctor Mac-Beth, I shall. But only because you seem like someone who'll persist in annoying me until you have your way."

"Ahh, methinks the castle cook has a rare wit and an uncommon perception regarding the heart of a man!"

"And you have a verbose side you've hidden well until now."

"Hmm. Well, I guess my little speech about Saint Edward wasn't as impressive as I thought. But I know your game, Jane. You're deliberately trying to get me off the topic at hand. Fields of gold, madam, fields of gold!"

Jane laughed, but sobered as soon as she began to speak.

"I grew up not far from here. My father was a freeman who farmed about 30 acres. Mostly oats and rye, but my mother and I tended a large vegetable garden, and our harvest provided many a fine meal to the lord of the manor," she said proudly. "Our land was bordered at the north by the Thames, and each evening Mother and I would sit on its banks and watch the sun go down. Just Mother and me. She called the sparkling waters a field of gold."

"What did you talk about?"

"Nothing. We usually sat in silence, although not always. She was lost in the past, I suppose . . . and I was lost in the future wondering what fields of gold lay ahead for me."

"So they are a yearning?"

"Yes."

Jane turned and looked at him frankly, having difficulty but knowing that there was no other course just then. His green eyes demanded truth and not merely a little trust.

Patrick reached for her hand. "For what do you yearn, Jane?"

"A life of quietness. A man who loves me. No more loneliness. No more regret." Her heart was thundering madly. The artery in her throat throbbed. She looked away, grabbing hold of her emotions, but not letting go of his hand.

Patrick said nothing. She was relieved that he continued to stare at the river.

"Do you yearn, doctor?"

"I used to."

"But no longer?"

"I haven't the time. I'm afraid all my innocence is gone, Jane. I see only today, and truly believe that that is all there will be."

Only today.

" 'Tis a pity then," she said quietly, then perked up a bit. "But at least you've made me see one thing. Maybe it is better to yearn!"

He smiled. "If one yearns, it means one hopes."

"There's always a reason to hope, Doctor MacBeth."

"I trust you are right, Jane."

They sat in companionable silence, side by side, until the sun plunged completely below the horizon. Both were well aware of the encroaching darkness, but neither wished to move from the ethereal protection of each other's presence. They were lonely. They both knew it. And all Jane wished to do was lay her head on his broad shoulder and feel his warmth beneath her cheek.

⋞⋟ ⋞⋟ ⋞⋟

"Tell me more about this cook's boy."

From her window Lady Alison looked down on the couple, while Percy prattled on behind her about the cuffs of his tunic and the terrible job his tailor had done.

It was getting too dark now to see with any clarity what was going on down there. But Alison knew. Her heart told her.

"As I was saying, he's nothing more than the son of a servant," he sniffed. "Nothing more."

"But why the interest?" Alison asked herself more than her son.

"*I* think it's most peculiar. There's all manner of qualified people in the region who could replace Skeets without all this training. But," two sniffs, "I suppose Uncle has his reasons. Most peculiar."

Alison's eyes remained on the scene below.

"Yes, most peculiar," she echoed. "Hurry down now, Percival, and fetch the doctor again. He's down on the wall not far from the keep, come—" Percy walked to the window, accompanied by more sniffs. "See there? Go now and do as I ask. Hurry! I'm not feeling well at all."

"As you wish, Mother."

Lady Alison quickly backed away from the window and ran in place as hard as she could, as fast as possible, working up a sweat and a reddened face. When she heard the voices of Patrick and Percy in the passageway, she laid herself prostrate on the bed, gasping and wet with perspiration.

❧ ❧ ❧

Jane quietly returned to her room, the hand which had rested fleetingly in Patrick's radiating a tingling feeling all the way up her arm. Her face was flushed, her eyes glowed. Inside her chest, her heart broadened and she felt giddy—the girl she had never been when age would have allowed such sweet fancies.

In her mind's eye, she continued to see his unique silhouette against the glowing skies. The flaming hair and the memory of his green eyes beseeching hers thrilled her. And his voice. The lilting accent, the sincere tones. It washed over her, cleansing her with its caring.

She loved him.

It was that plain. That simple.

Automatically, Jane chided herself. She hardly knew him. And he was an esteemed physician. Surely, if he exhibited any amount of interest, there could only be one outcome.

And that simply wasn't an option.

She would rather continue life on her own than as any man's mistress, even if that man were King Henry himself! Besides, Patrick still exhibited an aura of mystery. As willing to open wide his soul as she was to expose her own secrets. That aspect of his eyes which reflects the soul was covered by a gossamer veil, revealing enough to see Patrick but not enough to see what had made him the man she was coming to know.

"Mother?" Nicholas's voice filtered through the gloom.

"Tiring day?" She began to remove her overgown.

"Yes. Mother, I'm sorry I walked out on you. I've been trying to think of a way to apologize for three days now, in a way that might save my pride. But there is no way of getting around it. I was wrong to defy you and cause you pain. And yet, I'm struggling, Mother. There's so much responsibility now."

Jane sat down on the edge of the bed next to him. "We just need to learn where we fit now, don't we, Nicholas?"

He nodded. "Mother, I'm frightened. What if you're right? What if all of this is nothing more than the passing fancy of a nobleman? 'Tis true that someone better could come along and the earl will point his finger at me and say, 'Back to the kitchens with you, lad.'"

Jane leaned over and put her arms around her son. She felt rebuked, for in her anger at his insolence she had allowed herself to cause doubts in her son's mind. How hard she had worked to make Nicholas believe he could conquer England if he would so choose! And how quickly she placed a stone of doubt on the careful construction of his spirit.

"There's no need to be frightened, Nicholas. God will care for you. You are one of His sheep. I wish I bore more assurance in regard to our employer, but who knows which way the winds of whim will blow around men such as he from one day to the next?"

"You're right. That bears little comfort to my soul."

"Perhaps not. But if you work hard at your studies and become indispensable to Skeets, learning his job most thoroughly, chances are great that you will be retained in the honorable position you have received. What I was trying to tell you before, son, is this: You will not gain his lordship's continued favor by humor and smart remarks. Respect, hard work, and responsible behavior will win the day."

Nicholas smiled in the dim light and hugged her closer to himself. "You are a wise woman, Mother."

"No, dear Nicholas, I'm not. I learned my lessons the hard way. But you can do better than that."

She arose from the bed and blew out the lamp.

⋙ ⋙ ⋙

At that precise moment, Lady Alison Hastings stormed into her brother's solar.

❧ THIRTEEN ❧

"What do you think you're doing, Alexander?" The older sister, eyes narrowed into malicious slivers, crossed the room quickly for someone supposedly ill. The earl's writing table shivered under the single forceful pounding of her fist.

He merely looked amused. "Writing a letter."

"Don't be inane!" she sneered. "You know perfectly well what I am talking about!"

Alexander de la Marche was completely accustomed to his sister's regular tirades. They should be cause for consternation, but he chose to not let them worry him. She was his older sister, after all, the mother of his heir, and to be quite honest, he pitied her. Years ago her eldest son, upon assuming the title of Lord Hastings, had proceeded to banish Alison and Percy from the castle and the surrounding lands. Besides, her diatribes were usually about such incidentals that he chose to let her have her way most of the time.

"Truly, sister, I'm not sure what transgression has been charged to my already-lengthy account this week, so you might do us both a favor and speak plainly on the matter." He set down his pen and turned toward her in his chair. "Why don't you have a seat on my bed?" His mouth shook just barely, trying not to grin. "I heard the good doctor had to pay not one, but two calls tonight."

"All right." She spit the words out and sat down, her brother's soft words calming her a bit. "Now, what's all this about the cook's boy?"

"Nicholas?"

"Yes, Nicholas, the cook's boy—who else would I be talking about?"

He shrugged, baiting her. "Well, Alison, I employ many cooks at Marchemont who've given their spouses sons."

"Answer me, you impudent witling! *Percival* is your heir, and you've never showed him such interest! We've lived here with you for ten years, and you've done nothing to help him grow into a man or to prepare him for his future role. I will not allow him to be ignored by you any longer, Alexander, do you hear me? This silly, bewildering diversion you've begun with the cook's boy must stop!"

Alexander stood to his feet, trying desperately to hold his anger in check. Maybe a warning was in order here. "Alison, Mother taught us many things, one of which is the old adage to not bite the hand that feeds you. You'd do well to remember that."

"Don't preach to me, little brother. I didn't waste precious strength to be subjected to old, ridiculous axioms."

"You want to know the answer to your question, Alison?"

"I wouldn't have asked it if I didn't!"

"Hear me well, then. I will give you the answer if and when I choose and not before. Remember to whom you're talking. I've suffered you so long because you've made yourself such a pitiful creature with your false illnesses and that prattling, simpering son of yours always hanging onto your skirts!"

"I will not hear you talk about Per—"

"I'm not finished. My reasons for educating 'the cook's boy' as you so magnanimously call him and raising him to a higher station are mine alone. I certainly don't owe you or that effeminate son of yours an explanation. Now leave me before my anger leads me to do something drastic." He turned back to his writing, then stood to his feet. "On second thought, I'll leave. After you've infested the room, Alison, I feel in desperate need of fresh air. You'd best be gone and sequestered back up in your room by the time I return."

The earl strode past his older sister, leaving her standing alone in the center of his room. Mouth wide open in shock and disbelief, it was one of the few times Alison Hastings failed to voice her thoughts.

Down the steps of the keep Lord Alexander hurried out into the bailey and up to the gate house. Geoffrey stood to his feet with a salute. "M'lord."

"Open the gate!"

"Yes, sir."

"Andrew!" Geoffrey called to the other guard on duty, a man who had just arrived from out on the manor two days before. "Raise the portcullis!"

The two men turned the giant crank, and the large iron grill slowly raised to an open position. They ran to the drawbridge mechanism and did the same, watching the end of the great planked bridge descend to its resting place on the other side of the moat.

Soon the earl was walking by the moonlit banks of the Thames, remembering his younger days, his indiscretions. Alexander sat transfixed for an hour, the moon rising to its eleven o'clock position. He wasn't a man who needed days to come to a conclusion about anything. His mind was a fearsome thing. Sharp. Grasping easily the information fed to it by his keen, voracious senses.

Percy mustn't assume his title.

Ever.

There was no way around it. He had to do something, and there was only one course of action he would take.

Mind made up, he went back into the castle and summoned Skeets to his solar.

Skeets's clothes were undoubtedly thrown on with haste. He had decided not to work Nicholas until the wee hours of the morning, for he needed the rest himself. "But, m'lord, I'm sure the lad sleeps now. To your instructions I work Nicholas to the point where most fellows his age would be fainting with exhaustion."

"How does he perform under such stress?"

"His eyes don't even water," Skeets said proudly.

"Brother Boniface tells me he is excelling at his studies. 'Tis true it took him a couple of weeks to get used to such learning, but the monk swears that Nicholas has the makings of a re-markable intelligence."

"Naturally, your grace."

The earl looked up sharply. "You know why I'm doing this . . . really know . . . don't you?"

Skeets nodded firmly. "I've been here at Marchemont since before you were born, m'lord. There isn't much that I miss or don't remember."

Lord Alexander puffed a sigh of relief. "You'll keep silent."

"Of course."

"You knew it when you hired her, didn't you?" The earl smiled and clapped his hand upon the older man's back. "You've always served me well."

"And you've always been kind, a solid lord. But I believe that you should soon reveal to Nicholas the reason he has been elevated so quickly. He doubts your intentions."

"He does? Why?"

" 'Tis something Jane told him about the whims of nobility."

Lord Alexander laughed out loud. "She's absolutely right. But Nicholas has no need to fear where that is concerned. Just don't tell him that. I want to see how much the lad can take. Make him work doubly hard tomorrow."

"That won't be difficult with the tournament only four days away. Do you still want me to bring him to you now, sir?"

"No, no. Let the lad sleep. I've much pondering to do. Besides, he's due another riding lesson tomorrow."

"Shall I have Richard take him?"

"No. I'll do the honors myself."

"Yes, sir." The steward turned to go.

"And Skeets! Write another letter to my nephew in Hastings and tell him that I think he really should make amends with his mother."

"Yes, sir. With pleasure."

❧ ❧ ❧

It was a sober Nicholas who met Lord Alexander by the steps of the keep the next morning.

"Did you sleep well last night, Nicholas?" he asked, laying a hand on the young man's shoulder.

"Yes, m'lord."

"And your mother as well?"

"Uh, yes, of course, sir."

"Good. Here come the horses. Are you ready for more of a challenge today?"

Challenge. It was Nicholas's favorite word. His eyes lit up, his mother's warnings forgotten, and he replied with bravado, "I'm always up for a challenge, sir."

Lord Alexander smiled appreciatively. "That's the kind of talk I like to hear from you, lad."

"Sir?"

"It shows me you will indeed be able to accept the challenges of your future position."

"Thank you, m'lord."

They mounted the horses. Nicholas again riding Jasper as they made their way slowly through the bailey, over the drawbridge, and out into the meadow. Nicholas had been riding for

almost two weeks and was already feeling quite comfortable galloping along, but he had not before attained the speed at which
they were traveling now. So he bit down, firmed up his jaw, and
with a great deal of determination caught up to the earl.

As soon as Nicholas made it alongside the thundering Bedivere, Lord Alexander slowed his horse to a canter, and then
to a walk. Nicholas did the same.

"Good work, son," the earl complimented him. "I knew you
could do it."

"After that pretty speech I gave back in the courtyard, I
knew I *had* to do it or forever play the fool!"

Lord Alexander laughed. "Let's talk for a bit, shall we? What
do you know about me?"

"Not anything other than the usual, m'lord."

"Hmm. It is one of the crosses that a nobleman must bear.
Never really being known but by a few people, yet coming in
daily contact with many."

"There are crosses found no matter what station a man finds
himself, wouldn't you agree, m'lord?"

"How so?"

"While you worry about stature at court, the workings of a
nation, a serf worries about firewood and food—things you take
for granted. And that serf takes for granted that there will be
peace from foreign marauders—the peace that men like you ensure for all of us."

"Very astute. It is true, our own difficulties seem larger than
everyone else's."

"Yes, m'lord."

"Lady Marie and I always wished for children. It's been quite
a cross all of these years. But now, I suppose it has ceased to
matter. Marie's well into her forties."

"At least you have Percy to assume your title." Nicholas
knew exactly what he was doing.

And the earl saw through it immediately with a derisive
laugh. "Having that nincompoop follow in my footsteps and

destroy everything I've built over the course of my life is something I'd rather not contemplate!"

"It must be uncommonly difficult, your lordship."

"How long have you lived at Marchemont?"

"Almost all of my life. It was just after my first birthday that we moved here."

"And where were you before that?"

"Mother says we lived about four miles away, down the Thames."

"I see. Do you love Marchemont?"

"She's all I know."

"Aside from that."

"Aye, I love her. I know almost every inch of her."

The earl smiled appreciatively. "Do you now?"

"Yes, m'lord. The passages."

"Secret and not-so-secret?" the earl laughed.

"Everything."

"Have you ever seen my solar, Nicholas?"

Nicholas shrugged. "Maybe I have. But it would have only been during one of your absences, m'lord. I'm a curious sort, but I'm not nosy."

"Is there a difference?"

"Certainly. Curiosity is a broader disease. You know, wanting to find out how the portcullis is raised, why the king likes France so much, who the first Roman was to step foot on Britannia. Nosiness concentrates on the small details of individuals' lives."

"That is true. So you know Marchemont well. But I'm sure there are a few places I could show you that you've never found."

Nicholas nodded eagerly. "I hope so. Did your father show you all the secret places?"

"Yes. He built Marchemont. He was a difficult man, and it wasn't easy to be his son. But he instilled a love for this place deep inside me. That is why you cannot fail me, Nicholas. I've chosen you above all others to protect Marchemont. To guard her."

"I will, m'lord," Nicholas said assuredly.

"How can I be so certain?"

"You're training me. I see now why it was so important you mold someone yourself, for after you are gone. I won't fail you or betray the trust you've placed in me."

Lord Alexander looked at the serious lad next to him and reined his horse to a stop. "Thank you, Nicholas. You've no idea what it means to me to hear you say that."

◈ FOURTEEN ◈

Construction around the tournament field, known as the lists, had begun two weeks previous. And there was a grand, conscientious din as carpenters pounded their hammers quickly and accurately, erecting the galleries which would flank both sides of the lists. A higher dais would seat the earl, the soon-to-return countess, and the more illustrious dignitaries who would attend the festivities, including King Henry. More stands were steadily rising as well for additional guests. And naturally, the castle walls would serve as a spectating post for many others.

Of an early morn Alexander de la Marche surveyed the activity with Nicholas from atop the walls. Two darkened forms against a pink sky, their tunics fluttered about their knees, and the same breeze ruffled their brown hair. They were precisely the same height.

Nicholas, still completely in awe at the entire tournament concept, spoke. "Quite a stir has run through London, sir. This tournament is the talk of everyone."

"'Tis true. Only recently has the joust been resurrected. It was outlawed for years. But soon after Henry took control of his throne, things began to go back to the old ways." Alexander remembered a recent event. "There was a tournament held in

121

Northampton last year, but those who wished to participate feared excommunication from the church."

"What happened?"

Alexander, who was loyal to Henry, spoke in glowing terms. "The king sought an ecclesiastical license from the pope. It insured the participants would not be excommunicated. In fact, he was so fond of the idea of the joust being allowed again that he sent all of his household knights letters which ordered them to attend."

"Then it must have been a successful gathering."

"Yes, it was."

"Were you there, m'lord?"

"Naturally."

"And did you participate in the joust?"

"I certainly did."

"Did you win?"

Alexander laughed. "No. Although I held my own for quite a while. My greatest power lies above my neck, boy, not necessarily below it."

"Mother told me that you were a man of remarkable intelligence."

His eyebrows raised. "She did? How could she surmise that from way down in the kitchens?"

"She says you are kind. And in her eyes, a kind lord is an intelligent one. After all, your serfs have never revolted on you, and for years you've helped to keep the peace of England intact with all of your foreign missions."

"Wise woman, your mother," Alexander joked.

"Yes, sir," Nicholas nodded soberly, his words not in jest, "she truly is."

"Walk with me around the walls a bit before you get on to the abbey. Help me to survey my little kingdom, Nicholas. And tell me of Jane Lightfoot."

❧ ❧ ❧

Jane wiped the sweat from her eyes with the back of her forearm, angry that this September seemed as hot as August had been. She had been looking forward greatly to the respite. But for now, she had her own little kingdom to survey. It was a mammoth undertaking to feed such a large group, and Jane walked briskly through the gate house to the meadow which lay on the opposite side of the castle from the jousting field.

Several great pits were being dug to cook the large quantity of meats that was necessary for the feasting.

"How is the project faring?" she asked the man in charge of the project—a burly, brutish type with a black beard, a bald head, and no sense of humor whatsoever. A man named Joseph.

"Fine. Why are you here?"

"To check up on *you*, Joseph," she joked, purely for her own benefit. "Actually, I came to find out when the first pit will be done. We need to get started with some of the beef."

"I said we'd be finished by sundown, and nothing's changed. I don't add on extra time to safeguard a project, Jane. I simply work my men harder to make sure my word is good."

I'll bet you do, Jane thought. "Fine. At sundown I'll have the fires started."

"Good day then."

"Same to you," she turned around, "Joe." The last word was spoken under her breath, for Joseph was the type who hated nicknames. "No fun at all," Jane muttered. "He's just no fun at all."

On her way back into the kitchens, she was detained by Skeets, who laid his hand upon her arm with a well-recognized sigh.

"Oh no, Skeets, what is it this time?"

"Lampreys."

Jane's face took on a pained expression. "Again? But the tournament begins in three days."

123

"Yes. But he wants the good ones, Jane. I suppose it's simply up to you. You said yourself that no one else can pick them like you can!"

"Well, I lied! Oh, Skeets, I don't have the *time* to go into London!"

"You'll simply have to find time, Jane."

"And m'lord wants them for his supper tonight, doesn't he? Of course he does."

"You've surmised correctly."

"What time is it?"

"It's a little after nine o'clock."

With a sigh, Jane reached behind her back and began to untie her apron. "All right. I see I've little choice. I'd better tell Gregory what needs to be done."

Skeets's eyebrows raised, and Jane hurriedly said, "Not that he doesn't know already, it's simply that—"

The steward held up a hand. "No need to explain, Jane. I'm aware of the work you do."

"Thank you, Skeets. And Gregory *is* learning. With this tournament he's being sorely tried. I'd better hurry. Is there a barge available, or do I have to walk up to London Bridge?"

He handed her a small purse of coin. "There's a barge."

"Thank goodness."

Jane rushed into her room, put on her second-best gown, washed her face, and tidied her hair. Running out of the kitchen, she fetched a large basket and swung it on her arm. Gregory accompanied her to the barge, listening intently to her instructions. He assured her dinner would be on the table at eleven o'clock as usual, and that she could rest easy, enjoy the respite.

Once she was on the water, the breeze began to cool her off, and she realized that Gregory was right—the sudden errand was truly a respite, a sweet little gift from God. It was quite nice to be removed from the activity. The absence of the bustling hive she worked in was rather soothing. One could only take so much buzzing before she became ready to sting the first person who crossed her unnecessarily. And since she had no choice but to obey her master's orders, she felt no guilt whatsoever about her sudden enjoyment of her errand. It almost felt like a holiday.

Alighting from the barge at St. Andrew's Hill, Jane covered the quarter-mile distance to Cheapside. She hurried to the fishmonger's stall.

"Well, Mistress Jane!" he hailed her. "What brings ye in so late in the day? Why, the sun has already risen!"

She laughed with the scrawny blond man who had probably been born with the smell of carp and oysters on his hands. "Tell me you have some choice lampreys just waiting for me, Ben."

The quick shake of his head from side to side brought a cry of distress from between her lips. "Don't play with me, Ben. You *must* have them!"

"Truly, mistress, I don't. But my son may be bringing some in around noon. Can you wait that long?"

Jane was in a quandary. There was so much work to be done back at Marchemont. But the truth was, returning with no lampreys would be worse than letting Gregory do his job for one morning. "I suppose I'll have to. I'll be back at noon. Promise me you'll save them for me, Ben, that I'll have first pick."

"For you, Jane? Anything. If he has any, that is."

"Let us pray he does, or I may be pleading with you for a job come tomorrow!"

"Aw, ma'am, you're much too fancy for the likes of us market folk!"

"Too fancy, eh? That's the first time anyone's ever called me that, bless you greatly!"

Jane left the market, more concerned about the time ahead of her than her employment. *What am I going to do for two hours?* And then she remembered that Nicholas was at the abbey today. She would hurry down to Westminster. Chances were she wouldn't get to see her son, but a time of prayer in the quiet coolness of the old church would be more refreshing than anything she could dream of just then.

Back onto the barge and back down the river Jane went, feeling the same emotion she always did as the abbey came into view at the bend in the river. Solemnity. Awe. And a surprising joy always hailed her heart when her eyes rested upon the revered building.

The dim recesses received her in solemn welcome, as she knew they would, and she thought of all the labor that had gone into the building of such a place. Even in its shabby, year-worn condition, it was easy to imagine the glory the building once possessed. She pictured the strong hands of masons, their biceps bulging as they hefted stone and carved with chisel and hammer. And yet, she knew well there had been one mason in charge of the project, a royal stonemason. The castle cook wondered who that illustrious man was, what he had been like, what he would have thought had he been able to see his church, his masterpiece, built in only a 15-year span, so neglected, in such utter disrepair.

So sad.

Time was a merciless thing, it seemed. Decaying even the very rock of the earth. Destructive. Causing all objects to wax quickly and wane slowly by its very presence. Yes—the waxing part of the process could be very good, but the waning was inevitable, always peeping furtively round the corner, eager and sly, awaiting its moment to step in and take right over.

And Jane, still feeling that her life had not yet taken that certain turn, couldn't help but think that maybe, unbeknownst to her, it had indeed rounded the corner—that halfway mark of years, that crest of the wave.

Utilizing a side aisle, she walked to the front of the nave, past the choir and the transepts to one of the small chapels that surrounded the apse. She crossed herself and knelt, not knowing the words to say, but feeling the presence of God about her, and having a simple, yet complete faith that He knew her heart.

The crucifix above her was a hideous vision of pain, and she couldn't imagine subjecting herself to such agony for anyone other than Nicholas. But she knew that Christ loved her as much—more really—than she loved her son. Hence, His willingness to die. It was all rather astounding. And she could not tear her eyes away from the broken form of the Son of God which hung above her.

At length, the sound of whispers brushed softly against her eardrums. When Patrick MacBeth entered her scope of vision, Jane stood quickly to her feet, feeling somehow caught, not used to her exposed soul being seen by anyone but God. A woman walked close beside him, and they were intently engaged in conversation. But he failed to see Jane and continued on around to the other side of the apse, his attention utterly captured by the beauty of the woman on his arm. Her gown was exquisite, her face refined, her voice soft and low.

Jane felt angry.

Had he deceived her? Talking till the sun set over the land, opening their hearts—hadn't it meant the same to him as it had to her? Did he think of her at all moments of the day as she thought of him? Of course not! Look at the beauty—the elegant, lovely beauty with him now. She couldn't hope to compete with that.

Soon the anger was directed only at herself. Why had she thought for even a moment that a man like him would truly be attracted to a simple cook? He was a physician to some of England's most powerful men, well-esteemed, and intelligent. One of the few physicians who actually held a university degree in a time when practically anyone who felt like it could try their hand at doctoring.

You're a servant, Jane. A menial woman who toils each day merely to survive. You're nothing like his patients. You're nothing like any woman he knows. The woman he had been escorting would make any woman jealous. And the way she walked beside him was graceful, yes, but there was a familiarity to her steps as they meshed with his, an easy rhythm, a swaying harmony.

Is he married?

The thought horrified Jane.

The peace of the church disappeared, and Jane exited the chapel. Walking back down the ambulatory, she saw Patrick and the woman across the nave, closer to the door. All too aware she became of her plain brown braid, her utilitarian hands, her dusty shoes, and her practical, servile garments. Her head she raised higher, her chin thrust forward defensively, while inwardly her soul was slumped forward and slithering in disgrace out the great doorway. Unworthy. Unworthy. Unworthy.

Wait.

She had as much to lay claim to as anyone else. She realized this, and the thought raced through her almost explosively. She'd raised a son on her own, had risen in the ranks of the kitchen servants of one of the greatest earls in the country, had survived by her own labor and wiles. Those were not matters to be ashamed of! This woman... this... fairy princess... probably had no idea what it was like to suffer, to take responsibility for her own life.

There.

I may not be fine and dainty, but I am more woman than that type of person will ever be!

Patrick saw her as she exited and called her name. She turned back around and crossed her arms in front of her. "You should have told me you were married, good sir!"

And she walked down the path feeling quite good about herself and sick at the remembrance that she had fallen in love with this man.

hy are we stopping back at Westminster?" Jane asked the bargeman a little while later, a crock of lampreys (much to her supreme relief) now safely tucked in her basket.

"While you were in the abbey the doctor came by with a lady. He told me to pick him up on our way back. Lady Alison sent for him to see her this afternoon."

Jane sighed. It figured. Times like this when she stepped out on a limb of impudence, it always broke and sent her falling to the ground. She couldn't even insult someone who deserves it without having to answer for it soon after.

Why do I ever try such things? she goaded herself. *I never get away with it like others do.*

And there he stood, waiting at the top of the stone steps that led to the landing. Jane rolled her eyes in consternation. He saw that, too. She rolled her eyes again, at herself this time.

He sat down next to her with a laugh, and the bargeman pushed off the stone wall with his pole.

"Did you enjoy your time at the abbey?" he asked pleasantly.

"Apparently not as well as you did."

"I don't know, Jane. Your little drama at the end caused me to answer many questions."

"You deserved it, then."

"Perhaps I did. Aren't you going to even ask who she was?"

"It's none of my business whom you choose to keep company with. I just wish you had told me earlier about her, doctor, before I offered you the hand of friendship."

He rubbed his great chin. "Hmm. Friendship. Is that what we are, Jane? Friends?"

"I don't know. I thought so. But come to think of it, I really know nothing about you, Doctor MacBeth. So perhaps we aren't friends at all. Especially if you have a wife!"

"What do you want to know about me?"

"Pardon me?"

"I think you're absolutely right. You know practically nothing about me. So ask me anything, and I'll answer you as honestly as I remember."

"You have to remember to be honest?"

"No, Mistress Pedant, I was thinking more along the lines of you asking me to describe my early childhood or something like that." He motioned slowly with his hand, the circles just slightly quicker than the lap of the river against the barge. "Go on . . . ask. And just to get it out in the open, I'm *not* nor ever have been married."

"Well, that's some small relief. All right." Jane rose to the challenge. "Let me think. You were obviously born in Ireland. What part?"

"Dublin."

"And you've been in London for—"

"Fifteen years."

"I see. Where were you before that?"

He blinked. "Paris. 'Tis where I studied medicine."

Her eyebrows raised. She was impressed, but she would never let him see that. "And your parents, are they still in Dublin?"

"No. They are both dead. My father was a physician. Scottish. His family has produced fine physicians for many years."

"That's what they all say, doctor."

Patrick laughed.

Jane continued. "And your mother, was she Irish?"

"Where do you think I get my charm?"

"That you have such an attribute at all is highly debatable. Any brothers and sisters?"

"One sister. Two brothers. One is a priest in Belfast, and the other is a man of law in Edinburgh."

"My, my. You MacBeth lads are scattered all about, aren't you? Your mother would have certainly missed you."

"Spoken like a true mother. I try and get back to Ireland every now and again, though, to visit her grave."

"Still, 'tis not much time spent grieving the one who nursed you."

He looked at her, mouth open with mild incredulity. "I've always had a theory, and you are proving it to be true."

"What is that?"

"That when a baby issues forth from a woman, she automatically receives a highly developed ability to effectively distribute guilt."

"People who have done nothing wrong have no cause for guilt no matter who tries to place it on their shoulders."

"What do you know of guilt?" he asked suddenly, his tone harsh for him.

Jane winced. It had been a dangerous topic to get on. She should have seen that when it showed its face in the conversation. "This isn't *your* interrogation, it's mine, thank you, sir." She lifted her chin and looked down her nose imperiously.

His mood immediately cleared. "Oh, Jane, you can be such fun! All right, it is as you say. Continue, please."

"You mentioned a sister. Where does she live?"

"Here in London."

Jane was mildly surprised, though she didn't know why. And then she suddenly became embarrassed. "The lady in the abbey, she was your—"

"—my sister," he interrupted.

"I'm sorry, Patrick. Forgive me for speaking so hastily."

"There's nothing to forgive. The fact that you let loose the frustrations of your heart means a great deal to me. You see, Kathleen has been going through a terrible time. Her husband passed away only two months ago."

Jane remembered all her hasty judgments of the woman merely because she was beautiful. "Oh, Doctor MacBeth, I'm so sorry. What happened to her husband?"

"He was a wool merchant, taking a shipload of wool from Dover to Calaise. When he set sail the day was fine, but you know how fast storms can arise over the Channel. The boat went down, and all the crew with it."

"How terrible! The poor woman. Did they have any children?"

"Five."

Jane gasped. "What is she going to do?"

"She's moved in with me for the present. I think she wants to eventually go back to Dublin. Perhaps next spring."

"A woman should have her mother with her to help her through tragedy."

"Well, that's something you understand, Jane. I assume you are a widow and have had to raise Nicholas yourself."

Jane choked down the guilt at the forthcoming lies. "You make a sound assumption. 'Tis not easy to raise one child alone, much less five. And at least I have always had other things to keep my mind occupied."

"Such as?"

Jane crossed her arms over her chest. "Is it your turn to ask questions now?"

"It certainly is."

"I don't take kindly to too many questions. So just limit them from the time I came to Marchemont forward."

"All right. So . . . my previous question, then. What is it that keeps you occupied?"

132

"My work, of course, and with this tournament coming up so quickly I've barely had enough time to sleep!"

"But that isn't all that keeps you busy?"

"No. While the upper classes of Marchemont receive care from yourself, I tend to the servants and many of the villagers and peasants round about."

"So you are a healer?"

"As much as I can be. I use mostly medicines gathered from the forest and the meadows. I also assist with birthings and accidents of one variety or the next. That's the sum of it. No bleedings or leeches on my part."

"Interesting." His tone was a little too patronizing for Jane's liking.

Her brown eyes flashed. "You can dismiss it all you like, Patrick MacBeth, but at least I'm *there* for people like the smithy, and the farmers, and scullery maids. People that illustrious men like yourself wouldn't care to dirty their fine hands on."

"How do you know I don't do my share to help the poor?"

Jane blushed at her impertinence.

"If you must know, I tend to many of the monks at the monastery."

"Yes, *that's* a real gutter there."

"So . . . you despise me for my service to the upper classes?"

"No. I don't despise you at all. I only question your amused tones at someone who seeks to dispel a bit of the misery of the people you don't even know exist. Don't mock what I do until you're willing to find yourself in a filthy, refuse-strewn hut in the middle of the night!" She stomped her foot for emphasis on the planking of the barge.

"How do you know I don't understand their plight or am unaware of their miseries?"

"Hold out your hands."

He did.

"See? I haven't had such nice hands since I was five years old!"

"At least *you* don't have to care for Lady Alison!" he joked, ignoring her high-handedness. Immediately the tone of the conversation was changed.

Jane couldn't help but laugh. "Well, there is that. Are you on your way to see only her, or is the earl your summoner as well?"

"No. Just Lady Alison. Perhaps you're right. It may be true that I pander to the illustrious merely to fatten my purse."

"I never said that."

"No, you didn't. You've just made me think. You know, most of my patients aren't people I spend very much time with on a social basis. Just the earl and the abbot, really. The rest are just like Lady Alison to me, although not all the trouble."

"Well, more's the pity on the rest of your day, then."

"I was too harsh, I suppose. There are some genial men and women I tend to. Just because people are wealthy or important doesn't mean they're not good."

Jane looked deliberately skeptical, then laughed.

"In any case," he continued hopefully, "the day may not be a complete loss. Not if I can work out an invitation to supper. By the way, madam, your rabbit stew was indeed the finest I have tasted. If you have as magic a way with healing as you do with food, then your patients must be well tended to."

It was a huge concession on his part—a singular one made only for her, she realized, and she accepted the compliment with a gracious nod of her head. "Thank you, doctor."

The barge pulled up to the embankment, and Jane let Patrick help her down. Together they trod the path to the castle and through the gate house.

Patrick laid a hand on her arm as she turned to go toward the kitchen. "It was nice having this chance to chat with you, Jane."

"Likewise, doctor. It was most enlightening."

He bowed. "For me as well. You've given me much to ponder. Far more than you could ever realize. Thank you."

"So . . . will you become a physician to the poor and needy?"

He laughed. "Don't rush me, woman!" Suddenly he reached out and touched her face, for just a moment. "You really are the most extraordinary woman I've ever met, Jane."

"I'm a castle cook, doctor, and only that."

She turned away and walked toward the bustling kitchen. A future with Patrick MacBeth seemed absurd even then. But the feeling that had flowered throughout her mind, heart, and body was something she could never have foreseen.

꧁ ꧁ ꧁

Percy Hastings stormed into the wardrobe where Skeets and Nicholas were taking inventory of the spices. His normally pale face was red and blustery. The brown curls which sprung from a low forehead were in disarray, and his blue eyes were rounded in anger. His voice was low and dangerous.

Pushing by the barrels and chests, Percy took no note when he turned over a hogshead of wine. The piercing eyes were focused on one thing only: Nicholas. His hand fell naturally on the hilt of his sword.

"Leave us, Skeets. I will have words with the cook's boy."

❧ SIXTEEN ❧

Skeets hesitated. "But, sir . . ."

"You heard me!" Percy's deep voice ricocheted off the provisions around him. "Get out of here!"

Skeets cast Nicholas an apologetic glance but was forced to obey orders. Nicholas, weary and raccoon-eyed from lack of sleep, squared his shoulders. "That's all right, Skeets. I'll be all right."

Skeets shut the door behind him.

Percy sneered ferociously and then sniffed, gaining his composure with startling ease. "You'll be all right, will you? I'd say you are definitely doing all right . . . for a cook's boy."

Nicholas decided the best way to deal with Percy Hastings's dramatics was to remain silent. The young nobleman appeared to have come looking for a fight, and Nicholas had no wish to honor Alison's brat with his intended desire. Besides, Percy was the finest swordsman at Marchemont, diligently practicing at least three hours each day, fair weather or foul. And his hand had not yet moved away from the hilt of his sword.

"You seem to have been given an honor far above your birth and well beyond your natural inclinations and talents. It makes me wonder just what my uncle has in mind for you. He's always been a man of 'odd' tastes, if you know what I mean."

Nicholas still stayed silent.

"Nothing to say to that? I suppose not, for I've heard the same said of you. You two certainly make a lovely couple!"

Nicholas's eyes grew round, for his mother had taught him that when people falsely accuse, the finger pointed at you should rightly be pointed at themselves. Come to think of it, Nicholas realized he had never seen Percy make any advances whatsoever toward a woman.

Percy crossed the room to stand directly in front of Nicholas. His breath was stale, his hair smelled old and oily, and any traces of his effeminate ways were banished by his anger, his territorial protectiveness. The blue eyes deepened, narrowed, and in them Nicholas saw a radical fearlessness which overshadowed all the fine trappings of Percy's clothing. "Look in my eyes, boy, and remember this well. *I'm* heir to Lord Alexander. If you are wise, you won't forget that. Ever. For although you are being trained by my uncle to take over old Skeets's position, rest most assured that when I am in charge it will be back down to the kitchens with you. If you are that fortunate!"

Percy placed his two hands against Nicholas's chest, and the cook's boy immediately recoiled as the hands moved over his shoulders. The horror Nicholas felt was evidenced by his expression. Percy snarled some semblance of a laugh, removed his hands, then roughly pushed Nicholas over Skeets's writing table.

"Those who will not endure my affections will endure my scorn, Nicholas." The heir to the earldom of Lambeth tittered his laugh, once again playing the fop. But Nicholas had seen enough for a small fear to enter into his brain. Even still, his pride forbade him from letting Percy have the final say.

"It isn't the earl who's perverted, it's you." Nicholas rubbed the back of his head on the spot which had collided with a table leg.

"Jolly, isn't it? But it all comes round to this. I have every reason to be the next earl. And when my uncle dies someday, you'd better pack your things or prepare for the worst."

"Won't your mother be glad to rule Marchemont through you, then?"

Percy drew his sword. "You leave my mother out of this, guttersnipe! She's the only person who is good here in this dismal place."

"Your mother? Good?" Nicholas laughed, but his grin was soon replaced by a grimace of pain. He barely heard Percy's sword slide from its scabbard before his hand darted up to his cheek, which was bleeding profusely from the nick of Percy's nimble blade.

"She prays for my soul, boy. She only."

Percy sheathed his sword, straightened his hair and clothes, then left the room.

Skeets shuffled quickly back into the room and, seeing Nicholas on the floor, he hurried to help him to his feet. "Are you all right, son? What happened to your face?"

"Just a little nick. It's nothing serious."

"The earl shall hear of this!"

"No!" Nicholas cried. "No, Skeets. Let's just leave it at this. Please."

"Why? Lord Percy should answer for his reprehensible behavior."

"And I should be left with at least my dignity. Me running to the earl with the tale will do little to seal any respect I'll need around here in the future."

"Are you sure there's nothing I can do?"

Nicholas brushed off his tunic, straightened his hosen, and retied the lace on his shoe. "Yes. Percy and I will have many more battles in the future, sir. I believe I shall be able to hold my own against him someday."

"Choose your battles carefully, then. Percy really *is* one of the most deadly swordsmen in this part of the country. Don't cross him unnecessarily, for he's killed for the most petty of reasons before."

Nicholas could only guess what *that* entailed. He wanted desperately to ask Skeets about Percy's personal attractions, but couldn't find the nerve or the stomach just then. The hand which had sought to staunch the flow of blood from his face was red and sticky.

"Let's get you down to your mother, lad. She needs to bandage your cheek. It's still bleeding quite heavily."

"I must look a mess."

"Nothing that can't be mended."

Soon they were both in the kitchen, Jane asking altogether too many questions, cursing Lord Percy Hastings beneath her breath as "nothing better than a kitchen rat," and feeling that she was being highly unfair to the kitchen rats. But despite her verbiage, she worked quickly, cleaning the wound and bandaging it.

"I feel ridiculous with this bandage strapped round my head." He touched the clean strip of linen with his fingertips 20 minutes later.

"Just wear it until the morning to keep the dressing in place. You won't have to embarrass yourself after today."

"All right." His voice was surly—truly that of a 15-year-old.

"Cheer up, Nicholas, at least we will be in the wardrobe the rest of the day." Skeets patted his shoulder. "Maybe your mother has a pastry or two we can take back up with us."

"A fine idea, Skeets! The best medicine I know of! I'll send some up in just a little while. Mattie's got some baking right now. I'm sure you'll want them fresh and hot."

So the two got back to work, with a break for the little snack sent up by Jane about two hours before supper.

"I never had a snack sent up to me before," Skeets remarked, his tone jolly as he bit into a fruit pie, the sweet apple juice cascading onto his tongue.

"That's because you're moving up in the world, Skeets," Nicholas joked.

"Well, if this is any indication," he lick the honeyed syrup from the corners of his mouth, "I should have done this *years* ago! Your mother is a good woman, Nicholas. You must always be good to her."

Nicholas looked puzzled. "Why wouldn't I be?"

᪄ ᪄ ᪄

"Come quick, Mistress Jane, please!" Agnes's voice petitioned desperately from the other side of her door. With the tournament only two days away, there was still much activity going on. Jane had come in only minutes before at three in the morning to catch a couple hours of sleep.

Agnes's normally pink skin was ashen.

"What is it, Agnes?"

"It's little Jane, ma'am. Please, can you come?"

"Tell me what's wrong first."

"She just started this awful shaking. Like a devil had got into her. Joan is so frightened, and Mother, too."

"Does the babe have a fever?"

"No."

"Was she still shaking when you left?"

"No. It only lasted a few minutes."

Jane became frightened. She had heard of these seizures but had never had to deal with such before.

There was only one thing she could do at such an hour. Taking Agnes firmly by the shoulders, she looked into the girl's eyes. "Agnes, listen to me. We'll have to hurry. I must get dressed." *The child must have a fever!* she thought hopefully. *If she doesn't, I am at an utter loss.*

Jane quickly threw her gown on over her head. She grabbed her usual basket of herbs and medicines and headed out the door of the kitchen under a full moon. Geoffrey let her out of the stronghold without questioning her destination. He knew she took care of the sick. And she just had that look about her, which forbade questions or even simple conversation.

It was hard to say whether it was fortunate or unfortunate, but baby Jane fell into another seizure upon Jane's arrival. The tiny body quaked, rocking heaves, that seemed too slow, too mature, and reeking of a mortality unfathomable in one so pink and young. Her eyes rolled slightly back in their sockets, and the wee fists curled inwardly as they beat a ghastly, silent rhythm against the air.

Jane stood horrified.

"Can you help her? Please?" Agnes's mother pleaded. Joan was too upset to even speak, but stood there gasping for breath.

The sound of the woman's voice stirred Jane to action. She took the babe from her grandmother.

No fever!

Her mind was filled with panic as she felt the babe's forehead.

No fever!

"Please, Mistress Jane," it was Agnes's voice, "there must be *something* you can do!"

The shaking stopped. The babe lay still, her curved legs curling up to her smooth chest. Jane handed the baby back to the grandmother. There was only one thing to do. "I shall return by morn."

"Where are you going?" Joan was coming back around.

"To find help. This is beyond me."

"What if she starts quaking again?" the grandmother asked.

"Just do whatever it was you were doing before. I'm at an utter loss. I'll be back as quickly as I can."

Jane hurried out of the hut and into the dark night.

"Lord, forgive me," she whispered as she entered the forest a little while later. "I don't know where else to turn."

Deeper into the forest she trod, branches and leaves crackling loudly underneath her feet, the soft leather of her shoes doing little to dull the feel of the stones which protruded through the forest floor. September weather had finally appeared, and the early morning air was chilly. She wished now she had brought her cloak with her. Her haste had brought on a bout of forgetfulness—a condition unusual to Jane Lightfoot. But then this whole evening was turning into a very unusual evening.

She hadn't a clear idea how she would locate Tatty-Nan. The crone usually appeared unwanted, unsought, from what most people said. And indeed, that had been the case with their previous meeting. Still, she couldn't rely on chance to get her to her destination.

But she remembered a rhyme some of the servants' children chanted when they went about their play.

> East of the castle lives a woman old.
> She worships the moon, turns stones into gold.
> Into the woods, a mile you'll walk,
> Under the leaves to a great standing rock.
> Go left, God guide you, faint not if you can
> For in half a mile you'll find Tatty-Nan.

So Jane went north. The forest wasn't a quiet place. Nocturnal animals scurried about with their slick, long, pink tails and round, startled eyes. An owl hooted from a tree somewhere to her left. And the giant moon did little to shed light through the dense foliage. Briars snagged her dress with their sharp fingers, and branches reached low to grab at her hair. But when she thought of the newborn babe, she realized she had little choice but to go on and try to forget the cold and discomfort.

She came upon the standing rock—most probably the only remainder of what might have been a circle of stones raised by ancient druids. She looked left, and yes, there was a path. Jane sighed with relief and set her foot on the beaten earth.

Tatty-Nan might be thought of as a sorceress and foolish in most ways, but it was well-known that when it came to healing, there was no one more knowledgeable for miles around. She was sought by only the foolhardy, the irreligious, or those most desperate.

Jane tripped on a fallen log, regained her balance, and decided to rest for just a minute. She felt as if she had been walking for hours. Surely the rhyme was right. It had been accurate about the standing stone, but she could have sworn she had walked well over half a mile since coming upon the small monolith. Her face was pale and lined with stress.

Normally so competent and in control, Jane felt bewildered, anxious. "What am I going to do?" She placed her elbows on her knees and rested her head in her hands, rubbing her tired eyes.

She kept them closed for a minute, trying hard to concentrate on what to do next. There was no choice—she simply had to go on. When she raised her head, her eyes coming slowly into focus once again, a small figure in white stood before her.

"You've returned. I knew you would. But the spirits tell me 'tis not in homage to them that you seek me."

"I need your help."

"Follow me, then."

Several minutes later a camp fire was visible in the distance. It sat before a hillock from which a structure protruded. An odd structure this was, made of three mammoth stones—two up on their sides, and a flat one laid across the top for a roof. Having lived all her life in this general area, Jane had still never seen anything like this before.

"What kind of home do you have?"

"It's a cairn. A cairn of a great Viking who once lived in these parts ages and ages ago. Some say he was the son of Thor. His remains were spirited from this tomb hours after he was buried."

"Is it this man's spirit that speaks to you?"

The old woman nodded, her long hair swinging back and forth like kelp in a watery current. She smiled a toothless grin. "Yes. His . . . and others. But you do not hear such voices, do you?"

"No, thank the one true God."

Tatty-Nan laughed and coughed at the same time and pointed an accusing finger at Jane. "And yet it is to Tatty-Nan that you come in time of need!"

Jane said nothing. Of course she was ashamed inside, but she didn't want Tatty-Nan to see that. A futile gesture because the woman continued to laugh. "Don't worry, my dear, your priest will hear of your repentance in the morning, I am sure."

But Jane didn't want to admit to this night's activities to anyone, especially a priest. "Can you help me? There's a newborn who is having seizures."

"I know."

Jane wasn't surprised. "Then is there anything you can give me?"

"Of course! I can cure anything, Mistress Jane Lightfoot, anything!" She disappeared into the cairn and returned with a small vial of a syrupy substance. "Have her mother give her some of this when the sun rises and when the moon rises for three days. The babe must be facing east to catch the rays of light as she drinks the potion. That is of the utmost importance."

Jane took the bottle. "What do you want in payment?"

"Nothing, dear child. Just seeing your discomfort and knowing you've sinned against your God is my reward."

Without answering, Jane turned around and hurried to the hut of Agnes and Joan as swiftly as she could. When the sun rose she followed the instructions of Tatty-Nan in detail.

꧁ ꧁ ꧁

Throughout the rest of the day, Jane's eyes kept snapping to the door each time a shadow flickered on the lintel. Agnes didn't come around until the next day. The news was grim.

Baby Jane had stopped breathing the night before.

"I'm sorry," Jane said as she pulled the tearful girl into her arms.

"I suppose her little body just couldn't take the strain. I know, ma'am, you did all you could."

Lying in bed that night, however, Jane realized that Agnes's statement wasn't even close to being true.

"Mother?" Nicholas asked in the dark. "When you come upon a situation that you're not quite sure how to handle, what should you do?"

"That's easy, Nicholas. The first thing to do is pray."

"Is that what *you* do?"

"When I'm smart, it is. When I'm not, I figure things out on my own, and it has never done me any good, Nicholas. Never."

He lay quietly. So did his mother. But her heart was crying out for forgiveness yet again, as her mind wondered how she could have forgotten God so quickly in the face of adversity. And she was seeking to piece back together the trusting faith which had been shattered only last night.

⊶ SEVENTEEN ⊷

Today was the last day before the tournament. The countess would be returning, as well. Skeets was delivering most conscientiously on his promise to the earl. Nicholas had never worked harder.

"Mother?" The darkness was thick as they wakened to begin yet another exhausting day.

"Yes, son."

"Do you feel like talking?"

"I can always spare a few minutes for you, Nicholas. What is it you wish to talk about?"

He roughly pulled on his tunic and his hosen, and began to slip his feet into his shoes. "I'm almost 16 years old, Mother, and I think it's time that I know the truth about my father. Or at least more of the story. I know so little."

Jane's heart jolted, but she responded lightly. "You've always been rather direct, haven't you, Nicholas?"

"I'm serious, Mother, and I truly mean no disrespect. But there's so much you haven't told me. I'm becoming a man. I want to know where I came from. I want to know more about my father. Please, Mother, I want to know every detail."

Remembering the past night's transgression regarding Tatty-Nan, the last thing Jane wanted was to add another sin to her eternal account. Besides, Nicholas deserved to know the truth. It was the final reckoning she had been dreading for years.

She poured water in a basin. "All right, Nicholas. The truth. Your father was not a huntsman."

"Who was he, then?"

"I'm not sure—"

"You're not s—"

"Hear me out. I don't know, but not for the reason you think. It wasn't that I had coupled with more than one man during the time period of your conception. Your father was a stranger." Jane proceeded to tell Nicholas in nonspecific terms what happened on the night he came to be, and the consequences she suffered. "We met, we parted, and you, my darling son, were the result."

"So the stripes on your back are not from your father's anger, but from the sheriff's?"

"Yes. My father would never have whipped me, no matter how angry he had become. I'm sorry I ever told you that lie. Edward Lightfoot would not have been capable of such an action."

"It did seem odd to me."

"Your father was a noble stranger, a traveling lord. He did, however, give me a bracelet to remember him by."

"Do you still have it?"

"Yes. In the chest."

"I'd like to see it."

"I promise I'll show it to you soon. I'm sorry I lied to you all these years." She felt so guilty and hollowly ashamed. "You should be angry with me."

"Would it do any good?"

"It might make you feel better. It might make me feel better."

"I already do feel better, Mother."

"I don't understand, Nicholas."

"You just told me that I am the son of a lord. Don't you think that is just cause for gladness?"

"If you knew who your father was . . . yes."

Nicholas moved closer and kissed her cheek. "I'll find out, Mother. Someday I'll know. But tell me, please, why did you find it necessary to keep the truth hidden from me all these years?"

"For your sake as well as my own. 'Tis not easy to be illegitimate, my son. 'Tis harder when everyone knows it. I wanted to make sure you were old enough to realize this, after you had learned the value of a well-kept secret."

They put their arms around each other and held close. "I may not have always done the right thing, Nicholas, but I've tried to be the best mother I know how to be. I've always loved you."

"I know. You've been both mother and father to me. You love me, and I've always known that you're the only one who really does. And your love has been enough."

"Thank you, my son," Jane whispered into his hair. "Thank you."

❧ ❧ ❧

All the servants were assembled in the courtyard, waiting patiently as the litter carrying Countess Marie de la Marche, hung between two magnificent white horses, entered through the gate house. Returning to the walls of Marchemont was in reality like arriving at a miniature city. Lady Marie's eyes misted over as they took in the numerous outbuildings, particularly the chapel. Much missed. *A just penance*, she thought. It had been built upon her own initiation and charity.

She carefully alighted from the litter near the steps of the keep. Lord Alexander met her down at the bottom, bowing over her extended hand and kissing the backs of the fragile, slim fingers in a single chivalrous gesture. "My lady."

"My lord." The voice was soft, barely audible.

"Your trip was fine?"

"Yes, thank you."

They turned formally and walked up the steps and into the keep. Her prematurely white hair stood out boldly against his wine-colored tunic, so different from his own warm-brown hair. Lady Marie practically floated up the steps. Alexander's feet were planted firmly.

Once they disappeared into its interior, Skeets cleared his throat, and everyone dashed madly back to their duties. Now that September finally felt like September, the overcast sky blocked the sun, and the air was cool and moist. It seemed as if countryside, village, and castle collectively sighed with relief.

Jane was busy cutting up some chickens in the kitchen. All fireplaces were roaring. Over the pit in the middle, two sides of oxen were being roasted, the poor scullions assigned to the task sweating profusely. It was a warm job no matter what time of year.

"Take off your tunics, lads!" Jane called. "I can't bear to look at you much longer."

The two boys gratefully complied, removing their garments quickly lest the meat should burn.

Stephen appeared with a huge lump of dough that required kneading. "Almost ready, Jane?"

"Everything's on schedule. You?"

"Aye. Poor Mattie, I don't think she's slept for two days now."

"She's most conscientious," Jane agreed.

"And how is Nicholas doing at the abbey?"

Jane turned to Stephen. "I'm not sure. I haven't heard for a while. Other than Nicholas's one-word report. When I ask him, he always says the same thing. 'Fine.' That's all."

"Don't I know what you mean! My Jeremy is much the same. You have to pull any information out of him with a crook! Must be the age."

Jane wrinkled her nose with a quick nod. "I think you're right."

Gregory, emerging from the kitchen clerk's large closet, decided to sit with them and enjoy a bit of company. He looked like he had been enjoying a good nap. "The participants are arriving. Some of the untried knights are having a practice day today. They'll be hungry tonight, for certain."

"Oh yes, to be sure!" Jane agreed. "There will be ample amounts of food prepared for tonight's dinner. Did Skeets tell you what the final count was?"

"Final count?" Stephen's eyebrows raised humorously.

"As final as a headcount for a feast ever is," she said wryly.

"There will be 1800, not including servants," Gregory reported.

Jane pulled another bird off the pile of plucked chickens across the table and began to cut off the wings. Her hands worked so quickly they were almost a blur. "So that means we can probably count on another 300 at least who didn't bother to send a message."

The two men nodded. "There are going to be 30 knights competing."

"Really!" Jane's eyes now glowed as most women's did at the thought of a knight in his armor, sporting his colorful silks. "It promises to be quite a tournament, then?"

"Aye. And those men will be plenty hungry after a day of the joust! How are the pits outside running?"

"Fine. We've got so much beef it will be served on the joint, in stews, pottages, and pasties. I don't see how anyone coming will possibly go hungry."

"You do a fine job, Jane," Gregory said admiringly.

"Thank you. My father told me before he died that I should have been born a man."

The men laughed at the statement, and Jane did, too, but she was a bit chagrined, not having meant the statement as a joke at all!

꒐ ꒐ ꒐

The conversation up in the solar of the earl and the countess was stiff and stilted. It had always been thus. Lord Alexander, so far, after 20 years of marriage, had been unable to shear through Marie's hedge of piety. She tried to be dutiful by her husband, kind. But he did not own her heart. And the earl knew he never would.

"How was your stay at the convent?"

"Lovely, thank you." She walked past him to the window and looked down on the bailey and her chapel. "I believe I shall go and pray."

He made his warm voice sound as inviting as he could. "Oh, Marie, come, sit and talk with me. I'm your husband. I would hear more of your journey."

"I must go pray." Her voice held a soft panic, and she left the room.

Now at the window, Alexander de la Marche watched her emerge from the keep a minute later and walk across the bailey with several of her women. He knew she had blamed herself for their childless state. Hence all the chapels and convents built by her charity. She was always thin and sick from the numerous fastings. Otherworldy, ethereal.

Unashamedly sad.

Alexander was considering taking a mistress. Marie's sadness was becoming his own, and he had always prized his jolliness. He felt his own honorable intentions were swallowing him alive, and no matter which way he turned, a part of himself would continue to die. Maybe such quandaries were natural to the aging process. He didn't know.

The earl called one of his personal servants to him. "Bring me Nicholas right away."

"Yes, m'lord," the servant bowed, hurrying to the tournament grounds where Skeets was attending to the final details.

Ten minutes later, Nicholas appeared in the room.

"Did you ask her, lad?"

"Yes. And I believe she told me the truth, m'lord."

"Tell me everything, Nicholas. I need to know it all."

"So you *will* find my father for me?"

"I'll do my best."

❧ ❧ ❧

Jane pulled her woolen shawl tightly about her shoulders. The midnight breeze tugged softly at her loosened tresses. The river beckoned her with its sighing waters, dark and peaceful. Due to the tournament, the portcullis was up and the drawbridge was down. Geoffrey stood up from his seat with hopeful eyes. "Mistress Jane?"

"Good evening, Geoffrey. I was just going to take a walk. I'm overtired."

"Busy day?" He closed his eyes with exasperation. *Of course it was a busy day, you dolt!*

"Yes. Very. Will you be on guard all night?"

" 'Tis the shift I've received of late. Perhaps I'll be able to watch a bit of the tournament tomorrow afternoon. Will you be attending any of the jousts?"

Jane shook her head, the torch light hitting first her left cheek, then her right. "I'll be much too busy."

Geoffrey thought she was the most lovely vision he had ever seen. His heart jumped into his throat. "Jane?"

"Yes, Geoffrey." Her brown eyes looked directly into his, causing his breath to come up short. He forgot what he was going to say, and simply stared at her. She placed a hand on his arm. "That's all right. You can tell me whatever it was on my way back in."

Geoffrey nodded mutely, cursing himself while she walked through the gate house and over the drawbridge.

Jane widely skirted the encampment of the guests, the normally blazing colors of the tents and pavilions now muted in the pale light from the sickle moon. A bit of laughter emanated from two or three camp fires, but most of the visitors were sleeping soundly, resting for the practice jousts which were set to begin at nine o'clock the next morning.

The dark, rolling waters flowed before her, and she sat down on the bank in a copse of trees. Tucking her heels up close to her bottom, she used the skirt of her gown as a blanket to keep the infant autumn chill at bay. In her busy distraction, she hadn't attended to the river like she wanted. The last time she had been with what she thought of as her old friend had been the trip back from Westminster with Patrick MacBeth.

The thought of him sent more shivers running through her, but these were not chilly shivers—they were shivers of subtle heat and intense yearning. Jane almost wished she hadn't come now. It had been easy to forget about the emotions that had bloomed in her heart when she was busy with the preparations. But now, sequestered in the darkness, she saw Patrick's face all too clearly, remembered his soft voice all too fondly.

Are we friends, Jane?

She wanted so much more than that. But it was a futile desire—she knew that right well. Not only were they in different classes, but he seemed to have no compassion for people like herself. Was he a man to whom money and position meant everything? Did he always seek the best of everything? Certainly his clothes were fine, and his shoes, too. It rankled her inside, but not enough to overcome the attraction she felt for him. She did have the advantage going for her that she was the most unusual woman he had ever met. Or so he claimed.

What did he mean by unusual? she wondered.

"Jane Lightfoot, is that you?"

She quickly turned around but could not see the stranger in the darkness.

❧ EIGHTEEN ❧

Who are you?"

"It is Lord de la Marche, Jane."

She began to rise to her feet, the earl quickly offering his aid. "Forgive my presence. I will leave now, m'lord. Surely you don't wish to be disturbed here by the river."

She could see his features now. Comely, unusual. Ruddy and manly. His most keen feature, startlingly light-green, deep-set eyes, were dulled by the darkness. He smiled kindly. "Do not leave. You are the reason I've come."

"Truly?"

"Yes. Why don't you sit back down? I'll join you."

"If that is your wish, m'lord." Jane resumed her earlier position, and the earl sat down beside her. In all her years of service at Marchemont, she had never been this close to him. He smelled nice, which was a rarity in even the most noble of men. She couldn't help but enjoy the clean scent of him and the slight aroma of perfume mixed with the smells of wine and parchment. It struck an alarmingly familiar note in her brain, but she could not easily pull the memory up to the surface.

His voice interrupted her thoughts. " 'Tis a beautiful night. Autumn is my favorite time of the year. Is it yours, Jane?"

"No, m'lord. I'm a springtime type."

"You seem like a springtime sort of person. Always busy, bustling about. Like the plants coming out of dormancy, busy growing to feed others come harvesttime. Did anything bad ever happen to you in autumn to make you not favor it as highly as spring?"

She hesitated, recalling her father's initial reaction to Nicholas's conception. "Yes. But that was a long time ago. Thank you for the compliment, however, m'lord, as regarding my work habits. But how would you know of my industrious ways?"

"Skeets speaks highly of you. And your meals are so wonderful that I'm sure they can only come from industrious hands and a creative mind. I must admit that my invitations to dine are eagerly accepted, and it's not merely due to my abilities as host."

She said nothing. Neither did he. They watched the barges go by for several minutes, the boats and the ground upon which they sat the only things they seemed to have in common. If she had but looked at his face, she would have seen a troubled man. Jane finally broke the uncomfortable silence.

"Sir, may I be so bold as to ask of Nicholas's progress at the abbey?"

"Certainly. He does remarkably well. As he should. He has an uncommon intelligence."

"Why have you taken such an interest in him, m'lord? I don't mean to be disrespectful, but I am his mother, and I think that perhaps I might ask of you if he truly will be your steward someday."

"That and more, Jane."

"I don't know what you mean."

" 'Tis the reason I sought you out tonight. There's something you need to know."

"What? Is Nicholas causing you trouble?"

"No, no. Nothing like that. He's done nothing but please me with his performance. This goes much deeper than that,

Jane. You are aware, of course, that the countess has never given me any children."

"Yes, m'lord."

"It has been her great sadness and mine. I love children, Jane. I always have. And I never wanted them simply to have an heir. I wanted them to love and care for. To teach. To learn from. To be a father and experience all the wonderful joys raising children can bring."

"They bring a lot of heartache and work, too, m'lord!" Jane said pleasantly.

"True, you are right. But the joys outweigh the troubles, do they not?"

"Oh, yes. My Nicholas has been the greatest blessing of my life."

"Well, I found out recently that I *do* have a child. At least I think so."

"That's wonderful! Isn't it?"

"Yes. I think so. Still, while I'm quite sure he's mine, I'm not sure his mother will admit to it."

"M'lord, forgive my impertinence, but what happened? Perhaps a woman's perspective will help."

"That's what I'm hoping. All right, I'll tell you. He was conceived over 16 years ago."

"So he's Nicholas's age?"

"Yes. The reason I remember it so clearly is that I was traveling back from Dover. I had accompanied Lady Marie to the Channel because she was going over to Normandy. Her sister was about to deliver her first child."

"What did she have?"

"Who?"

"Lady Marie's sister. Was it a boy or a girl?"

"Oh, it was a girl. Anyway, I was about six miles upriver, and it was getting late. I was very tired, so my servant and I stopped to rest and take a little wine. It was then that I saw her."

"The mother of your son?"

"Yes. She was a beautiful young woman. I remember the way her shoulders glistened in the moonlight, and the way the water had soaked into her dark hair. It was long, smooth hair. And I don't know why she attracted me so . . . clearly she was a peasant girl."

Jane's mind began to turn. "So . . . she was in . . . the water?"

"Yes. I sent my man over to fetch her to me. I was drawn, Jane. Trapped. I knew it was wrong, but I was like a curious child, drawing ever nearer to a great precipice that could well be my destruction. My mind was shouting for me to stop, that she was just a young girl, innocent, unable to refute the seduction of a worldly man like myself. And my heart cried out, 'What are you doing, Alexander? This is not the love you seek. This is lustful passion!' Yet my body, my lonely body, which hadn't felt the loving caresses of a woman in years, any womanly warmth whatsoever, cried out, 'Take your chances, man. Avenge your loneliness!' It seems, Jane, that the voices of our bodies are all too easily heard over the other voices we hear inside of us."

Although Jane knew that by experience, she said nothing. She could hardly believe what she was hearing. A young girl bathing in the river a few miles downstream. Sixteen years ago. A boy child. *It can't be!*

"And so, I lured her to my camp. I gave her fine wine—something she had never had. I could tell she enjoyed it immensely. And I gave her more. Until finally all her defenses were down, and I took complete and utter advantage of her sweet innocence."

It must be! He must be the father of my son! Oh, Lord. Oh, Lord. Jane started to shake within. The world expanded, became large, out of focus. She knew only her hands as she stared at them, and his voice. That familiar voice. The scent of him. It all come rushing in so dreadfully clear. She wanted to die. "What happened next, m'lord?" Her voice was propelled by an automatic instinct within her brain—the part that wants to know all that the heart and soul would rather forget.

"I saw her safely back to her hut, and I gave her a bracelet. I didn't know what happened to her after that. Until years later." He was hesitant for a moment, and then he spoke slowly, as though he hadn't prepared her enough. "Jane, I know who you are. I know you must remember everything. Don't you? You are that girl, aren't you?" He pulled out a fine gold necklace that matched perfectly the bracelet stowed away in her room. "I am the father of your son. I know I am."

"It was *you!* Oh, m'lord, it was you!" She stated the obvious, her shame apparent. Her skin flamed with embarrassment as her pride was completely obliterated. The sin that had been so impersonal for so long was that no longer. And now, here he was: her employer, her lord.

They had made a child together.

It was too intimate to comprehend. And even as her shame birthed an anger, her heart sought to refute his claim. After all, just because he knew the story didn't mean he was Nicholas's father, did it? He could have learned the story from the real father. For that matter, Nicholas might have told him everything. He said it himself—he wanted a child more than anything.

She rose to her feet. "This is insane."

He rose to his. "I promise you it's not."

She felt woozy, her head seeming to circle about her body like a swiftly flying falcon. Alexander de la Marche put his arms about her to steady her. But Jane felt such a hot confusion that she could barely think. "It's all right, Jane. Truly it's all right," he whispered.

Jane, Jane! the inner strength that God had given to her so long ago in order that she might survive bullied itself through the fog of astonishment. Steady now. Steady. This would do Nicholas no good. She pulled away, throwing accusations in his direction.

"How do I know you speak the truth? It was all so long ago, m'lord. 'Tis common knowledge that you yearn for a son, that you despise your nephew. I don't know how you found out the details of Nicholas's conception, but it isn't impossible that Nicholas's father, whoever he may be, shared his confidence with you on a lonely night when the wine flowed too long. Words will not convince me, m'lord."

"Then look at this, Jane, and tell me he isn't mine." Alexander de la Marche unbuttoned the first four buttons of his tunic and pulled it aside. Jane gasped as the moon illumined the same birthmark upon his chest that Nicholas bore. It shone black in the scant lunar gleam. "Nicholas is my son, Jane. I was that man by the riverbank all those years ago."

There it was. As much proof as anyone could offer. All these years she had lived in his shadow, serving him gratefully, raising his son on her own. All these years the man who had taken advantage of her had lived within the same palisades as she. It was horrifying to her.

And her anger bloomed as she realized that in some strange way she now stood on equal ground with the earl. He had earlier admitted he had wronged her grievously. And she wasn't going to let him smooth that away because he was her lord. She would not waste this opportunity to say the things that for 16 years she had imagined herself saying, in the dark, when she couldn't sleep. Even if it meant banishment from Marchemont. "You think that little mark gives you the right to claim him now? You stole my life! You left me with nothing but a bracelet. A bracelet and a child. My child, m'lord."

"He's mine, too, Jane."

"Oh yes, that's fine enough for you to say. But it was I who raised him! It was I who was humiliated in the village square, stripped to my waist, and whipped for my fornication while you lived your life of ease and luxury."

"I'm sorry."

"That isn't all. I bore him with only my dear father to assist me. I suckled him and cared for him during many illnesses. I raised him to be the young man you've now taken an interest in. It was because of my love that he is worthy enough to be called your son. And so, m'lord, now that I've done the excruciating work of a mother, you believe you can easily step into any role a father has the honor of claiming? No! It shall not be!"

The whole time Lord Alexander stood patiently, listening to her tirade, knowing she had every right to say the things she did. As her lord, he certainly had the right to chastise her for them, but that thought never entered his mind.

But Jane wasn't finished. "Besides, I've no idea what you have planned for him, m'lord. Will he always take second place to Percy? Be doomed to running your family's earldom while Percy receives the glory? What is it you plan for him?"

"He's my son, my only son. Jane, from the day I first saw him standing in the courtyard with no tunic on, that fairy-bite in utter glory on his chest, I knew! Can you not see it? The hair? 'Tis mine. The form he bears is so like unto mine as well! And Jane, he's smart and responsible, a young man who neither shirks his duties nor pulls back in the face of hardship. I freely admit that *you* are responsible for the fine characteristics he possesses. I don't begrudge you that honor. But would you honestly keep him from a life of glory, of honor, of power, and of wealth?"

"If it turns him into another man like you, m'lord . . . yes."

He held the necklace toward her. "I remember, Jane. I remember everything. I'm sorry. I did you wrong, and I've been paying for it since it happened. Do you not think the countess's barrenness is God's judgment upon my sin? Surely *I* do. Please forgive me, Jane."

Tears threatened to come forward, but Jane held them in check with a will hard won. She wondered just how he had suffered over the years, but would not suffer her dignity to ask. "What are you going to do with the lad?"

"He will be the next Earl of Lambeth. He is the son of my loins."

"He is baseborn."

"He is my only son," the earl reiterated.

"Why, then, did you commence this future steward charade?"

"I needed to see what Nicholas is capable of. He is possessed of a shrewd intelligence, Jane. And, as I said before, is duty-bound and hardworking. He will inherit my earldom most worthily. I know that now, having seen him perform this past month."

"He is illegitimate."

"Look beyond that, Jane!"

"How can I? I've lived with it for 16 years!"

"I'm offering him the world. He feels it just beyond his reach, Jane. You know he does. Haven't you always thought of Nicholas as different from the other servants? Different from yourself?"

His words stung. "Yes."

"Then can you not see that this is his destiny? Why do you fight against this?"

"I don't fight against what you are willing to extend to Nicholas. I fight against you, m'lord. I fight against men like you who use people simply because they weren't born in a lord's bedchamber. Perhaps Nicholas is worthy of such an inheritance. But are you worthy of such a son?"

Jane pushed past him and started to leave, but a few feet away she turned back around and nodded once, slowly, defeated more by her station than by her own will. If the earl wished Nicholas to succeed him, ultimately there was nothing she could do. And in the end, she knew it was up to Nicholas. "It is as you say, m'lord. He is your son."

The castle cook went back to her kitchen and crawled into bed next to her noble son. Only then did she allow 16 years of pain and longing to fall from her eyes in the form of innumerable tears and galling sobs.

NINETEEN

Tuesday dawned cool. Its sky, full of congested clouds, gave every indication that it would eventually deliver rain to the participants of the tournament. But so far the gray expanse delighted itself in teasing all those who would be gathering on the field around five o'clock that evening.

Yet long before the sun proceeded to rise behind the clouds, a sleepless Jane arose from her bed at the sound of a knock upon her door. The air already had a morning smell, so she knew that her normal wakening time wasn't far ahead anyway. She pulled open the door.

"Skeets?"

"Sorry to disturb you, Jane. But I've a summons for you."

"Who?"

"Lord Alexander." There was something in Skeets's tone, some apologetic inflection. And Jane realized that he had known all along.

"Why didn't you tell me, old friend?"

"I couldn't, Jane. You know I couldn't. I've tried to make you and Nicholas comfortable over the years. 'Twas all I could do."

She nodded and turned back to slip on her gown. She quickly dragged a comb through her hair and tied her shoes to her feet. "All right. I'm ready. Did he tell you what he wants?"

"No. Well . . . yes, but I'm not at liberty to pass on the information."

"You never are, Skeets, but that hasn't stopped you before!" Her nervous joke fell flat between them.

"There's no need to pretend, Jane. I know you must be frightened."

"Frightened? Why would I be frightened about the fact that my son is entering a world he knows nothing about? That he has the likes of Lady Alison Hastings to deal with? That a heavy responsibility—one of a magnitude that I couldn't have possibly prepared him for—lies just around the corner? Frightened? Why should I be, Skeets?"

They walked out of the kitchen and up a flight of stairs into the side entrance of the keep. Up another interior flight, and Jane found herself in the great hall. A low fire burned upon the central hearth, and before it in his chair sat the earl, barefooted and deep in thought. The warm light flickered upon his jutting brow and reflected off his deep-set green eyes. Without looking at her he said, "Thank you for coming, Jane."

Jane remained mute.

"Come closer. I would tell you something." Jane did as he bid, and he looked at her, noting with compassion the red rims of her eyelids. His voice sounded distracted, however. "Our conversation of earlier must remain strictly confidential."

"Misgivings already, m'lord?"

"No. I just want to break the news gently to my wife and more gradually to Alison and Percy. My desire is to convince Alison's eldest to take them back with him at Hastings."

"I shall do as you ask. Besides, m'lord, anybody I would know to tell, simply wouldn't believe it!" This time her jest was genuine. And Jane felt the situation as truly real for the first time.

"You know you won't be able to stay here once my wishes are made public, don't you?"

"It is what I assumed. I certainly wouldn't want to be an ever-present reminder to all of Nicholas's humble matronage."

"I'm glad you understand. I will have a place made ready for you immediately." His tone was still distracted.

Jane fell to her knees, overcome with panic. "Oh, m'lord! Please! Let me stay on here at Marchemont until your will is declared. I'm not ready to leave my son just yet."

He looked down at her, his expression almost surprised that she was there. "Agreed. But you must still assume your duties as before."

"It's all I've come to know, m'lord."

"As you wish, Jane."

"M'lord? Might I make one request in regard to where I will be sent?"

"Certainly."

"I'd like to be able to see the Thames from my doorway."

He continued staring into the fire. "That is granted."

She stood to her feet. "And although I will not come to Nicholas at Marchemont, I pray you let him visit me often."

"Of course." He looked up into her eyes. "My intention has never been to remove Nicholas from you completely."

"Thank you, m'lord."

Lord Alexander turned to look back at the fire.

Jane leaned forward. "M'lord?"

"Yes, Jane."

"When will Nicholas be told?"

The earl nodded from side to side. He didn't know.

"Will you be needing me for anything else?"

He shook his head as though a decision had been made. "No, Jane. Unfortunately not."

❧ ❧ ❧

A lone figure strode through the gate house while Jane walked slowly back to the kitchen, head filled with confusing thoughts.

"Jane!" Patrick called through the dark morning air.

"Doctor MacBeth!" Jane hated to admit it, but just seeing him coming toward her made her feel so much better. "On your way up to see Lady Alison?"

"No. Actually, I'm here to see the countess."

Jane's brows knit. "Is she all right?"

"I don't know. I was sent for by messenger, telling me to come right away. The countess is not a good sleeper, and with the recent traveling, I'm hoping she's just having a hard time settling down as opposed to anything more serious."

"She's grown thinner." Jane remembered the observation she had shared with her kitchen compatriots upon the countess's arrival.

"Really? Well then, maybe an examination is truly in order. I'd better hurry, Jane. It was nice seeing you again. But then, it always is."

"And you."

❧ ❧ ❧

"Patrick." The countess gave the doctor one of her rare smiles and held out a thin white hand. "You came."

"Of course I did, my lady. How was your journey?"

"Tiring. Very, very tiring."

"Did you find what you sought?"

She shook her head. "There is no peace. Not in France, not in England. No peace to be found."

"God is a God of love, my lady. He wouldn't wish you to live your life in torment."

"But nevertheless, I am. I feel His judgments on me daily, hourly. And now with this sickness . . . My time to meet Him is coming, Patrick. And I fear my soul is far from ready."

"What more could any mortal do than what you've done? Surely the God we serve isn't vindictive and unkind, is he, my lady?"

"No. He is all-merciful. He loves us all. Poor, rich. Sick, healthy. Each and every one of us."

"Then you must take comfort in that. You must concentrate on His goodness and not on His judgments."

The countess's smile was gentle. "You couldn't possibly understand, doctor. You are not dying."

"It pains me to hear you say such words, countess. I'll determine whether or not you are dying. It's what you pay me most handsomely for." He smiled gently down at her.

"But we're all dying, doctor. Some of us are just taking longer than others to do it."

"Have you made known your suspicions to your husband yet?"

"No. I'm hoping to continue my life of prayer and not deplete my physical strength. If God is merciful, Alexander will simply slip in here one day and find me gone."

Patrick shook his head sadly. He had sent her to several of the best physicians in Paris, and they had found no remedy, had suggested no treatment which could help Lady Marie. She was growing thinner and thinner, and now her pale skin, once as fair and glowing as a pearl, was ashen and gray.

"I will pray more for you, Lady Marie, than I have been doing."

"Please do that, Patrick. Prayers such as yours are my only hope."

After examining her, Patrick sat with her for two more hours as she drifted in and out of sleep. Finally her state of repose remained constant, and he slipped quietly out of the room, down the inner steps of the keep, and out underneath the newly-pink sky. A front of clouds was moving in from the west.

It was true that he sympathized with the countess far more than she realized. He knew no peace either. He tried not to think about the past, the destruction, the hate. And the future was merely the thought of more "todays" coagulating in a pool of futility. It was a bleak picture. Atonement was elusive for his deeds of yore. As much as he tried to make up for the acts of his youth, nothing helped. Maybe Jane was right—maybe his deeds of kindness needed to be meted out to those far below his social station, those who couldn't afford the help he could give. In that he might find peace. It surely was a proposition that should bear much thought.

His deep preoccupation continued, and so, when Jane hurried from the kitchen to the outside with a large bag of feathers, they literally collided with one another. Caught momentarily unawares in a storm of swirling feathers, they both burst into laughter.

T<small>HEIR</small> laughter settled down quickly as they were both so tired.

"Doctor MacBeth!"

"Jane."

"Are you all right?"

He simply shook his head in exhaustion and delusion as they brushed the feathers off their shoulders and from their hair. Jane quickly pulled up some water and put the dipper into the bucket. "Here," she held it out to him, "drink a little. You look as if you could use some refreshing."

"Thank you." He drank a few sips and returned the dipper. "Jane, are you busy?"

Jane thought about the day ahead of her. Of course she was busy. The tournament was set to begin at five o'clock, dinner at 11 beforehand. But his pale face and tormented expression caused her to shake her head. "I can certainly spare a little time."

"For a friend?"

She smiled. "Yes, for a friend. Let me just take this water back into the kitchen for the scullions to drink. No one thinks to draw water for them."

Back in no time, she ushered him out of the bailey and around to the cooking pits. At least she could see if things were as they should be there.

"You seem melancholy, doctor."

"Aye, perhaps I do. But before we say another word, there's one thing I wish to ask you, Jane. Since we have admitted to our friendship, would you please call me Patrick?"

Jane didn't know why, but she suddenly felt shy. "All right, Patrick," she whispered. They walked slowly along, and the smells of roasting meat, fish, and fowl rose delectably from their destination. Patrick was too preoccupied to notice, but Jane did. The smell of good food never ceased to please her. "What is it that troubles you?"

"It is the countess. She is very sick, Jane."

"How terrible! Does the earl know?"

"No. She doesn't want him to know. She plans to put a brave face on until death is imminent. I know she seems a quiet, pious sort, Jane, but the countess is a warm, wonderful woman deep inside."

"I'm sure she is."

"Earthly appetites hold little significance with her, 'tis true."

By now they were walking in tandem, steps in perfect coordination with each other, a rhythm of comfortableness theirs to claim. "The poor woman. I will keep her secret safe, Patrick."

"Yes, thank you. Do you remember when I told you that every day was like unto the other before it?"

"Of course."

"It's true. The countess just proves it. Jane, it doesn't matter if we seek to please God utterly, to serve Him with our entire being, and to give Him all that we have. In the end we're just as dead. And every day leading up to that day was like the day before it. Living. Eating... breathing... sleeping."

"If we're lucky," Jane smiled, and Patrick nodded.

"Luck has absolutely nothing to do with it, as well you know. It's all futile, isn't it? Look at the countess's life. She is pious and noble, caring dutifully for the poor. She's given her life to God, and now she's dying, Jane. And dying alone. No children.

A husband with whom she cannot share the fact that she is dying."

" 'Tis a sad tale, and one that I wish I could understand myself."

His voice lowered and he stopped, turning her to face him. "When I was sitting at her bedside waiting for her to sleep, I saw myself, Jane. I saw myself dying before my time, with no one to comfort me. No child to hold my hand, no wife to cool my brow and brighten my despair with a kiss or two. And it frightened me."

Jane didn't know what to say. She merely laid her hand on his arm.

"What do you see as your future, Jane?"

Jane shook her head from side to side. "I try not to think about it, Patrick. For mine looks much the same. It is when I rely on my faith. The Lord has not failed to provide for me yet. His grace has always been clearly made known."

"Even in the death of your husband?"

"Even then." *How can I keep lying like this?*

"How did you bear it?"

"There are worse things in life," she said truthfully about what she had been through. "I don't mean to sound callous to my own sufferings... past sufferings, that is. 'Tis best, I've found, to try and forget about such things. Or at least put off the sadness until I am alone. Patrick, you've so much to be thankful for. A good practice, the many patients who rely on you for their care."

"But each night I go home to an empty bed, Jane. And each day is just like the one before it."

"Then you must change your view of life, Patrick. As far as your empty bed and your desire for a death surrounded by those you love, *you* are the only one who can do something about that. But to do such, you must learn to open your heart."

"My father was a hard man who demanded perfection, science, and little whim. My mother was a woman of little personality and no dreams. But there was a time when my heart was opened far too wide. But I won't go into that now."

Jane impulsively slipped her hand in his, squeezed twice, then let go. "I could never know too much about you, Patrick MacBeth."

He stopped again and looked hard into her eyes. "Do you mean that, Jane?"

"With an open heart."

"So that's how it's done?"

"Yes. And I must tell you that it is something I'm not used to doing, either. At least on so personal a level. My healing exposes my heart regularly. But that's different. And the loneliness which drives me to open myself to you is nothing compared to the troubles I've seen in the village when they call for my services. Loneliness is but a pittance in the coffers of human pain."

"I don't believe that, Jane. I've seen much death, and whether we are rich or poor, death arrives in the same chariot. And when he does come, 'tis much easier for the dying if they have someone watching them go, waving them on, wishing them luck. And then I think of Lady Marie. She of all people should have a hand to hold as she passes through the veil, but she chooses not to. The pity, the sadness I feel right now, Jane, is sore. What a waste—what a dying, pitiful shame."

"You grieve for Lady Marie, but you must realize that she understands the pain of others, Patrick. She dies knowing she did much to alleviate their sufferings. And in that she dies not lonely, but surrounded by the soul gratitude of the people she's touched in her lifetime. She will not be alone."

"You see things in a beautiful light, Jane Lightfoot. I wish my eyes had vision such as yours."

"I simply try and see things as they are. Pity not the countess, for she would not wish for such. Just make her end comfortable and continue her work after she goes."

"What do you mean?"

"There are many people in London who need your care. You could make a difference."

Patrick said nothing. By this time they were past the cooking pits, and all the way to the Thames. "Jane, you are an extraordinary woman. I don't know how you've become so wise, yet I thank God that you did."

Jane dropped her eyes, but Patrick put his fingers under her chin and raised her face to his. He bent his head and brushed her lips softly with his own. A whisper of contact. A sweet, gentle thrill. "Thank you, lady Jane."

Jane opened her eyes. "Why do you call me 'lady'?"

"Because you *are* one. You're gracious and kind and good and so very, very fair. If anyone deserves such a title, sweet madam, it is you."

He kissed her one more time—a longer kiss, but no less tender, savoring her sweetness. Then he tucked her hand in his arm, and they walked toward the barge together.

"So tell me now, Patrick MacBeth, is one day truly just like the rest?"

Patrick took her small hand in his large one. "No, Jane. I suppose the days that are different are the turning points. I'll be back later on for the tournament and dinner. Will I see you?"

"Probably not. I *am* just a servant, you know," she joked.

"No, Jane, not just a servant."

Jane waved as the barge pulled away from the shore, then ran back to the kitchens as fast as she could. But the rest of the day, caught up in her work, she relived the moment over and over again when his lips touched hers, and she felt her heart open wide under the tender kiss he gently bestowed from the innermost portion of his lonely heart.

Such hope was new and so needed. And she felt it ravage her heart in a heady melee with the broken dreams that had once claimed the victor's crown therein. And hope conquered. She didn't know how they would come together. Indeed, was not sure whether that was part of God's divine plan. But she dared to hope that someday it would be so.

Fields of gold, Jane. She heard the words in her mother's voice and knew they were out there. Real. Attainable.

Fields of gold.

❧ ❧ ❧

From her solar, her hands clutching hard the velvet of the drapery, Lady Alison watched the loving kiss that Patrick gave freely to Jane. The scarlet of the soft material mimicked the angry flush that rose from her neck up over her face. For years she had been trying to lure Patrick MacBeth to her bed, and now she realized that the man she dreamed about in torturous, wanting dreams had a penchant for robust commoners.

She walked over to her looking glass and examined herself closely. Yes, it was true, she wasn't looking any younger these days. Her beauty had faded ... when? A change in tactic was in order.

And if that didn't work, maybe Marchemont simply needed a new cook.

❖ TWENTY-ONE ❖

Lady Alison was back at her solar window when Nicholas and the earl started out together. It wasn't their usual day to ride, but since Nicholas's studies at the abbey were suspended for the short duration of the tournament, Lord Alexander sought out the lad's company.

A soothing balm, he thought, *before the din of the next three days threatens to shatter my peace of mind!* And that was exactly what Nicholas was to him. Someone real, healthy, alive, and young. A part of himself. Looking upon him now gave him the sensation he would have had if he had raised Nicholas—to cradle him as a baby, feeling the soft, living skin that encased his body, and listening to his son's heart beat its steady, rhythmic pace. And to know that at least *something* was going right in the crazy world in which he found himself.

So they rode, down the Thames toward the archbishop's palace. Lambeth Palace. Both were quiet, concentrating on relaxing, oddly enough, knowing it was the last chance for several days. Soon, however, they were galloping quickly, enjoying the speed and the sense of release they felt as the horses thundered beneath them. It was freeing. They were at the mercy of these powerful beasts, equalizing them with every other man who was on horseback at that moment.

Time flowed by with the Thames, and still the two pushed themselves, sweating and joyful. Lord Alexander had thrown off his melancholy after the brief interview with Jane, and now he was ready to act like a father. At least in secret. Finally, the earl pulled on his reins, slowing down Bedivere. Nicholas did the same to Jasper.

"Let's cool off a bit, eh, Nicholas?"

"That would suit me well, m'lord."

The earl laughed at Nicholas's flushed cheeks and sweat-streaked face. They walked down to the river, leading the horses, and soon Nicholas was out of his tunic, splashing water on his upper body, arms, and face.

"Good idea! Even if I do have to be subjected to that fairy-bite again!" the earl exclaimed, removing his own tunic and undergown, accompanied by Nicholas's boyish chuckle. The two men were kneeling side by side next to the river, their movements perfectly coinciding with each other.

Alexander de la Marche laughed. "If my Lady Marie saw me now, she'd be horrified!"

"Mother would be as well!"

"At least I can tell Marie *you* started it all."

"And as usual, I have no good defense against my mother."

"What son does?"

Both stood to their feet, and Lord Alexander took advantage of an opportunity which might never occur so naturally again. He turned his son to face him.

Nicholas's eyes immediately rested on the birthmark.

"Remarkable, isn't it?" the earl said.

Nicholas didn't know what to say. He didn't want to presume anything, but . . . there it was, exactly like his own. There was no necessity for him to speak just then, for the earl began.

"It's something I've always been proud of. Like you are of yours, Nicholas." He pulled his undergown over his head. "Do you remember when you asked me if I would find your father?"

Nicholas nodded.

"I had a talk with your mother right after that. She told me about the traveling lord who was your father."

The earl told Nicholas the tale of his conception from his own perspective, and he related the proofs of his paternity. The birthmark, the physical characteristics, the bracelet. "I had to talk to Jane. And when she conceded that her memories coincided with mine, I knew it was true, that you are my son."

Nicholas still didn't know what to say. The man he had come to admire more than any other was claiming to be his father. He felt all his arrogance skitter away in the face of true humility. He remembered saying to his mother, "I am half noble." But now all he felt was illegitimate.

Is he accepting me? What does he have planned for me? I am his bastard. I can be nothing short of an embarrassment.

"What do you have to say, Nicholas?" The earl couldn't read the young man's face. And he suddenly realized that maybe Nicholas didn't want a father around. That he resented the lies.

Nicholas dropped to his knees. "I have only one request, m'lord."

"Yes?"

"Would you please at least extend to my mother and me the privilege of a quiet exit from Marchemont? I realize this must be an embarrassment to you. To find out you have had an illegitimate son all these years cannot be easy to accept. Perhaps we can keep this quiet until we find positions elsewhere."

Clearly, the boy wasn't thinking straight, but the earl rushed to reassure him as any father would the son he loves greatly. "Oh, son!" He pulled him to his feet. " 'Tis not like that! I've told you because I cannot contain myself any longer! I know that you're mine, my own son! Do you realize what that means to me? How many years I've longed for a child? I love you, Nicholas. And I tell you this not because I want to be rid of you, but because I want to be your father, because I want you to love me like I love you." He pulled Nicholas roughly into an embrace, both a bit bemused and uncomfortable with such, but so thankful for it. Finally they pulled apart.

"How can this be?" Nicholas still couldn't believe what was unfolding.

"I don't know, my son. I don't know why all this has come about now, at this time in my life, but I am thankful, Nicholas."

"My father. I have a father. And you are that man." He looked bemused. Then the veil lifted and he returned to his father's arms, and this time they both felt completely at ease.

꧁ ꧁ ꧁

An hour later, Nicholas stood beside the earl on top of the walls. Several squires exercised their knights' horses on the field below. It was only nine o'clock and Lord Alexander wanted to survey the tournament field from a higher vantage.

The green turf of the lists appeared lush beside the waving, summer-dry grasses around it. Nicholas's eyes glowed at the sight of the colorful tents. The squires who weren't exercising their employers' horses were busy polishing armor or darning the silks which would be placed over the horses and the knights' armor. They sat on straw mats, the pieces of armor stacked neatly in baskets beside them.

"Will you take part?" Nicholas's lips were parted slightly in anticipation of the excitement which would start that very day.

Lord Alexander's eyes glowed. "I'm of a mind. If only to show off for my son."

Nicholas readily accepted the new love of his father, and freely offered up his own. "M'lord, what did you *really* think when you saw the fairy-bite on my chest?"

"I immediately starting calculating how many years ago I had been with your mother."

"You didn't dismiss it as a coincidence?"

"How could I? Nicholas, if I could have designed a son in form and character and charisma, it would have been you. Still,

I did realize it could have been a coincidence, but I didn't want to approach your mother about it, if indeed that thought even entered my mind at that point. I told myself I was a bit overeager, that a birthmark does not a son make!"

"But didn't you install me as apprentice to Skeets soon after that? Did you find more proof?"

"Not really. Our physiques are similar and our hair color. But you favor Jane more highly than you do me."

"Then why did you put me in with Skeets without being positive?"

"I knew that either way I would benefit. Even if you weren't my son, it was time for me to start training someone to take over for Skeets someday. Percy is a buffoon, Nicholas, as I've said many times. I admired your pride and your spirit there by the stables that day, and I knew that if anyone could stand up to Percy, it would be you."

"Thank you for your confidence in me."

"Oh, you deserved it, son. You deserved it. After that I realized that I needed to get to know you better if I was to find any other similarities between us, any characteristics I might have handed down to you. And the more I grew to know you, Nicholas, the more impressed I became. It was under my orders that Skeets worked you to your limit, but I had to see what manner of man you would become.

"Finally, I realized the only way to truly find out if you were indeed my son or not was through your mother. That is why I had you ask her the true circumstances surrounding your birth. After hearing your report, I knew that you were truly mine."

"I'm glad you remembered her, m'lord."

"So am I." The earl's words were soft with embarrassment and full of regret. "She raised you well. And for that I am grateful."

"You will take care of her, won't you?"

"I promised you I would, Nicholas. She only asked that she be near the river."

Nicholas smiled. "It makes perfect sense. Anything of import that has ever happened to Mother has happened on the banks of the Thames."

❧ ❧ ❧

As expected, the kitchen bore a distinct resemblance to a whirlwind.

"Three more days! Only three more days and this will all be but a memory!" Mattie called above the din, to which everyone cried in mock imitation of tournament viewers, "Huzzah!"

"Did the wine from Bordeaux arrive in time?" Jane asked Gregory. Poor Skeets had been wringing his hands waiting for the anticipated import.

"Aye, yesterday. And the Gascon shipment as well. Which is a good thing. The last bit was already going bad. Skeets told me Lord Alexander was served a cup of wine at Lord Belford's that was so bad it smelled sour, and looked so thick and flat that the earl actually closed his eyes, clenched his teeth in preparation, and drank it down shuddering."

Jane shuddered herself. "Sounds like he was forced to filter the stuff rather than drink it."

"Better that than be discourteous," he said mockingly. "Oh well, at least down here in the kitchens if something's rotten we call it rotten!"

"Does that include beef?" She raised her eyebrows.

"Well, if that wagon load hadn't been rotten to begin with, after you'd set your hand to it, Jane, it certainly would have become so."

Jane threw a turnip at him.

She missed, hitting Mattie directly on her backside.

The kitchen roared with laughter!

"No free-for-alls today!" Gregory quickly shouted. "We cannot spare the food!"

180

The staff quieted down immediately.

Jane and Gregory continued talking. "You've done marvelously in preparing for the tournament, Gregory. Think you're ready to really be the clerk?"

"Aye, Jane. I actually enjoyed this week, especially since I was given enough time to observe the way things work around here, get a feel for the rhythm of what you've had set in motion for some time now."

"You'll not be going back to your old ways, now will you?"

"No, no. You shall always have enough spices for your delectables, and your meat will never be rotten."

"You indeed declare good things, sir." She bowed her head quickly. "And now, I've got to send a couple of boys round for some more of the oxen that's been roasting this morning."

"Are the swans ready?"

"They certainly are. How much longer until dinner will be served?"

"An hour and a half."

"Nice chatting with you then, Gregory. Off we go!" Jane hurried off in one direction, Gregory the other, both barking orders as they went. Of course, Jane's voice was almost twice as loud.

⋇ ⋇ ⋇

The royal barge drew closer, and all craned their necks for a view of the resplendent young king who lounged beneath a purple and saffron-colored pavilion held up by gilt poles. Courtiers lined the barge, along with many ladies and lords garbed in a myriad of splendid colors, the ladies' silken veils fluttering gracefully from their headpieces.

Henry III was a young man who appreciated the finer things in life. While the king was infatuated with all things European, many of his barons and earls were disgruntled. But he also had

181

a loyal contingent as well and was careful to make sure that he kept them on his side.

He alighted from the barge dressed in regal splendor of crimson and gold. His festive mood was immediately evidenced, the aura of a fresh breeze seeming to emanate from him as he laughed heartily and joked with two of his favorites. A falcon, intense eyes darting precociously, sat on his gauntleted hand. Lord Alexander was there to greet him with a bow, saying something for Henry's ears only. The king responded with three giant ha's and a hearty whack between the earl's shoulder blades. Henry's herald stayed close behind, keeping away anybody who sought a royal audience without permission. Protocol for speaking with the king was very rigid and precise, and the herald took his duties seriously and did his job exceedingly well.

King Henry invited Lord Alexander to walk beside him to the castle.

All the other courtiers walked to the festivities as well, but that did not squelch their zeal or the excitement that naturally surrounded such a day. The tournament was a grand spectacle, to be sure. And the fact that it had been outlawed for so many years made it that much more tantalizing and infinitely more romantic.

But first, dinner.

A manly affair at that. The noblewomen were served upstairs with Lady Marie, and the more illustrious men, as many as could find seats, were served in the great hall downstairs. Truly, it was one of the grandest banquets that had taken place at Marchemont for many years.

The procession began, heading first for the lord's table, which that day stood beneath a multicolored canopy. A household officer on horseback led the procession, followed by William, the marshal of the hall, carrying his officious white staff. The servants followed behind, platters heaped with the wonderful offerings from Jane's kitchen.

The tables had been set beforehand, covered with cloths and equipped with wooden spoons. Silver cups were placed at Lord Alexander's table, and wooden ones everywhere else.

Through the air an incredible din vibrated, and the smells of the food made the men at the lowest table feel more hollow than before, knowing they would be the last to be served.

When the first course was served, the almoner said grace, and before the echo of the final "Amen" floated off, all had grabbed their spoon or taken their knife from the small pouch attached to their belt. And if the din was great before, it was nothing compared to now. Dogs barked underneath the boards, and King Henry's falcon, as well as several more, published their piercing cries from their perches behind the benches. Men shouted to be heard, and so the noise grew greater and greater. But that was all part of a banquet.

The first course was a marvel. Liver and kidney pottage, larded boar's head, duck, mutton, pork, swan, roasted rabbit, and several varieties of savory tart made under Mattie's strict supervision. Geese, capon, partridges, and veal were offered as well. Over 2000 eggs had been used in preparation for the feast, and the cheese which came in from the country was already venturing to run out too soon. Jane had dispatched a boy earlier that morning to get more from several of the neighboring manors.

While the first course was being consumed, the kitchen servants were busily putting the finishing touches on the second course and working furiously on the third. Jane was placing the stuffed chickens on several platters. Stuffed with a mixture of egg yolks, dried currants, cinnamon, mace, cubebs, and cloves, there certainly wouldn't be any of these precious prizes left over, she knew. Pheasant were also arranged for transport from the kitchen and up the steps by the serving men and women. But Jane was especially proud of one of the pottages, which contained almonds seethed in a meat broth, minced onions, and small parboiled birds, sparrows, linnets, starlings, magpies, and jackdaws seasoned with cinnamon and cloves.

Leche was served, as well as more pottages for the third course. And a viand royal—a sweetened wine concoction made with mulberries and honey—was offered alongside more partridges, beef dishes, roasted cranes, spiced port liver, and the most special dish of all: peacock, its skin sewn back over the roasted flesh, complete with feathers, head, and tail.

Anyone who wasn't eating ran from task to task, the servers becoming quickly exhausted. A banquet for the king was a most magnificent affair.

At least there's only one such meal as this over the next few days! Jane, glistening with perspiration, looked optimistically on the situation and shouted orders at the top of her lungs.

In fact, it was noisy all over! The bailey was filled with dining guests as well, all enjoying themselves beneath a cloudy sky. Laughter accompanied the meal, blending in with and almost drowning out the dulcet tunes from the minstrels' instruments. A celebratory feeling bound men and women together as they ate their fill of the delectable meal.

But Lord Alexander and King Henry were having an interesting conversation despite the din.

The young king took a sip of his wine. "Have you seen the Lady Chapel that Richard of Barking is building onto Westminster Abbey?"

"Yes, sire. 'Twill be a beautiful addition, I am told."

His luminous brown eyes sparkled above the rim of his cup. "It is wrong. They're going about it all wrong."

"Sire?"

"He is planning on using the same tired Romanesque arches. It will be another Norman disaster in architecture."

"Do you not like Norman architecture, sire?"

"It pales when compared to the Gothic architecture coming out of France. We are giving him a bit of help with the project. But it could be so much more."

"That is good news, sire. Are you of a mind to take over the project yourself completely?"

The king looked delighted at Alexander's conjecture. "We wish to do exactly that. If we can incorporate what they've done and are doing at Notre Dame, we should think it a most successful project. Those flying buttresses are inspiring, are they not?"

"Forgive me for my ignorance, my lord. But wouldn't the two styles of architecture seem most peculiar when seen alongside one another?" Alexander was indeed planting seeds with his friend Richard of Barking in mind.

"Yes. That is why it is taking us so long to decide whether or not to take on the project completely. If we build the Lady Chapel, we shall wish to rebuild the entire monastery. Of course, the funding for such a project will be immense."

Lord Alexander smiled appreciatively. The king could play his own games as well. "You may count on me for heavy support. I've well loved the abbey for many a year, my liege."

"Are there others who would like to contribute?"

"I am sure we can be very persuasive regarding the matter to all manner of men."

"A good man you are, de la Marche. We value you highly."

"Thank you, sire."

Very soon after that, the meal ended. Exactly four hours from when it had begun.

Sitting at a table below the dais, Patrick MacBeth received a summons to come upstairs.

᪥ TWENTY-TWO ᪥

The tournament was a *plaisance*. Not a matter of war or a fight for honor. Alexander de la Marche had assembled the men for sport, pleasure, and the entertainment that naturally stems from such an event. For the joust, armor would be worn, but during the other forms of hastilude—mostly hand-to-hand combat with blunted spear or sword—the participants would wear padded leather cuirasses. All in sport for sport's sake, no malice, but each knight dreaming of a little more glory and a much heavier purse when he left the lists for the last time.

But a certain knight, whose squire was busily polishing his slick black armor, had a vastly different idea of the purpose of this tournament. He sat in his tent, staring at the flap which swung softly in the wind. And thought of the events which had led him to this day. Some were glorious, some were not. He had no regrets. Only a need for more of everything. More wealth, more fame.

᪥ ᪥ ᪥

"Come, come, Alexander!" King Henry chided the earl as they climbed the steps of the escafaut. " 'Tis why we came! To see you participate. You must. Please don't make us issue a royal behest!"

Lord Alexander laughed, and a knight from the region of Dover, Sir Ronald Rey, shouted from the lists, where he was exercising his horse. "The host must do his guests the honor of fighting in their midst."

"The fellow is correct." Lord Alexander bowed to the king. "I shall do as you command, my liege. But I must warn you, these old bones never stop readying themselves for their final resting place. I wouldn't expect too much."

"We won't," Henry said without malice. "Our household knights are the finest in England. The rest of you will have a difficult time besting these challengers."

"As you say, my liege! As for the rest of the comers, I may be able to give them hints as to the subtleties of my field." He raised his eyebrows, and the young king laughed and waved him on.

That was the way the tournament was to be played out, upon the king's insistence. Six royal household knights—the challengers, against the rest of them—the comers. Excitement was sure to descend upon not only the participants on the field, but upon those who congregated together around the field.

"It all reminds me of the old tales of the gladiators," Jane said back in the kitchen. "You realize most of the people out there wouldn't be attending so eagerly if they didn't expect someone to get hurt!"

" 'Tis the way of all of us," Mattie quipped. "When someone else is ailing, we can't help but be glad it isn't us."

Agnes joined in. They all had their theories. "It's all about the excitement, if you ask me. Those ladies out there are dreaming of those knights and the possibility that the same arm which wields the lance will drape possessively across their own shoulders someday!"

"I have to agree with you there!" Mattie nodded. "Have you seen some of those knights? Manly gents, all of them. And some of them are as fair in the face as they are in form!"

Jane clucked jokingly. "Listen to the two of you. Agnes I can understand, but you, Mattie? You've been a grandmother for ten years now! Such talk!"

"A good-looking man is a good-looking man, Jane Lightfoot. Don't you even try to pretend to us you don't notice them. Especially with that handsome Doctor MacBeth lurking around the kitchen more than a man of his means should!" She and Agnes stood looking at Jane, their arms crossed over their chests.

Jane laughed. "All right! All right, you two. Your point is well made and well received. He's most comely, is he not?" she winked conspiratorially.

"Tall!" Agnes said.

"And all that red hair," Mattie remarked approvingly. "Makes me wonder—"

"What?"

"Oh nothing, Jane. You'll think me a foolish old woman!"

"What? You're wondering what it's like to run your fingers through his hair, aren't you?"

Mattie turned away in embarrassment and traversed the kitchen to check on something in the oven.

Agnes still stared at Jane. "Well?"

"Well what, Agnes?"

"What is it like?"

"When I find out, I'll let you know. I promise."

The two laughed girlishly together and continued their duties, getting ready for the supper which would take place after the activities.

Meanwhile, more nobles filed into the upper grandstand, vying for the best seats, while in the lower sections of the sloping galleries burghers and substantial yeoman did the same. The posturing was more violent in the lower portions, and the two marshals of the field, armed with war-ready weaponry, rode up and down the lists, their very presence keeping the commotion down to a hearty minimum and the violence almost nonexistent. To be sure, several men went home with a headache caused by a pommel of a sword or knife. But a basic atmosphere of good-will pervaded, and others took their places around the field, eagerly waiting for the joust to begin.

The darker clothing of the commoners in the lower grandstand contrasted with and enhanced the riotous colors worn by the noblemen and women above them. The green of the lists and the splendor of the nobility, separated by the browns and grays of the lower citizens, was a pleasing, balanced spectacle of color and composition.

The joust was the first event of the tournament. Battle with swords, spears, and other weapons would begin on the next day during the Grand Melee, that wonderful free-for-all battle, which possibly could (and most probably would) lead to the death of a participant, though many precautions were taken. It was one of the reasons the tournament had been outlawed so many years before. And probably why it was so well attended now.

Ah, the Grand Melee. It was this particular event in which one participant had a keen interest. A Condottieri he was, a mercenary knight with no loyalties to any particular country. He was a man for hire, an excellent, brutal soldier who had made a fortune from kings and princes all over Europe. As his squire strapped on his exceedingly shiny black armor, Phillipe de Malveaux eyed Alexander de la Marche with greedy eyes. He would be richer yet before the sun set tomorrow evening. And that thought rang a decidedly pleasing tone to his greedy ears. The knight was a mysterious fellow, unknown to most of the participants and looked upon a bit warily. To be certain, he had gained a reputation during the fifth crusade ten years before when he took the cross. But Phillipe de Malveaux wore the cross undeservedly.

Perhaps most of them did.

And the games began.

To the flourish of clarion and trumpet, the heralds rode upon the field to call out the rules of the tournament. Their voices bounced off the air, some attendees hearing fine, others leaning forward, cupping their ear with a curved hand and nudging their neighbor saying, "What did he say? I didn't quite get that. Do you know what he just said?"

The idea of Marchemont's tournament was this. The challengers must fight all comers who wished to do so. And each who wished to face a challenger must touch the blunt end of his lance to the challenger of choice's shield. For this day of jousting, all lances would be affixed with a small wooden disk at the pointed end.

When all knights present who had splintered three lances during their jousts would be gathered, King Henry would declare the winner of that day's events. And for that illustrious fellow, a prize awaited in the stables of Marchemont. A mighty war horse. His superior strength and battle cunning was a noble prize to any man gathered that day. The knight would receive him as a share of his booty. Then, the honor of choosing the queen of love and beauty from the realm of ladies present would be bestowed upon him as well.

Each lady sitting eagerly in the upper galleries, dressed so fine and so beautifully, knew right well that she would be the chosen, of course.

The heralds continued to lay forth the rules. The next day the Grand Melee would take place, and once again, the king would decide which knight carried himself most magnificently. He would be crowned by the queen of love and beauty as winner of the lady's favor.

And finally, the third day would be a day of contests for the amusement of the populace from the surrounding area, and London, too. Archery contests, bull baiting, knife throwing, and other games.

Already the countryside round about was crowding in with all manner of people. News had flown about, and wandering minstrels, dramatic bands, and troops of gypsies and wanderers had set up camp. Camp fires burned, and half-naked children cartwheeled and somersaulted about, running with dusty legs and feet through their camps. Looking out from the walls, Skeets estimated that 5000 to 6000 people had gathered for the excitement.

"Thank goodness we don't have to feed them all," he said later to Jane, who could only agree wholeheartedly.

Back at the lists, the heralds finished their business and rode off the field to the cheers of all present. The marshals of the field rode solemnly forward to the center. Once there, they parted ways, and each rode to the opposite end of the lists. Armed, motionless, their piercing eyes missed nothing.

At the right extremity of the lists, nearest Marchemont Castle, an enclosed space held all the knights who wished to face the six challengers. It was a barrage of color and insignia of all manner. Falcons, clenched fists, lions, snakes, turrets, and various weaponry exhibited themselves in embroidery upon their silks. Lances thrust through a sea of colorful feathers that adorned their great helms. Women cheered from the grandstand, waving their scarves. Everyone chattered as to whom they thought would be the winner of the event. The cloudy sky rendered the scene highly visible, and the colors stood out in splendor against the gray backdrop.

Six knights exited the barricade, riding in single file. They had won the initial casting of lots and were the first to combat the king's knights. The said knights waited in front of the royal grandstand for the comers to touch their shields in challenge. All six stopped in front of the household knights and made the challenge almost simultaneously. Each group rode to the opposite ends of the lists under the watchful eyes of the marshals of the field. There they lined up, their armor now shining as the late-afternoon sun began to burn through the clouds. Alexander de la Marche sat proudly upon his stallion, Bedivere, surveying the turf which stretched before him with a trained eye. Bedivere pawed at the ground, eager for combat.

Richard, the Earl of Gloucester, and Sir Ronald Rey began the joust. The din from the crowd rang tumultuously. Sir Ronald held his lance aloft, showing off the prizes he had garnered from the prettier participants of the crowd, many silken scarves tied around its painted shaft. Sir Ronald was a favorite at court, and he typified the chivalrous knight with his wide smile and courtly, almost effusive gestures. And yet, he was depended upon most heavily by the king. He was composed of more substance than just bluster and fight. He bowed to the audience and began to prepare himself mentally.

The Earl of Gloucester, though not so heavily endowed with silken snippets, could put on just as good a show as Ronald. But in a different manner. He rode his horse magnificently around the field, turning the beast with quick stops and starts, and so reaping the praise of those all around the lists. He lifted up his helm to show his face, and shook his lance and shield with a frightful yell of intimidation. "Aaaarrrrrrrr!"

The crowd roared their appreciation.

The two combatants slowed their horses, turning to face one another. Lances poised, helms over faces now frozen in harsh concentration. Their lances were weakened to shatter upon too great an impact; nevertheless, it was a dangerous, deadly sport in which the two men had chosen to compete. A fall from such an impact, at such a speed, could easily break a man's neck.

Again the trumpets and clarion eructed their shrill sounds. Both men dug their heels into their horses' flanks and charged toward the other as if all their honor was contained in the victory of this single joust.

ﻬ ﻬ ﻬ

Patrick knocked on the heavy wooden door, his heart pounding. "Come in, Patrick," Lady Alison said upon hearing him. He shook off the feeling with several forthright shakes of his head, lifted the latch, and opened the door.

"Close the door."

Lady Alison's voice was different. Deeper. Stronger. Swollen with a tone he had never heard in it before. It was larger, more potent, yet menacing in its seductive overtones. It mirrored the spicy perfume which the room had metabolized, making the scent a part of its very essence.

He quickly surveyed the room. The heavy curtains were drawn against the late-afternoon sun, and they kept all but the loudest cries of the tournament at bay. Candles, at least 30, burned through the dimness in a sultry fashion. Patrick should have closed his eyes against the scene before him. He should have walked out the door and never gone back.

But he didn't.

For lying on the bed strewn with flower petals, a shimmering undergown of the finest silk molding to the curves of her body, was the woman who had called him. Blond curls caught the glow of the white tapers. Alison's lips parted slightly. The woman in her early fifties looked closer to Jane's age.

"Patrick," she hummed smoothly, holding out her hand to him. "I knew you'd come."

Feeling hypnotized by her appearance, almost drugged by the perfume, Patrick walked toward the bed. And Alison arose swiftly, gracefully, walking toward him as though on air, each step a floating movement. Even as those outside battled for supremacy, Alison was making a deadly charge of her own.

᪐ ᪐ ᪐

The lances clashed as the two combatants made contact. The Earl of Gloucester's lance hit squarely on his opponent's breast, and Sir Ronald Rey tumbled off his horse. Victory number one for the comers.

Two more knights took to the field.

Those waiting in the enclosure at the end of the lists cheered wildly as Gloucester danced his horse in a sideways step, his feral cry a parting legacy to the next man who readied himself for combat.

※ ※ ※

Patrick tried to shake off the sluggish feeling he was experiencing as Alison crossed the room. He forgot she was his patient. His sinful nature enjoyed the thought of this woman walking toward him. The voice of conscience wasn't speaking overly loud just then, either.

But Alison was taking her time. Savoring the moment. Forbidding her seduction to play itself out *too* quickly. She stopped roughly a foot away. The perfume which she had dabbed on several minutes before his arrival wound its way from her smooth neck to assault his senses.

Her eyes were beguiling, their startling blue shade deepened by the dimness of the room, the irises catching the candle light in a most bewitching manner. "Wine?"

Patrick nodded despite himself, watching her as she walked to the table and poured him a glass of the finest wine from Gascony. She held the goblet out to him. But first she took a tiny sip, a gesture of intimacy as her eyes locked onto his.

"Drink." Her voice was husky and smooth, its velvet tones cloaking and just shy of smothering.

Patrick felt compelled to obey, downing the heady wine in four swallows.

TWENTY-THREE

Come." The temptress took his hand and led him toward the perfumed bed. "You will be mine."

But Patrick stood his ground at that request, the wine not quite taking hold of his morals yet. Lady Alison became inwardly frustrated, knowing the portal of success in a carefully planned seduction such as this was but a small opening, a narrow avenue in a dangerous city. She must work quickly.

⚜   ⚜   ⚜

The next knight representing those who dare challenge the household knights was not favored by the lists with a victory. Beneath his armor, Percy, untried in the joust, perspired in profusion, unable to wipe away the beads of sweat which collected in his hair, ran down into his eyes, and skittered down his back and chest.

The blare.

And they charged, not in quite as thunderous a manner as the previous two sets, but in a dangerous shuffle, all the same. Their horses' hooves tossed clods of grass and dirt into the air, and both men squinted beneath their helms, awaiting the impact.

The clash!

Unexpectedly, both horses rode away riderless, much to the amusement of the crowd. Percy seethed inside his armor and began counting the minutes til the Grand Melee when he could unsheathe his beloved sword.

ᵛᵎᵄᵛ ᵛᵎᵄᵛ ᵛᵎᵄᵛ

"What are you doing, Alison?"

She pouted, her reddened lips forming a delectable little red bow. "I only wanted to thank you, Patrick. You've made a new woman of me." She pulled her shoulders back and threw back her head, shaking her tresses.

It was an Alison that other men had seen, but never Lord Hastings, or any man of import. Lady Alison Hastings was a woman of feverish pitch when someone she wanted walked into her life. And she had wanted Patrick for a long time.

"Did you enjoy the wine?"

"Yes."

She locked her gaze into his, blue eyes melting with green. A sigh escaped from between her lips when his large hands encircled her waist. His eyes became flat, a heated stare, no longer Patrick. The time had come. The drugs had taken hold.

Patrick's head dropped, and his arms crushed her against him as his lips claimed hers. Alison wound her arms around his neck desiring only to own Patrick MacBeth, body and soul.

ᵛᵎᵄᵛ ᵛᵎᵄᵛ ᵛᵎᵄᵛ

"Huzzah!"

The spectators roared their approval as two more knights clashed before their expectant eyes. A mighty clang splintered the autumn air, and the colliding force of the joust splintered the lance of one of the knights, always cause for an exuberant cheer from the crowd.

"Huzzah! Huzzah!"

One more for the challengers.

❧ ❧ ❧

Alison's eyes closed in rapture. She was where she had wanted to be for three years. His kiss brought on memories of the first time she had seen him. He had paid a social call to her brother, the two laughing over a cup of wine in the great hall.

His accent was honeyed and soft. And she realized immediately that she wanted to hear him say her name in passion. *Alison. My Alison.*

Ah, yes. 'Twould be a wonderful thing. Unfortunately, her more subtle advances had not proved successful, and her "illnesses" had begun. And now, the third tactic she employed seemed to be working quite well.

Like a charm.

She pulled one arm from his neck to finger the necklace she had put on earlier that morning, and with the other arm she pulled him down onto the bed.

"Jane, oh Jane," Patrick muttered in his now-drunken stupor, failing to notice Alison's sudden stiffening and subsequent relaxation. She would take him any way he came to her. Having drugged his wine and lured him unscrupulously into her bed, she wasn't going to start being choosy. Besides, a common cook was the least of her worries. Humble women like Jane Lightfoot could never prove a match for a woman like herself. Highborn. Intelligent. Used to getting everything she desired.

Alison kissed him ferociously. Her heart beating high, like his. Her mind full. Patrick responded in kind, incapable of knowing that this would change his life forever.

❧ ❧ ❧

Finally, Alexander de la Marche prepared to take his turn. The cries were sonorous, ringing over the countryside. And Nicholas stood with the other servants, breathing through his mouth with expectation.

My father.

He thrilled boyishly at the thought that he had come from such a man. How he wanted him to win his joust! But he didn't cheer as loudly as he wanted, for fear he would cry out in his joy the word *father.*

Lord Alexander bowed chivalrously to the ladies, his lance bearing the white scarf of his countess. He had offered the weapon to no other. After placing the slit-eyed helm over his head, his eyes caught Nicholas's, and the boy could see them crinkle at the corners from the smile beneath the heavy steel.

Philippe de Malveaux looked upon his opponent with eyes steely gray. He positioned his lance and shield and readied himself for the impact as the horses thundered forward at the signal. But the time for him to do the job he came to do was not yet upon him.

Closer the horses drew to one another, their nostrils flaring, their hooves pummeling the earth in a virulent tattoo.

Lord Alexander aimed his lance at his opponent.

Nicholas cheered despite himself as the two men rode hard and fast on a near-collision course.

❧ ❧ ❧

"Patrick. Oh, Patrick."

An ugly passion pervaded the close air of the room with its own sordid perfume. Alison knew the time was close, oh so close.

❧ ❧ ❧

"Huzzah! Huzzah!"

The crowd yelled again the traditional cheer, all standing on their feet as the earl's lance hit the black knight's chest dead-straight. His lance splintered. Back off the horse the Condottieri tumbled. And the spectators' cheers rose to a hysterical pitch.

But the black knight rose to his feet, a large grin, unseen by the masses, warming him yet further inside the forged suit of armor.

Soon.

ఞ ఞ ఞ

Hurry Alison! she thought frantically. *You haven't much time!* Much to her chagrin, the now-unconscious weight of Patrick's body came down on her.

Dead weight.

And she cursed herself and her tendency for overprecaution.

The drugged wine had proved too much.

But Alison smiled just the same and began to undress his unconscious form. For when Patrick awoke, naked and in her bed, he would believe that the act had indeed taken place.

"You're mine, Patrick MacBeth," she said tenderly, her lonely, ill-touched mind firmly believing that no one could love him more.

ఞ ఞ ఞ

And the jousts continued. The six household knights remained undefeated, except for Phillipe de Malveaux, unhorsed by Lord Alexander, and Ronald Rey. Daylight turned to dusk, and great torches, which lined the perimeter of the field, were soon blazing against the darkness.

But at the end of the day, Richard of Gloucester, bellowing his primal cry, seized the honor by unseating the last of Henry's knights. The prized steed was led onto the field, gold bells ringing cheerfully on his harness and reins.

The Earl of Gloucester led the horse by the reins and proclaimed his 13-year-old daughter, Roesia, the queen of love and beauty. The blushing young maiden assumed the empty throne that sat opposite the king's on the other side of the lists. Shouts of approval from the crowd rang against the galleries. The final lauding of the day. There would be no more contests until the morrow collected them all in its fleeting embrace.

Back to the castle they filed for the evening festivities. Dancing, music, and games. All would change into their most beautiful garb, secretly comparing themselves to one another and coming up clearly superior, vain lot that they were.

Lord Alexander, still clad in his leather cuirass and looking very virile with breeze-flushed cheeks and sun-bleached hair, called Nicholas to himself, and they walked up the path together. "Sorry I failed to win the horse for you, my son."

"You fared well today. If your foot hadn't slipped out of the stirrup on the third joust, I'll warrant you'd be riding that horse back to the stables. Your opponent might have acted more chivalrously toward your predicament."

"Don't *ever* rely upon the chivalry of others, Nicholas. It's all a game, like anything else, and used only when such courtesies suit the purpose of him who wields them. Hear me well: There is no such thing as a truly chivalrous man."

Nicholas felt a bit disappointed, but he didn't say so. He assumed instruction such as this was all part of being a son. "Some of the younger knights, they seemed to have chosen lances too heavy for them," he observed, wanting to continue the conversation with Lord Alexander.

" 'Tis true, and a worthy observation. I'll give you another tip, Nicholas, for someday soon you'll learn the art of the joust. *Don't close your eyes upon impact.*"

Nicholas laughed. "Of course not."

"I speak seriously, my son! The biggest obstacle a jouster must face is learning to keep his eyes open. For some it is because they are concentrating so much; others simply cannot help themselves. Visibility is the key to mastering the joust. And, as I see it, 'tis the key to mastering life as well. Keep your helm on correctly and your shield low enough to keep your view free, but high enough to protect your body."

"So the joust is much like life, sir?"

Lord Alexander thumped him on the back. "Yes, Nicholas, yes. The lessons we learn, our accomplishments, become much like our shields. They can protect, but used unwisely they can blind as well. Remember that. See as much as you can see, Nicholas. Never let any man block your eyes. And never, never block them yourself. Now, Skeets is waiting. 'Twill be only a matter of time before you take your place at such festivities upon my dais."

"Yes, m'lord." Nicholas bowed and hurried toward the castle.

Lord Alexander watched him stride forward—a long, strong gait belonged to his son. His green eyes held as much paternal pride as if he had been given the privilege to raise Nicholas from birth. He thanked God silently, quickly, that such a youth bore his blood, if not his name.

But someday that would no longer be the case. The Earl of Lambeth would tell the world that this young man was his son, and accept him they would. It was one of the benefits of power and wealth, and he would use them most thoroughly to ensure Nicholas a proper place in the illustrious kingdom that was England.

❧ ❧ ❧

"Did you enjoy the day, my son?" Jane's brown eyes sparkled into Nicholas's.

" 'Twas a marvel, Mother, truly a marvel."

"Someday you, too, will be a knight, Nicholas." Jane was slowly getting used to the idea of mothering a nobleman.

His tone was serious. "I know. I will make Father proud."

"I'm sure you already do. And you know you always have my affection."

Nicholas inwardly rebuked himself as he walked to her and placed his arms around her slim shoulders. "It has sustained me since I was born. And will continue to do so, Mother. You'll always be my heart's first love."

Jane choked down the tears. "Thank you, my son."

Later, once the covers were over them and sleep was almost nigh, Nicholas turned to face her. "Mother?"

"Yes, Nicholas."

"At times I feel daunted by all that is going on around me, all that will someday be. Am I a coward?"

How wonderful to be the mother of a man, Jane thought, *to be the sole recipient of his fears and wants. Wives are made for dreams, mothers for sorrows.*

"No, son. You're simply becoming a man. 'Tis true your present circumstances are extraordinary. But all of us feel these fears, this heavy admission that failure may follow us at every turn. A man of brave heart admits these fears and goes on despite them to carry out his God-given tasks. That is what I see you doing, Nicholas. You're learning well from both Brother Boniface and Skeets. And behind the backs of everyone but me, you're becoming a most dutiful son to your father."

"But I'm so frightened at times."

"Fear makes not a coward, son. A man perpetually unafraid is either touched in the head or sheltered from obtaining his manly potential. But a wise, strong man recognizes his fears, counts the costs, and moves forward with courage and discretion. That is what I see you learning to do, Nicholas." She leaned forward and kissed his forehead. "Sleep now, my son. You are a noble creature, and I love you so."

Nicholas smiled slightly in the darkness. "You say that, knowing we will soon be parted."

"That changes not my heart, my son. All sons leave home.
We're just doing it the other way around. How much longer before your father proclaims you his heir?"

Nicholas nodded from side to side, his tones getting sleepy.
"I'm in no hurry. Life may be busy, but therein lies the peace.
Percy could prove to be a formidable adversary. My inheritance,
I fear, will not be so easily won as I would hope."

"Strength and courage," she whispered, "and wisdom. Those
three together will guide you. And our Lord will not forget you,
Nicholas. He will impart what you need to succeed."

But Nicholas was already asleep. So Jane stalwartly applied
the advice to herself.

৩৯ ৩৯ ৩৯

That night, down in the knights' encampments, horses and
armor were bestowed upon the victors by those whom they had
beaten in the joust, "according to the laws of arms." Some of
the victors chose to take the offerings of those they had defeated—most took gold for the armor and horse, a ransom for
the goods.

Having been unhorsed right away, Phillipe de Malveaux
sat in his pavilion as his squire polished his armor and brushed
his magnificent black steed to take to Lord Alexander.

He chuckled to himself, knowing that Lord Alexander, as
host, wouldn't dream of taking them from him.

❦ TWENTY-FOUR ❦

Patrick walked the streets of London until the sun began its ascent into the pearly blue of the morning atmosphere. Unseeing. Loathing himself. Yes, the wine was drugged.

The wine was drugged.

The wine was drugged, but that fact didn't make him feel anything less than foul. For even before the narcotic could take effect, Alison's own allure had drawn him away from all decency.

Alison Hastings! He could hardly believe it. *Ten years his senior!*

It had been surprising to see her as a temptress. Her appearance was beautiful, it was true, and the pearlescent skin and surprisingly lush lips took him unawares. It was the wine's fault. The wine. The wine!

Oh, Jane! I've betrayed you! He felt sick at the thought, seeking someplace else to lay the blame. But the blame could rest only one place.

You took that step forward, Patrick, before the wine was offered, before you even smelled the heavy perfume.

He had only himself to blame. Caught in the trap of a temptress the likes of which had never before beguiled him.

How will I ever tell Jane?

And Patrick did what most men do with their most loath-some deeds: He drove it back into the corners of his mind that only he knew existed.

But nevertheless, he continued to haunt the streets, mentally flagellating himself for his lack of self-control. There was only one thing to do. He had to extricate himself from the service of the de la Marche family. It would prove to be a heavy financial burden, but he saw no other way out of the situation.

"Sir, a bit of help for the poor? Would you please, sir?" The soft voice permeated his thoughtful stroll. He looked down. At his feet sat a young girl, perhaps seven years old. She was begrimed with the filth of the streets, and yet he could see that underneath the layers of dirt she was a pretty child.

He reached into his pocket for a coin and handed it to her.

"Bless you, good sir." She tucked the treasure into a little pouch tied around her waist.

"Bless *you*, little one." He knelt down on his haunches and gave her a simple smile. Worth more to her than all the coins given her that week.

"What is your name?" he asked.

"Mary, sir."

"And how do you feel today, Mary?"

"Fine, sir. We had a meal last night."

Patrick blinked when he thought of the great banquet, much of which went to the dogs, just yesterday at Marchemont. "Have you any aches and pains?"

"No, sir. But me brother, he does. Quite regularly."

"Have your mother bring him by Westminster Abbey next Monday morning. Take him to the infirmary, and I will see to his needs. I am a doctor."

Her eyes grew round. "Oh, sir, thank you all the same, but we can't afford to pay a doctor!"

"I know. Come anyway. What do your parents do to make a living?"

"Me father is dead, sir. And Mother cannot rise out of the bed until at least the afternoon each day."

"Why?"

"Don't know. But she leaves us all night after we're in bed. Takes the earnings from my pouch." She leaned forward and whispered, "I usually try to keep some of it out to buy Tom and me a little bread. But if she finds out about it, I get into terrible trouble."

"Well, you do right to do that, Mary. Here," he reached into his pouch and pulled out a crown, "you keep this hidden. It should feed you and your brother for quite some time."

"Oh, sir! Thank ye! Thank ye!" She scrambled to her feet, having never held that much money before.

"Then will you bring him round to the abbey?"

"I will, sir. Course I will! Thank ye!" she said again, and ran down the street, her rags fluttering about her spindly legs and arms.

Just penance, he told himself, as he reentered the world of self-disgust from which Mary's presence had briefly pulled him.

❧ ❧ ❧

Back at Marchemont, the castle servants roused themselves early preparing for another busy day. The king preferred to sleep at his palace but was back for more feasting and the second day of the tournament. This was the most enjoyable day for all present.

The Grand Melee.

It was the most uproarious, riotous event at any tournament. A free-for-all of sword and various manner of knightly weaponry. Some on horseback, others on foot. All breathing heavily and roaring their loudest. Grunts. Stops. Starts. Slipping feet. Weapons thrown from their wielders' hands.

Confusion.

Wonderful, life-threatening confusion.

All the implements were dulled, and participants, clad in linen cuirasses, grunted and groaned, struggling hand to hand, seeking the advantage. But most assuredly, a strong arm and a thick skull were the two most necessary elements to fighting in a melee.

The sport's objective was not to wound or kill the knights on the opposing team, but merely to capture them for ransom. In some tournaments the melee was far more expansive, the playing field literally extending for miles around, through village and town, through farmers' fields and grazing land. But much to the surrounding residents' gratitude, today the battle would be confined to the lists. A small skirmish by two knights in a cottage's vegetable garden might render a slender winter for its inhabitants. And Alexander de la Marche would have none of his people suffer for the mere sport of others.

Again the music sounded. Again the marshals of the field rode to their appointed posts. Again the heralds read the rules for the day's event. And the knights, now divided into two equal teams, flowed onto the field, a river of vivacious color and superior horseflesh. The plumage on their helms waved fluidly mid the breezy sunshine and the loud, sibilant roar of the spectators in the scaffold.

"Listen to them out there!" Gregory said to Jane as they walked around to the cooking pits for a quick check on the progress of the meat. "Must be nice to take an afternoon off to watch such sport."

"I wouldn't know!"

"Me either, Jane!" He looked up with mock exasperation, and they continued their stroll to the pits.

Back at the tournament, the knights separated and moved to opposite ends of the lists. Each team lined up in double file, ten men across. The horses shifted their feet restlessly; eye contact was made from across the field as each man on the front line promised to unseat the man opposite him. The men behind them would pick up whatever sport was left.

The crowd grew silent.

Danger clung to every particle of air.

Each heart accelerated. Swelling.

Nicholas watched, noticing a strange knight being counted among the contestants, one who had not jousted the day before. The red silk of his surcoat shone a ruby brilliance in the sun. No emblem was embroidered thereon. His identity remained a mystery. And the cylindrical helm with its menacing, rectangular slit in front of the wearer's eyes did little to enlighten the crowd as to who the newcomer was. On the back line, he held his lance with strength and confidence, his posture firm, yet supple. Ready.

The trumpets blared, and all the knights struck their horses' flanks with their spurs.

Forward.

Fast.

Hard.

They met with a clash that was at once so loud and confusing, no one watching could ascertain any action in detail. Loud. A cacophony of slamming armor, splintering lances, shields shattering on impact, grunts, yells. It resounded in a mortal din, bouncing off the castle walls, the forest. The noise catapulted across the Thames itself.

When the dust cleared and the noise settled to an even roar, a sanity of sorts returned. Almost half the men had lost their mounts. Some were scrambling to their feet, others lay wounded, and the quickest were already standing, pulling their dulled swords from their scabbards and kicking fallen lances out of their paths as they strode purposely toward their rivals. And the great clamor began again, of swords clashing and men shouting, while the more severely wounded were dragged from the lists or limped off on their own.

The battle zigzagged over the field, first the household knights and those who had joined them for the melee pushing the comers back, then the opposite way as Lord Alexander, royal-blue silk surcoat draped over his linen cuirass, advanced furiously, the unidentified knight fighting by his side. The man in red matched Lord Alexander's sword, stroke for stroke, against his own foe. With more skill, actually. He was an expert swordsman. And many in the lists conjectured just who this outstanding warrior could be.

"Onward men!" Lord Alexander shouted loudly above the frenzy, still seated on Bedivere. "Are we dogs that we should not make this day ours?"

The comers shouted their assent and bolstered their spirits with the heady wine of hand-to-hand combat. The unnamed knight fought more ferociously. His sword was remarkable. Of eastern workmanship. Obviously obtained on a crusade. This made the crowd even more curious. Wouldn't they have heard of such a fighter who had challenged the infidels who had stolen the Holy City? Even Percy, fighting on the same side as his uncle, had to respect this newcomer's prowess.

"Who are you?" Lord Alexander shouted above the din.

"The Red Knight!" the warrior answered with a shout.

"Ha!" the earl laughed. "Fight on, man! Fight on!"

"Huzzah!" the spectators shouted their approval, and the battle intensified as swords arched through the air and whirled in a dance of strength and might. The field thinned out dramatically as men were vanquished on either side and held as hostage by the other team to the side of the lists.

Frenzied and hot. Each man fought harder and with more intensity, promising a shorter melee than one in which indifference plays a role. Phillipe de Malveaux kept his eye upon Alexander de la Marche, working his way in his direction. After dispatching with his present combatant, he threw down his sword and pulled another out of his scabbard.

Minutes later, only ten men were left on the field, each the aggressor. The blue of Alexander's silk stood bright against the black of de Malveaux's surcoat. The earl jumped off the horse and confronted the Condottieri on foot, blocking his sword effortlessly and with skill.

The Red Knight dismounted as well, deciding to fight Sir Ronald Rey on equal footing. Without utterance, they continued the fight, but Rey knew it was a matter of time before he would be paying this man in red a ransom. Percy was fighting against one of the household knights, his blade a living, wonderful thing, a poetry of pain.

Meanwhile, de Malveaux swung round, and the tip of his sword sliced through the silken tunic. Alexander was taken aback only for a moment when he realized his opponent's sword was sharpened and battle-ready. His muscles tensed with the realization, and his intake of breath was sharp. That wince of time was all de Malveaux needed, and with a speed born of a dark, ill intent, he thrust his sword into the body of Alexander de la Marche.

TWENTY-FIVE

Crimson soaked through blue as Phillipe de Malveaux pulled his blade free.

"M'lord!" Nicholas yelled. Having never taken his eyes off his father for an instant, he leaped over the barrier and into the fray. He weaved through the frenzy, looking vulnerable, yet all the braver for it.

The Red Knight, keen of ear, heard the cry, and turned his head toward the earl. Lord Alexander crumpled to the ground. De Malveaux tried to remount his own horse, but he hadn't counted on the mysterious newcomer who leaped forward and grabbed the Condottieri around the ankle, pulling him off the horse.

When de Malveaux's eyes met those of the Red Knight, he became frightened for the first time in his life. His last view was the rage and the pent-up power of wrath he saw through the slit of his adversary's helm. They were green jewels glimmering a warning, foretelling of imminent death.

The blow was swift, precise, and forceful. Beneath his helm, De Malveaux's head was severed from his body. Percy stabbed the man through the heart for good measure.

⋆ ⋆ ⋆

Nicholas threw himself down by the earl. "Help him! Somebody!"

The Red Knight hurried over and said quietly to Nicholas, "Did you see what happened?" He lifted up the silken garment to expose the white linen cuirass, the front almost completely red with Alexander's blood. He was still conscious.

"He stabbed him, sir."

The earl spoke. "Yes, that's right. It was no accident. Get me back to the castle. At once. And let us begin praying that infection doesn't set in."

Nicholas's eyes grew wide with fear as the knight called for a litter to be brought. He lifted the earl into his arms and carried him off the field. "We must hurry, my lord. You're bleeding heavily. We must staunch the flow."

"It is as you say, I'm feeling weaker with every second. Please, sir knight, I do not wish to faint in front of such a gathering. Take me in all haste."

Nicholas stood back, eyes wide.

A litter arrived a moment later. King Henry's litter. It meandered along the path to the castle, the Red Knight inside with a now-unconscious Alexander. Nicholas watched as they departed.

Skeets was soon by his side.

"Come. He'll need you now."

"But how can I be—"

"Just be available in case he calls for you, lad." Skeets placed a strong hand on his shoulder. "Your reaction now will show him whether or not you are worthy of following after him. You can sit in the passageway outside of his solar."

"Skeets, do you think he'll die?"

"He isn't dead already. There's some hope in that. Come lad, hurry. There isn't much time. Remember, he needs you now, even if you aren't in his presence."

Nicholas determinedly accompanied Skeets up the path.

When the litter pulled up to the steps of the castle keep, the first one out was the Red Knight, his helm now removed, his identity no longer a mystery. Patrick MacBeth gently carried the earl up the three flights of steps and into his solar.

కికి కికి కికి

The encampment of knights was in a state of uproar as all talked about the outrage committed by the Black Knight.

"It puts a stain on all chivalry!" several claimed. But Sir Ronald Rey and his two compatriots, Sir Justin and Sir Niles, were busy looking through the deserted encampment of the Black Knight on the orders of King Henry himself. That it was left in haste by the sought-after squire was clearly evident. Baskets were overturned, the straw pallet upon which the Black Knight had slept was already rolled up, but not tied.

"Why do you think he waited?" Sir Niles, a stocky, swarthy man shook his head.

"The Black Knight was clearly counting his losses. He didn't want to do anything suspicious, and, if his squire broke camp during the melee, it would have been cause for, at the very least, observation."

Sir Justin, a beautiful young blond man, agreed. "And it leads me to believe he must have been hired by someone to kill the earl. Obviously, he was paid handsomely enough to leave this all behind."

"My guess is that the squire left long before the melee even started. Which means he knew what was to happen, which means he may know how and where and by whom the Condottieri was hired," Ronald surmised as he rubbed his chin. "Come then, let us be off. Into your hauberks, men, and onto your mounts. We'll find this squire soon enough."

" 'Tis why the king called for *us!*" Niles said proudly. "There are no better trackers in all of England! If anyone can find this unworthy squire, it will be us!"

217

❧ ❧ ❧

Patrick pushed up the sleeves to his tunic and wiped the sweat from his brow. The task he was about to undertake was one of the least to his liking. Grabbing a pile of rags, he picked up a hot rod from the fire.

Jane was by the earl's bedside. She placed an inch-thick stick in his mouth and put Lord Alexander's hand in her own. "Bear down on me, m'lord. Feel free to squeeze my hand as hard as you can."

Patrick's face was solemn as he walked toward the bed. "Forgive me, sir," he bowed, "for the pain I will cause you." And before the earl could even flinch, the red-hot rod was jabbed inside the wound. Lord Alexander bit down on the stick and squeezed Jane's hand until she thought all her bones would break. But she held fast.

Several seconds later it was over.

Patrick dressed the wound, and Jane soothed the earl by wiping his brow, cheeks, and neck with a cool cloth scented with rosewater. After a draught of sleeping herbs, he was resting soundly.

"The best thing for him," Jane said.

"Thank you for your help, Jane. There's many a man that can't stand the sight of a cauterization."

"I've done many myself."

He looked surprised. "Have you?"

"Of course. And I must say, your technique is very good."

"Thank you." He bowed with a smile and ushered her out of the earl's solar. "A compliment from you, I see, is something I should take most highly."

"I don't give them out frivolously, that much is certain. And now, Patrick, if you will excuse me, I have to get back down to the kitchen. If there's anything else I can do, please let me know. You know I'm always glad to help."

She hurried down the steps, practically feeling Patrick's admiring gaze as she disappeared from his view.

❧ ❧ ❧

The tournament rattled on in a more rickety fashion now, and the staff continued to work at a pace born of a busy fury, but all joy was gone from the service.

"Only one more day to go," Jane sighed, as she cubed some pig meat that night for a savory pottage that would constitute a small part of tomorrow's dinner. "Do you think he'll be all right?" She couldn't help but feel doubt.

"Of course he will!" Stephen said forcefully.

"I hope so."

Her reasons for such a hope were so different from the others in the kitchen. Her fellow servants knew they would find no kinder lord, or work in a wealthier, more upstanding household outside of King Henry's. But Jane's reasons went far deeper, and Nicholas confirmed them when he came to bed that night, deep circles drawn by worry beneath his eyes.

Jane immediately held him to her when he climbed into the bed, letting him weep softly. But sooner than she expected, his tears ceased. "Do you think he'll be all right, Mother?"

She sighed, not willing to lie to Nicholas ever again. " 'Tis not for me to say, my son. Truly we must pray for his grace."

"My father."

"Yes. Your father."

"It would be a cruel working of the divine to have given him to me only to take him away before the world knew I was his."

" 'Tis not for us to question God, son."

"Why not? I don't understand how He could let something like this happen. If He's as powerful as you taught me He is, He could have stopped the Black Knight, Mother."

"He could stop a lot of things, Nicholas. But He doesn't. Sometimes God just lets us make mistakes. And I wish I could tell you why. But if we can greedily accept the good God gives us, we must accept the adverse. You want to be strong, don't you?"

"Yes."

"Then realize that true strength comes only through pain. In my heart, I believe your father will live. Perhaps God will use this not only to strengthen you, but his lordship as well."

"Mother, will you take the time to go to the chapel and pray for him tomorrow?"

"Yes, I will, Nicholas. I'll gladly do that for you. Why do you not go yourself?"

"I'd rather not." His statement told of inner struggles and battles that lay ahead.

"All right."

The darkness of the room soon mellowed their consciousness, and mother and son slept, despite the many questions which whispered in the passageways of their minds.

ﷺ   ﷺ   ﷺ

The next afternoon Lord Alexander slept deeply. He had experienced a bad night of it.

"It's worse than I feared." Patrick's brows were knit.

"He vomited earlier in the day," Skeets volunteered the information.

"I wonder if his liver is becoming too hot."

"Sir?" Skeets looked puzzled.

Patrick tried to explain. "It is thought that the stomach is like a great caldron, Skeets, which cooks the food by heat which comes from the liver."

"After he vomited, he did seem to feel better."

"Let's try and get him to drink some more wine. It should aid him. Help settle his stomach."

"All right." Skeets called one of the young women who were attending the earl, ordering her to give him as much wine as she could get him to drink. "It probably won't be much," the steward turned back to Patrick, "but at least it will be something."

Just then Lady Alison breezed in, wearing a look of concern like an ill-fitting garment. She placed a familiar hand on the small of Patrick's back. "How is he?"

Patrick moved away and around to the other side of the bed. "Not as well as I had hoped, my lady. Skeets told me earlier he passed a fitful night. I'm trying to make him as comfortable as possible."

"What are you giving him?"

"Something to stay off a possible infection. I've ordered that he be given more wine upon awakening."

"Fine. I'll see to it myself."

"Thank you. This is most disconcerting, I must say. Last night he seemed to be doing much better. Didn't he take a little food?"

"Yes, he did. Perhaps that is the problem?"

"What do you mean?"

Lady Alison turned to Skeets. "Skeets, would you please leave us alone? You, too!" she barked in the direction of the serving girl.

Skeets bowed and was gone.

Lady Alison circled around the foot of the bed toward Patrick. She gazed at him with adoration and expectation, as she put her arms around his neck. "Let's not talk about Lord Alexander. He'll be fine."

"Alison. This isn't the time or the pl—"

"Nonsense, my lover."

"Alison, what happened the other day—"

"It was wonderful for me, too, Patrick."

"No, Alison, that wasn't what I was going to say."

"Then let us dispose of words altogether. Kiss me, Patrick."

"No, I can't. Please, Alison, it was all a dreadful mistake. I haven't been able to stop thinking about it the past two days."

"Neither have I."

"But my thoughts are filled with regret."

Her eyes flashed, and she pulled her arms from around his neck to place her hands on her hips. "Do you love another?"

He couldn't answer that question, yet, could he? Love? 'Tis true he thought about Jane Lightfoot almost constantly, but love?

"I don't know."

"Who is she?"

"I'd rather not say."

"Why? Because she's a common servant?" Alison's voice lowered in haughty disdain.

"What do you know of this?" His alarm was instantaneous. He hated to admit it, but the invalid Alison was easier to deal with—so much more predictable.

"I've seen you together. Thrice. Upon the walls. Coming off the barge. Down at the river." She chuckled. "I thought you were a man of fine tastes, Patrick."

"Lady Alison, I didn't come to argue with you. Please, your brother lies here in agony. Let's hold off on this conversation for now. In fact, let us pretend nothing has ever happened between us. I liked you so much better the way you were."

With a pitiful attempt at dignity, she held her head high. "There can be no telling, I suppose, what a man will find attractive. Perhaps you like an easy bed with no commitment. In which case, 'tis something I would never deliver." Conveniently, Alison not only made herself a woman of virtue, but she also believed it to be the case. "We shouldn't be discussing these matters anyway. My brother lies sick."

Patrick shook his head in exasperation but was glad the conversation was turning.

"I sat with him last night, you know," she volunteered the information. "He took a little wine from the cup I offered, and soon slept."

Patrick ignored the last bit of information Alison offered, much to her chagrin. "Has he eaten anything?"

"The cook sent up some lovely soup, which he ate earlier this morning. Mayhap she used rotten meat. It was after that when he vomited."

"Then that is most probably what it was. Just a bad meal."

"Terrible timing on the part of that cook of yours," Alison said dryly. Patrick ignored the barb.

"Will you sit with him while I go make up a poultice for the wound?" Patrick asked.

"Yes." She took her brother's limp hand dramatically. "I'll do that for you, Patrick."

Patrick nodded his thanks and hurried down to the kitchens.

"Jane!" he called as he entered the building.

"She's down in the chapel, sir," Stephen offered. "Just took a little time to pray for his lordship."

"Thank you."

He found Jane in the cool recesses of the small church. The sounds of the concluding day of the tournament were going on as the final round of the archery competition came to completion. And whilst Lord Alexander was far from the only one wounded in the melee, the fact that his wounds were inflicted so deliberately put a damper on the rest of the festivities. Even King Henry declined to come on the final day, preferring to stay in Westminster.

Patrick stood beside her. "Jane?"

She turned and smiled sweetly at him, saw his concern-weary face, and immediately placed a hand on his arm. "What is it, Patrick? His lordship?"

"Yes. He fares not well at all. He's got a fever now, and I fear the wound is becoming infected. I've come down to make up another poultice."

"I've done it for you already. I made up a plaster of wound-wart. There's nothing like it when it comes to—"

"I know that, Jane!" Patrick sounded exasperated, and his physician's pride exhibited itself once again.

Saying nothing, Jane hurried to the kitchen and retrieved the plaster. "Here you go then. Wait...there's something else you might try. Cow's parsnip."

This was something Patrick had never heard of. "What does it do?"

"I just boil the seeds and root in oil for a little while, and if you put it on the wound as well, it will stop it from seeping and smelling."

"All right. It's worth a try. I'll send someone down for it shortly. Thank you, Jane." He reached his hands out to hold her by the shoulders, and quickly he kissed her on the mouth, a familiarity found within the kiss that was comforting and thrilling in its trust.

"You know I'd do whatever I can to help you, Patrick."

"Yes, I do. That is what I was thanking you for. I'm sorry I was such a sod a minute ago."

"You're under much stress. It's all right. I understand."

He quickly left, Jane silently offering up one last, heartfelt prayer for the lord in the keep. A cold wind began to blow around the castle.

❦ ❦ ❦

Patrick's long, powerful legs swiftly negotiated the narrow, circular staircase of the keep. The woundwart plaster was contained in a small wooden cup, a spatula for slathering on the wound protruding from the paste.

Lady Alison sprang to her feet as he entered Lord Alexander's solar. "He's awakened!" she cried. "He just opened his eyes and asked for Nicholas."

"Nicholas?"

"Yes," Lord Alexander said, a weakened lightness to his voice. "Would you fetch him for me, sister?"

She turned to one of the serving girls and ordered Nicholas brought, much to her chagrin.

Lord Alexander pointed to the bowl. "What do you have there, Patrick?"

"Just a plaster for your wound, my lord. Jane sent it up for you."

The earl smiled. "Yes. Jane. What of my wound? How does it look?"

"I will check it now."

"Good."

Patrick exposed the wound on Alexander's abdomen. The flesh was inflamed; the wound oozed and festered. "He certainly didn't know much about anatomy to stab you where he did. I don't believe he hit any major organs. But you are feverish, and the wound seeps, my lord. I fear infection has set in."

"Do you mean to tell me I bore the pain of cauterization for nothing?"

Lady Alison's eyes lit up, but she quickly turned her back to pour fresh wine into the cup.

"Let us pray not. Do you have any idea why this happened, my lord?" Patrick asked as he signaled to a maid to bring over a bowl of fresh water and a clean rag.

Lord Alexander began his short tale. "Patrick, I saw it in his walk as he advanced before me that he was after more than just a good fight. And when I realized his blade was honed, I knew that I was about to settle an old score of some kind."

"Old score, sir? Who?"

"I don't know, but an occurrence such as this is not unusual when this many fighting men, and of such high caliber, join together for sport. As far as I know, I do not have any quarrels with the man personally. He could have easily been hired by someone."

"You did unhorse him, sir."

"Well, yes. I did that."

"It was probably that which made him seek out revenge. Perhaps he was a very small man inside that great black armor."

"Perhaps. One never knows just who is hidden inside their armor. Still, I think he was probably hired by someone who cares not for the policies of the king and myself."

"There are more disgruntled barons and lords around than content ones," Patrick agreed.

"In any case, I must say I'm thankful you were there so quickly, even if you were the mysterious Red Knight."

"Who told you?" Patrick asked, for Lord Alexander had succumbed to unconsciousness before his trusted physician had removed his helm.

"No one. I recognized your voice. Your accent betrayed you to me almost immediately. Although I don't think Nicholas realized."

"I've spoken little to the lad."

The earl lay still after that, wincing as Patrick thoroughly examined the wound. Lady Alison watched in fascination, her pink tongue licking her lips.

"How do you feel now?"

"Tired."

"Your fever worries me, my lord. I'm going to have Jane make up for you a decoction of chamomile. She also is preparing something which will hopefully stop the infection in your wound."

"She is a good woman."

"Very accomplished in the healing arts, I must admit. After this, my lord, you may find you shall be using her services and not my own."

"It wouldn't be such a drain upon my purse!"

" 'Tis true."

"But then again, I do believe I shall always want you for my physician, Doctor MacBeth. You give me medicine for my mind as well as my body merely by your pleasant and erudite conversation. There's precious little of that around *here!*" He threw a look in Lady Alison's direction, then closed his eyes. "I should like to sleep a little, I believe. I suddenly feel tired."

Patrick covered up the earl. "Sleep is what you need. I will leave the wound open to the air for just a while until Jane sends up her decoction. In fact, I think I'll go down now and see if it's ready."

Lady Alison stepped forward. "I'll continue to stay with him, doctor."

"There's no need," Lord Alexander said, opening his eyes again. He looked at Patrick. "Didn't I already ask someone to send Nicholas up?" The earl was feeling more and more irritable.

"Brother, he's a busy lad, and you need to rest," Alison asserted herself. "Besides, I just received word he's at the abbey today. If you want some company, I'd be glad to call Percy to your side."

"No! Please. I'd rather not . . . you're right, Alison, I need to rest."

"Let's leave him alone then, Alison." Patrick took her arm. "I would speak with you."

"All right." Despite his spurning speech earlier, she liked the feeling of his hand under her elbow.

They left the room as the curtains were being drawn against the afternoon sunshine by a sweet-featured maid. A sleepy dimness enhanced the sick-room qualities of the chamber. And the servants moved about silently, as though levitating just an inch above the ground, their movements fluidly quiet, their speech, when necessary, hushed.

"Do you know when the fever began?"

"Sometime during the middle of the night, I assume."

"Yes. They always seem to start then."

"Are you really that worried? Is there a chance he won't recover?"

"There's always that chance, Lady Alison. Let's just hope Jane's medicines work."

"Doctor, I'm not feeling well myself. Perhaps you can attend to me now as well?"

Indeed, Alison was a bit pale. But Patrick knew he must tell her of his decision. " 'Tis true, you don't look well. But in light of what happened the other night, Alison, I think it is not wise for me to continue on as your physician. I know of several good men in London who are capable and who would give you proper care." His voice sounded calm and so entirely devoid of emotion.

A livid, throbbing anger blistered her heart. The malevolent expression in her eyes almost caused Patrick to acquiesce.

Almost.

He turned his back on her. Alison stared feverishly at his back, not moving at all. But her mind was moving along at a furious pitch. She couldn't live without this man. The strong hatred Patrick had witnessed was not for him.

No.

For when Alison found out he was the Red Knight, her infatuation for him had grown tenfold. It had been worth it to watch that magnificent knight on the field and realize he had shared her bed only the day before.

There was only one thing to do. She had to make him see her for the woman she really was—a woman who would give her heart and soul to him, who would worship him only, be everything he could ever need in his life.

But as long as Jane Lightfoot was a part of Patrick, that would be impossible.

❧ ❧ ❧

A light rain began to fall as Alison, a green velvet cloak holding out the autumn chill, prepared to go out for a walk.

"Where are you going, Mother?" Percy had asked as he helped her into the outer garment.

"For a bit of a walk, Percy darling. I think that Doctor Mac-Beth is right. Being forever confined here in my solar cannot be a good thing. If I don't start tending to my own health, I fear I shall rue the day."

"Would you like me to accompany you?"

"No, my love. Just a little walk will be nice. I have some thinking to do and won't be good company. You know, your uncle may not recover from this grievous wound."

Percy nodded but didn't say anything.

"Well, off I go!" Her voice was too cheerful to be Alison's, but Percy didn't notice. It was almost time for his training.

"Have a lovely walk, Mother."

And so she found herself in the woods. She knew the way well to her destination, but she usually trod these paths under the cover of night. In truth, Alison had been accustomed to walking this way ever since she was a little girl—ever since she had found the secret passage behind the tapestry of Daniel in the lion's den, which hung in her room. It led out of the castle and into a tunnel which came up directly in the woods. No one ever saw Alison crossing the meadow, no one ever saw her outside the castle walls except for the very occasional trip to London.

But she came out frequently.

Alison had one friend she could claim. An old woman who had found her crying at the age of eight when father had begun to take an unnatural interest in her. An old woman who had taught her that life is cruel, and you had best be even more cruel if you wished to survive. A woman who had taught her never to bare her soul to anyone, never to let even those closest to her know who she really was.

TWENTY-SIX

By the time Alison arrived at the cairn, her cloak was covered with beads of rain. Tatty-Nan was not at home, but Alison was well-acquainted with the ancient burial mound. A ring of torches stabbed the ground in readiness for tomorrow night's ceremony. It was to be a full moon. Chanting and dancing would take place by the few who adhered to the "old religion" and looked upon Tatty-Nan as their high priestess.

Alison entered the great mouth framed by the three large slabs of rock. But the dwelling did not end with the rocks which protruded from the hill. It went farther into the earth, the hill being hollowed out, its walls made of smooth stones. The bodies once buried inside the cairn were long since decomposed, the bones scattered by wild animals, and all that was present now were Tatty-Nan's belongings, illumined by a dim lamp that hung from the ceiling. Herbs, plant bark and root, dried animal parts, cooking pots, and manuscripts written in an unknown tongue to any but those who prayed to the "old gods," littered the medium-sized room. On a table sat other implements of her craft: a boline or dagger, a chalice, and a wand. Tatty-Nan's pallet, a pile of rags and straw, huddled in the corner next to a bucket of water with a dipper.

Alison settled beneath the lamp, next to a haphazard mound of scrolls, and began to read as she awaited the return of her mentor. Spell after spell was skimmed by her eyes, and she smiled at each one. Tatty-Nan had taught her long ago to read the ancient language. The religion they practiced together was a collection of the dark sides of many ancient pagan religions. The old woman had never liked any one religion as a young woman, so she dissected them, taking the "choice" portions from each one to satisfy her own ideas of what pagan worship should be. Tatty-Nan sacrificed regularly the small forest animals to appease "her" spirits, which she claimed spoke to her regularly. And Alison followed her path, always searching for something that was never quite within reach.

The old crone appeared an hour later. "My lady!" Her pitted smile was wide with pleasure.

"Hello, Tatty-Nan." Alison always remained formal with the ancient woman. Perhaps it was bred by her noble circumstances, perhaps it was bred by the small amount of fear she held for the sorceress.

Tatty-Nan had a squirrel in her hand, hanging from its legs which she had tied together. "Awwww, ye can do a bit better than that for this old woman, can't ye?"

Alison smiled.

"There, love. That's a bit better." She threw the squirrel into a wooden cage. "Now, what brings ye to Tatty-Nan in the middle o' the day! Ye are troubled, that's for certain."

" 'Tis Jane Lightfoot."

"Ahhh, the cook at Marchemont. And what trouble can a simple woman such as Jane brew up for a great lady like yerself, eh?"

"I'm sure you can figure it out yourself if you try," Alison said dryly, taking the cup of mead Tatty-Nan handed to her.

"It wouldn't be somethin' to do with the fair Doctor Mac-Beth, now would it?"

Lady Alison nodded.

"Weel, now. I suppose she cast a spell of her own on the good man who's stolen your heart?"

"Yes."

"And you have come to the conclusion that he can never love you as long as she is there to steal his affections."

"Yes, that is exactly right."

Tatty-Nan groaned as she sat down next to Alison and began to pull the leaves from a large bunch of featherfoil she had gathered earlier in the day. "She's cast a spell on him in her own way. 'Twill be uncommon hard to work against that."

Alison sat up straight. "What sort of spell?"

"True love."

"That's not what I want to hear, old woman!"

Tatty-Nan cackled and wheezed. "But you must know the truth so that you can effectively deal with the situation at hand."

"What can I do? I want Patrick. Since I became a woman, I've been in search of a man exactly opposite of my father."

"Your father was a weak, spineless man! Do not speak of such vermin!" Tatty-Nan's eyes blazed. Just as quickly, they returned to their placid state of simple brown, and she put a tender though crabbed hand on Alison's arm. "There is only one way to deal with your problem. My child," her voice was warm and coercing, "I could cast spells or make potions to rid you of Jane Lightfoot, but there's only one way to effectively remove her from the heart of Patrick MacBeth forever . . . and that is death."

"How?"

"Come, girl, you know the way of it!"

"I don't understand, Tatty."

"Then I shall explain, and it will all be much easier than you may suppose."

🙘 🙘 🙘

The next day all the pleasure seekers broke camp, gathering their mountains of belongings and heading home. The archbishop of Canterbury had agreed to preside over the meals for what remained of the tournament. But now all that was past.

The traveling minstrels had moved onto fatter fields, those seeking amusement had quickly fled the dry, tired field they had made of the meadow. The once-waving grass was now clotted and bedraggled, pocked by the telltale signs of many camp fires.

The servants breathed a sigh of relief, even though they were busy trying to return things to normal. Soon the household would move on to one of the earl's other residences while this one was cleaned, the old rushes removed and new ones spread upon a freshly scrubbed floor. The moat would also be rid of its foul contents. But until the earl was able to travel, that would be impossible. It seemed stifling because of the extra grime, and yet they were free of the cacophonous strangers who had littered the hall, the bailey, and practically everywhere else for the past four days.

The kitchen staff had already slowed down to the normally frantic pace they were used to living with daily. Tonight's meal would be much more simple. Several pottages and only two selections of meat.

Jane was spicing the contents of the great caldrons when a weary Patrick entered the busy room. "You look tired, Patrick. Sit down at the table there."

Agnes and Mattie raised their eyebrows at each other. A nonverbal "See there?" erupting between them.

Patrick was glad to accept Jane's invitation. Yesterday evening the earl had succumbed to delirium. His fever hadn't stopped raging. And Patrick hadn't left his side since he had arrived the previous afternoon to put on the new plaster of woundwart.

"I can't believe it's already been two days since the accident," Jane remarked, setting down a cup of her honey mead in front of him.

He took a long draught of the sweet drink, draining the cup as much from the delight of its contents as from his extreme thirst.

"How is he doing?"

"No better. I was hoping to get some more of the cow's parsnip you gave me yesterday."

"Yes, I've got some ready for you."

"Thank you, Jane." He pushed his cup toward her.

"More?"

"No, dear lady. Much as I wish for just that, I must keep a clear head."

"Then you should take a little food." She set a trencher down in front of him, and soon it was laden with two slices of fresh bread, some slices from a joint of beef left over from dinner earlier that day, and some turnips. Patrick wasted no time consuming the food and felt much refreshed after he had finished. He suspected it was being near to Jane as much as the pleasure of a full belly. She sat with him the entire time he was eating.

"I heard an interesting tale here in the kitchen today, good doctor." She picked up a piece of his bread and took a bite, setting it back down on his plate. It was a gesture of great intimacy, and it pleased him. He bit off around the spot immediately.

Their eyes met.

"And what did you hear, good madam?"

Jane leaned close, her shoulder brushing his. "Skeets tells me there's a side to you I've never seen."

"Are you referring to my participation in the Grand Melee?"

Jane nodded. "Well? I think all those questions I asked you on the boat would have surely invoked a tale of your battle experience! What do you have to say for yourself?"

"Nothing, Jane. My days of knighthood are long since past. It's something I'd rather forget about."

"You were truly knighted?"

"Yes, but not here in England. In France. I forsook the 'Sir' after I came back to Britain. I'm a physician now."

"Yet you participated yesterday. Why?"

Patrick MacBeth shrugged. " 'Tis a mystery to me. For the first time in years I felt young, alive, virile once again. The tournament called to me for some reason, and I had to see if I could still compete. I think it must be having you in my life, Jane. You have a way of making a man feel strong, as if your own strength is challenging me." The rage inside of him from the tryst with Lady Alison was another, more potent reason. He needed to get it out of himself somehow.

"Did you compete much when you were younger?"

"Yes. Mostly in France and Germany."

"So I have much to learn regarding just who Patrick Mac-Beth is?"

"Oh yes, Jane. You have much to learn."

She hugged his arm close to her side. "Believe it or not, Patrick, that gives me much comfort. I must say, it thrills me more than I'd like to admit to find out you are such a man of physical strength. And here I thought you were a simple physician."

"No man is a simple anything."

"That's true enough. But I must give you a piece of advice, and that is not to mix your battle skills with your medicinal ones."

"What do you mean?"

"Don't you think you bled the Black Knight a bit much for his own good?"

Patrick laughed. "Oh, Jane. You are good for my heart. I do believe it's needed a medicine like you for quite some time."

She removed the plate from him and set down a pear tart. "Here's a little something to round off your meal, and then back upstairs with you."

"So soon?" he complained good-naturedly.

Her eyes became serious. "He needs you now. I'll meet you on the walls when the bells of the abbey toll for evensong."

"With something like that to look forward to, I can go easily up to my task." He stood to his feet, licking the last bit of honey from his fingers.

"Till evensong, then." Patrick's hands sought hers, his thumbs rubbing gently on the backs of her roughened hands. "You're so good for me, Jane."

"I know," she whispered. "Till evensong."

He left, and Mattie and Agnes hurried over. "You're holding out on us, girl!" Mattie blustered.

"I'm doing no such thing! He just came down for a bite to eat, that's all."

"As you said the other day, Jane Lightfoot, I've been a grand-mother for ten years, so I've lived a long time. I know two people in love when I see them!"

Agnes nodded. "He's quite taken with you, Mistress Jane."

"Well," Jane said smugly, not indulging their curiosity one whit, "perhaps he is just that!"

Mattie and Agnes talked in private later on. "Think of it. A man in love with Jane. And such a fine one. It's almost too wonderful to believe," Agnes gushed.

"She deserves it, Agnes, most certainly. Raising that son by herself all these years. We'll throw her some party when he proposes, as much for me as for her."

"What do you mean, Mattie?"

"I've been attempting to put her together with one fellow or another for years, and all for naught. 'Twill make my life much easier to put down the task of making a match for Jane Lightfoot! Unless, of course, you're interested in finding someone yourself, Agnes?"

Agnes looked shocked. "Me! Why—"

"Come now, girlie! I've seen the eyes you've made at Gregory."

"Nonsense! He's 15 years older than I am!"

"Handsome, though."

"Yes he is, but—"

"And surely you've noticed the eyes he makes at you."

"Why no, I've never noticed any such thing, Mattie!" Agnes had to admit, however, that the news was quite welcomed.

"You just leave it all to me, Agnes. I'll have you two fixed up in no time at all!"

❦ ❦ ❦

Percy inspected his fingernails in a sunbeam that drained across his mother's bed. "Terrible thing, this stabbing."

"More terrible than you can perhaps realize," his mother sighed. "How do you feel, my love, mayhap only minutes away from inheriting what is due you?" *And me,* she thought.

"I'm trying not to think about it. Even for all he's ignored me these past years, Mother, I cannot help but respect my uncle. He's been a great leader."

"And that should be an encouragement, for you've watched him. Now you must try to emulate him."

"Yes, I suppose that following his example would be a good thing. But, I must say," he sniffed, and began shining his fingernails on his gown, "there *are* a few things I would change around here immediately."

"Such as?"

"Finding someone else besides that cook's boy to follow Skeets. I was thinking of looking for someone more educated. Someone from Paris, perhaps."

"What a good idea! Even paying someone with such credentials will be less costly than educating that kitchen rat."

"Precisely, Mother."

"And while you're about that business, you might go about finding a new cook. A French cook. We'd be the envy of everyone except the king."

"I don't know, Mother. From what I hear about court, Jane Lightfoot puts on as fine a meal as any French—"

"Enough! I was simply surmising that if you demoted Nicholas, a proud woman like Jane Lightfoot would never stay around long to bear the effrontery."

" 'Tis true. But Uncle is far from dead. And I have to admit to you, Mother, that I am bored with all this waiting."

"Well then, I've something to which you might attend for me. I've a message to send to London, and I trust no one but you to take it."

He stood to his feet. "All right, Mother. Where do I need to take it?"

"Just a moment. Let me think while I'm writing this."

The quill scratched on the parchment and she wrote quickly, her pen leaving bold, undisciplined strokes on the creamy expanse. Quickly dumping sand on the paper, she blotted the ink. Then, scattering the sand on the table, leaving a mess for someone else to clean, she folded the message and sealed it with brown wax.

"Here. Ride as fast as you can and take this to the proprietor of The Traitor's Head."

"Where is it?"

"Near the Tower."

"Oh yes, I know the place. To whom should I give it?"

"The innkeeper. His name is Owen. He shall know what to do with it."

"Can you tell me what this is all about?" Percy put the message in a small pouch which hung from his embossed leather belt.

"Not yet, my son. Just be a good man, and go as quickly as you can!"

Percy kissed his mother on the cheek and followed her orders. Like always.

❧ ❧ ❧

The squire was leading the small band of knights on a merry chase. But they were soon to close in on the man who had changed his identity with each town he had passed through. The squire had been a bit loose-lipped during the tournament, bragging to another squire of the innkeeper's daughter he had bedded the day before the tournament had begun. And so, off they went to The Traitor's Head. They had learned from a serving wench there that a man had rented a stall for his horse before the tournament started, had paid in advance, and sure enough, came back for the horse three days later in quite a hurry to be gone.

"He had them big kind of eyes, sir," she explained as she served them all some ale. "You know, the kind that look all round and as if they might just *pop* out of their sockets if the wind blew at them sideways!"

"Any other distinguishing features?"

"Nah. He's just a wee man. But other than that, all I can really remember is them eyes. Now, his horse was a beauty."

And now it was two days later, getting late, but they were still on his trail. So far he had been disguised as a boy, a priest, a merchant, even a nun, but to little success. His only real ally was the fact that he had almost a day's head start, having left the tournament hours before the Black Knight had rode his horse onto the lists. Sir Niles grumbled irritably, "I don't know why he bothers with those disguises if he's not going to get rid of the horse!"

They came to a lonely farm cottage several miles later. All lamps in the humble dwelling had been extinguished, and a flustered cottager hurried to the door, which shivered from the hearty rap of Sir Ronald's fist.

"Open up in the name of the king!"

"Yes, m'lord. Yes." The old man opened the door a crack, but was pushed inward when Sir Justin shoved the door open completely.

"Have you taken in any guests tonight?" Sir Ronald demanded.

"Why yes, sir. Just a woman. Truth be told, I think she's a bit addled. And there's naught o' wonder of it. She's the ugliest wench I've ever laid me eyes on!"

"That's our man!" Niles triumphed.

"Pardon me?" The farmer looked confused.

"Take me to his . . . or her, room."

"Well, she isn't in here, your graces. She preferred to bed down in the barn with her horse. And I just as soon let her!"

The knights hurried back outside, but the barn held no man, only a cow, a goat, and a donkey. The squire could be seen riding down the road, the horse running as though his tail was on fire.

"We've got him now," Ronald smiled with delight.

"Long live the king and his wise decision to employ us!" Niles said, and the men jumped onto their horses and began to pursue the "lady" down the road.

꧁ ꧂ ꧃

Jane knocked tentatively on the door to Lady Alison's solar. "Come!"

She pushed open the door to the prettiest room in all of Marchemont Castle. She drew in her breath at the luxury. The tapestries hanging on the walls, the beautiful dower chest near the window. And the massive bed, made of maple wood and carven with flowers and fruit. Two great black iron candlesticks, complete with burning candles illumined the splendor of the room. Jane felt ill at ease and utterly out of place.

"You sent for me, m'lady?"

"Yes. I have a terrible headache this evening. Terrible. And Patrick . . . er . . . Doctor MacBeth is too busy with my brother to tend to me. I was hoping you had something you could give me."

"Why, of course I do. 'Twould be an honor to serve you. I shall be right back. What part of your head is troubling you, m'lady?"

"All of it."

Jane inwardly sighed. "As you wish, m'lady."

Minutes later she was administering a decoction of butcher's broom to Lady Alison. "There you are, m'lady," she said in a voice that was kinder than anyone had spoken to Alison in a long time. "With a good night's sleep, you'll feel better come morning."

"Thank you, Jane."

"Shall I come check on you in the morning?"

"Please do." Alison closed her eyes.

Jane turned to go.

"Wait!"

"Yes, m'lady?"

"Are you always this nice, Jane?"

"M'lady?"

"Never mind. Just leave me to get some rest! Come in the morning."

"Yes, m'lady."

Jane hurried from the room. The chapel bell was tolling.

Lady Alison watched her disappear around the corner, and she breathed a sigh of relief. Yes, she had done the right thing, she believed now. As long as Jane Lightfoot was present at Marchemont, so kind, capable, and gentle, Patrick MacBeth would never be won.

She pulled her covers up to her neck, simultaneously snuffing out the small flame of regret that very soon Jane Lightfoot would be no more.

TWENTY-SEVEN

"Patrick, how is his grace?"

"My lady, he fares not well. And I am just as frightened for you. You must bolster yourself. Do not give up just yet."

The countess had dropped even more weight the past five days, and she hadn't risen from her bed since yesterday. "Oh, doctor, I should have given up a long time ago. I feel I just cannot go on any longer. 'Twould be a good time for me to go, while Lord Alexander will be none the wiser. Leave me now and let me rest, my good man. I will do my best to stay until at least tomorrow." She smiled weakly and closed her eyes to sleep.

The bell for evensong tolled, and Patrick exited soundlessly from the room.

❧ ❧ ❧

The Thames was latticed by the moonlight, and the stars shone a gentle light on them as they spoke in hushed tones.

"Is he doing any better?"

"The fever continues, but the cow's parsnip is doing the wound well, Jane. I shall remember that in the future."

"So it's still too soon to tell if he will make it?"

"Unfortunately, yes. Who knows how far the infection has spread in his body? If the fever doesn't break within a day, I shall fear the worst."

"Then I must continue to pray for his grace."

"Yes, and you must pray for the countess as well."

"Is she faring more ill than before?"

"She cannot rise from the bed. In fact, she refuses to do so."

"Why?"

"She's given up now. Just before we met, I was at her bed-side. She said she would die soon, while her husband was still sick. That way it would be a peaceful passing without him having to know she was ever ill."

"That's the most selfish thing I've ever heard of in my life!"

Patrick looked up at her quickly. "How can you say that?"

"Perhaps her presence with him would be what he needs to cheer him, to bring him back from the gates of death. Oh, Patrick, she's never loved him. I see that now. She's been too steeped in a false piety, a vain humility, to be a wife."

"What are you talking about, Jane? You've no right to judge her like that. She's the most charitable person I've ever met."

"To everyone but the man God gave to her to be a wife to."

"You sound like you know more about their marriage than I do! I never thought of you as quick to judge, Jane."

"I know Lord Alexander de la Marche in a way you never could, Patrick."

Jane knew the time was upon her. It was so right—the lead-in was so perfect. The river shone below, and she remembered the night of the seduction and knew that if she was ever to be truly happy with this man who sat beside her, she would have to tell him the truth.

Jane looked hard into his eyes, then stared at the ancient river. "I've been lying to you about Nicholas's father."

"I know."

"How?"

"I'm not sure. I know you well, Jane Lightfoot. Don't ask me how."

She said the words softly. "Nicholas is not the son of a man I married in my youth. In fact, I've never been married. Nicholas is the only known son of Lord Alexander."

Patrick hid his shock, but barely.

"It is the reason he's being educated now, why there's the pretense of him someday becoming the steward."

"And your position as cook—is that a pretense as well?"

Jane knew exactly what he was referring to, but she asked him to clarify it. "Do you speak of my relationship with the earl?"

"Yes. You are a lovely woman, Jane. And you seem to know much about the earl's longings and desires as far as the countess is concerned . . . "

Jane laughed aloud, immediately diffusing the tension that had begun to build. "Oh, Patrick, you don't think that the earl and I are—"

"Isn't it a natural conclusion?"

"Well, yes," she chuckled, "if you're thinking with your heart. But use your head, man! I really am a simple cook. You don't think if I was the earl's mistress I wouldn't demand more from him? My goodness, feeding him all day and attending to his physical desires at night? Oh, Patrick, if I were to defame the morals I've built up over the years, I'd certainly expect more from the earl than that!"

Patrick looked at her. "I should have realized—"

"No, you shouldn't have realized anything. I think there was a little jealousy coming through on your part!" she teased. "In fact, I *know* there was!"

"And?" His tone was only slightly defensive.

"And it pleases me greatly," she whispered. Feeling embarrassed, however, she continued the conversation. For the next hour they sat together as the moon sailed higher into the night, throwing its clear, cleansing light onto the Thames. She told him everything, the words flowing forth in a rush, only tempering when Patrick asked a question for clarification. The traveling lord. Her pregnancy. The public whipping. Father. The birthmark. The day by the stables. Her fear of losing her son forever to his illustrious father. Patrick put his arms around her, seeking to be of some comfort.

They sat that way in silence for a little while. Jane feeling spent, miserable. Patrick not quite knowing what to say. But finally he spoke. "I'm sorry you had to go through such misery, Jane."

"I brought it all upon myself. Every day I've paid for my sin in some small way or another. The payment has grown large again now that Nicholas is the heir of Marchemont. But I made it through before, and with God's help, Patrick, I will continue to persevere. So you see, when I hear of the countess removing herself from Lord Alexander yet more, it pains me. For his sake.

"What he did was wrong. My reaction to his advances was wrong. But I can't help but believe if the countess had loved him as a good wife ought to love her husband, my life would have turned out a lot differently."

"And yet, you have Nicholas."

"My only consolation. So now, Patrick, the question is how you feel about me now that you know the secret of my past, now that you know I've lied to you. That I've lied to everybody. You cannot trust me, you know."

Patrick breathed in and pulled her a bit closer, placing her cheek against his chest and running a comforting hand up and down her back. "Oh, my love, I can trust you utterly. You were protecting your son. I could never fault a mother for doing that. And as far as what happened between you and the earl, that was a long, long time ago. You've punished yourself for these many years. I will not add another stone to those which you've thrown upon yourself."

"Forgive me for lying, Patrick. And I so wanted to be the perfect woman for you. I don't blame you if you walk away now."

Her heart twisted painfully, but she turned a brave face on it.

Patrick took his arms from around her and held her face between his hands, knowing he dare not judge her for past sins when his own were so much fresher and newly black. "Jane, it was all years ago. Perhaps it would matter to some men, but not to me." He put his arms around her. "In a way, I'm almost relieved."

"Why?"

"I thought you were too good to be true. Indeed, I thought I had found the perfect woman."

"And what's wrong with that?"

"Nothing. If you're a perfect man. And I'm far from that, my love. Perhaps one day I shall explain more fully." His eyes were tender, pure, and honest in their loving expression as he leaned forward and kissed her softly.

"I love you, Jane."

"And I you." Jane smiled at his admission, thrilled by its prospects. A man of Patrick MacBeth's quality loving her. She never would have dreamed of such.

"The question is, lady Jane, what are we going to do about it?"

"Enjoy it for now. I'm in no hurry for things to change."

"You're not ready to leave Nicholas yet, are you?"

She shook her head. "I don't know when the earl will proclaim him as heir. He has to deal with Lady Alison and Percy first. And I'm sure the countess will be most distraught that the son of a castle cook will be the next Earl of Lambeth."

"I don't believe he'll have to worry about that. Countess Marie will be gone within the week. And if the earl fails to survive his wounds, Percy will assume the title."

"Yes. And then life will continue on as it did before."

He kissed her softly. "I hardly think so, Jane. At least not if I have anything to do with it."

They sat in the darkness, both wondering what the future would be. "The earl has been muttering Nicholas's name ever since he fell into a delirious state. Now I know why. You must be proud of your son, Jane."

"Yes," she looked at her new love frankly and openly, "yes, I am. I just have one further question to ask you, Patrick," she said, changing the subject.

"Certainly."

"Now that we've declared our love, may I run my fingers through your hair?"

His great laugh echoed in the darkness, and he grabbed her hands in his and ran them through himself. "There! Do you feel better?"

"Much!"

They laughed together and held each other tight, basking in the joy of their briskly beating hearts.

꒰ꕤ꒱ ꒰ꕤ꒱ ꒰ꕤ꒱

Patrick went back to the keep to check on Lord and Lady de la Marche in their respective solars before getting a bit of sleep in a spare chamber as Jane made her way down the steep steps of the wall to the bailey. The moment her foot negotiated the last step, landing on the turf of the courtyard, Geoffrey, still on late guard duty, called to her.

"Mistress Jane! There's a lad here for you!"

Jane gathered up her skirts and quickly negotiated the distance to the gate house. There stood a small urchin of seven or eight years clad in country clothes and wearing a look of concern on his face. Jane had never seen him before.

"How can I help you, lad?"

"I've come from Agnes's hut. It's her mother. They need you something terrible."

"What's the matter?"

"Dunno. Agnes just told me to hurry."

"Why didn't Agnes come herself?"

"Dunno."

"All right. I'll be right there. Let me get my things."

Jane went directly to the kitchen and gathered a basket of common remedies which might prove helpful. She gathered her woolen shawl from her room and would have told Nicholas where she was going, but he was already fast asleep, looking like the babe she had given her heart to so long ago. "How I love you, Nicholas," she whispered softly, taking an extra second to caress the curve of his cheek with her fingers and kiss his forehead. He smiled in his sleep.

Geoffrey let her out of the gate house.

"What happened to the lad?" she asked.

"He hurried back to wherever it was that he came from. Who was he?"

"I've never seen him before. I guess he's a relative of Agnes's family. I'd best be off quickly. Hopefully, I won't be too long."

"It seems a shame that the tournament has ended and you're cut short a good night's sleep again!" Geoffrey was sympathetic, and much more verbally apt than usual.

"It's always the way, isn't it?"

And she was off, briskly walking across the meadow, her shawl pulled tightly around her shoulders, annoyance turning down the corners of her mouth. She knew God had made her a healer to help others, but just then she was so tired she felt no joy in the cool breeze which blew through her now-loose hair. The night had turned chilly. She had felt it up on the walls, but now it seemed even colder, though nothing like winter.

She had much to ponder as she walked. And soon her spirits were cheered when she remembered that above all else Patrick loved her. It was a thought she could barely comprehend. And yet, life was so uncertain. The earl's life was an uncertain commodity. If he died before claiming Nicholas as his son, they would be back to where they were four weeks ago.

Four weeks?

Jane could hardly believe it had only been such a short amount of time since Nicholas started training under Skeets. Life had been moving along so quickly. Four weeks since she had met Patrick, and already she couldn't imagine life without him.

If the earl died, she would have to find other employment elsewhere. *After that episode in the wardrobe with Percy, I can't imagine Nicholas will be keeping his present position.* But where would she go? She hadn't received a marriage proposal from Patrick. Perhaps he didn't have such grand designs for their relationship. And when she was thrown back down to the status of a mere castle cook, and one that had an illegitimate son at that, she couldn't believe the doctor would actually marry her. Would he?

She pushed the thought aside, not willing to let doubts destroy the memory of the time they shared up on the walls just a little while before. She had a lot to tell Mattie in the morning!

The woods stood before her now, a dark belt across the landscape, and she breathed in deeply, walking forward. Poor Agnes. That entire family had borne so much lately. It was hard to understand how they had even begun to cope with such heartache. And yet, Agnes still worked hard down in the kitchens and with a smile on her face. But inside her heart, she must have been crying most of the time. Jane knew how *that* was.

Her foot crunched onto the forest floor. It was just a ten-minute walk to the hut from here. She breathed a sigh of relief. Hopefully, she would be back home and in the comfort of her room within the hour.

A great hand clamped down over Jane's mouth. She tried to scream but could not. She was gagged with a length of soiled wool, her feet were bound and her hands were tied, and no matter how hard she tried to fight against her captor, he was too strong.

When she was clubbed on the back of her head, Jane succumbed to a world blacker than the forest had ever held.

Thrown over a saddle and led deeper into the trees, away from Marchemont, away from Nicholas, and most certainly away from Patrick MacBeth, Jane was abducted with all haste away from the vast estates of the Earl of Lambeth.

The abbey bells were tolling midnight.

❧ TWENTY-EIGHT ❧

King Henry sighed.

Through the window, dawn cast a rosy glow on his patrician features. He shook his head and cupped his bearded chin in his hand as he rested his elbow on the carven arm of his chair.

"Well, I suppose there's only one thing to do. The squire must be hung forthwith, and the rest of the matter must be dealt with very delicately."

Sir Ronald bowed. "Shall I go to Marchemont?"

"Not quite yet. Let us see how Lord Alexander fares. My last report was that infection had set into the wound. I have every intention of dealing with this deplorable situation, but if he is going to die, let it be in peace, without the stain of his own betrayal marring it."

"And if he lives?"

"You will go directly to Marchemont and make an arrest. Until then, send a messenger across the river to find out how the earl progresses . . . or digresses. Under the present circumstances, I hate to admit that I know not which scenario is preferable."

"As you wish, my liege." Sir Ronald bowed once again amid the gaily-stenciled room. The firelight catching the hooked nose made him appear predatory, the warrior he was.

253

Then, with a flourish of cape as he turned, the knight was gone to do the bidding of his king.

King Henry stared out his window, watching the still-dim waters of the Thames. Civilizations had come and gone on the island of Brittania: the Britons, the Romans, the Saxons, the Normans, and now it seemed as if they all were just beginning to meld together into a new breed of Englishman. The transformation wasn't near to being complete. There were still Saxon nobles who would have been glad to invoke the spirit of Hereward the Wake, that great Saxon lord who had led a resistance against William the Conqueror. And there were nobles with strong, unbreakable ties to Normandy.

Henry knew his love for all things French did little to mend the tear. *And yet*, he shrugged, *I am who I am. A lover of all things beautiful, all things fine.*

But the Thames had always been there. Dark, unchanging, life-giving, beautiful, deep. It didn't seem to matter which civilization inhabited the isle—the Thames served them and ruled them in her own way, her creeds never changing, her ways constant and not dictated by man.

Henry sighed.

And cupped his bearded chin in his hand as he rested his elbow on the arm of his carven chair. Dawn cast a rosy glow over the land.

෴ ෴ ෴

"This would be taking a lot less time," the hired assassin grumbled to himself, "if I didn't have to stay off the roads. But then, I don't make the rules of these things. I'm just paid to carry them out."

Jane stirred in front of him where she lay across his lap.

"Oh, up with the sun are you? Heh, you must have been more tired than you thought you were, poor mite." He spoke as one speaks to a child. His voice was warm and friendly, and at first Jane was extremely confused.

"Not to worry, though, girlie. We'll have to stop soon for something to break our fast. I know of an inn nearby. I'll keep to the forest, leave you, and be back as quick as you can sneeze. You'll be uncomfortable in your bonds, but there's nothing to be done for all of that, not until we get to the river."

The river? Jane thought and tried to twist her neck to see her captor. *What river?* To no avail—the angle was impossible to negotiate with a stiff neck. She decided it was better to save her strength.

"Real soon it'll be, Mistress Jane. And then we'll eat something together. Of course, it's not on that lady's orders, but sometimes a man's got to carry out his job in his own way. As I see it, in the end a man's got to answer to himself."

⸎ ⸎ ⸎

"You look tired, sir, if you'll pardon my saying so."

Patrick held up a hand. "You're right, I'm sure, Geoffrey. It's been a long night, but I do believe that the earl's condition is now on the rise."

"Thank goodness! We had heard the wound was infected."

"Yes, but it seems much better this morning. Jane made up a plaster that worked beautifully."

"That's our Jane!" Geoffrey said proudly.

"Yes. She's been most helpful. I'm sure we could sit here and laud her all day, Geoffrey, but I have neglected my other patients for too many days. I must head back to London, but I will be back to check on the earl this afternoon."

"As you wish, sir."

Just then, the men noticed a solitary horseman coming down the road from the direction of London Bridge.

"Ho! Who comes?" A guard shouted from up on the walls.

"A messenger! Come from the king to find out the condition of the Earl of Lambeth!"

Patrick stepped forward as the man reined in his horse at the gate house. "I am Lord Alexander's physician. I will give you the message to take back to King Henry. Tell him the infection seems to be subsiding, but it's too early to tell whether or not it is permanent or merely a temporary stay. But his condition has indeed improved since last night. Tell the king if he so desires, I will send a messenger this evening to report to him."

"I shall, sir. Thank you." He turned his horse around and was galloping back up the road toward the bridge.

"Well, Geoffrey, I'd better get along then."

Agnes came through the gate house.

"Hello, Geoffrey," she said cheerfully.

"Hello there, Agnes. I trust all is well at your house?"

The girl looked puzzled. "As well as can be expected, I suppose, Geoffrey. Why do you ask?"

"As Mistress Jane went there last night, I naturally assumed something was wrong."

At Jane's name, Patrick stopped and turned back around.

"Whatever do you mean, Geoffrey? Jane wasn't at our house."

"But didn't you send a boy round to fetch her?"

"What boy?"

"Oh, I don't know. He appeared to be about seven years old. Not much more. He came by close to midnight requesting she come with all haste to your hut."

Agnes's eyes grew wide. "Are you sure it was to our hut she was summoned?"

"I'm positive. I went off duty for a few hours to catch some sleep. I just assumed she came back during that time. I'll go check with Nicholas to see if she came back."

Patrick laid a hand on his shoulder. "That's all right, Geoffrey. I'll go back myself."

"But what about your patients, sir?"

"Never mind them. I must see if Jane's all right."

❧ ❧ ❧

Somehow, Jane had fallen back asleep. Perhaps it was the rhythm of the horse. Perhaps it was her captor's surprisingly lovely baritone that hummed softly down from his wide, garrulous mouth. Or perhaps it was instinct. A way to store up the strength needed for when it was time to escape this paradoxical man who had taken her from her home.

But now it was time to wake up.

"Jane!" he nudged her between her shoulder blades. "Girlie!"

Her eyelids fluttered open. All she saw was the forest floor and the flanks of the horse, and remembrance quickly flooded through her. Her captor dislodged his legs from beneath her abdomen and dismounted from his horse. He lifted her down and set her on the leaf-strewn ground.

Checking to see that her hands and feet were bound tightly, he took another length of rope and tied her around her middle to a tree. Once satisfied that she wouldn't be going anywhere, he rose to his feet. "I'll be back shortly. There's an inn not far from here where I'll fetch us something to eat. And then, I'm sorry to say, it's back on the road for us. I've got to get us as far away from Marchemont as quickly as I can."

Jane watched him mount his horse and ride quickly away.

She waited. Wondered. Tried to think who would possibly do this to her. This man certainly had nothing against her personally. Who did?

"I'm just a cook," her heart whispered to God, feeling desolate, hungry, and thirsty, "just a simple castle cook." She tried her best to figure out who would do such a thing to her and couldn't help but wonder if it was the ultimate act of penance she was to endure.

ere," he said, pulling down the cloth that gagged her, "drink a little of this."

"Thank you..." she looked at him with uncertainty, but she knew there was only one way to handle this situation while she was incapable of fleeing or fighting. Jane had learned a long time ago that most men responded to warmth and kindness. "I'm afraid you know my name, but I don't know yours."

She took a sip from the skin of water he held to her mouth. And then began to drink greedily.

"No one knows my real name but my good mother."

"Then at least give me something to call you by. Or I shall have to make up something myself."

"I'm open to any suggestions. As I see it, a man's name says lots of things about him. So whatever I am to you, then so name me."

Jane drank some more. "First, tell me why you've abducted me."

"It's what I do for a living."

"I figured as much. But who has aught against me? I find this quite bewildering."

"I believe it's what they call an affair de coeur, girlie."

"Someone's doing this for love?"

He nodded.

"Who?"

"I'm forbidden to say."

"Oh come, come, you're to kill me eventually. I can't imagine I've been tied up and taken away for no other purpose than to be tied up and taken away!" If her arms hadn't been bound, she would have crossed them.

"Pardon me for all the discomfort you're being handed out, but I've got to do my job. As I see it, if a man's going to enter this line of work, he'd better not take any chances. But then, life is just like that all around, isn't it?"

"I'd hardly label you a cautious fellow," Jane said wryly.

"Oh yes. I'm very cautious. It's the difference between a professional and a ruffian."

"I'll concede you that. You are in earnest about your crime, not just sporting about it." She was starting to enjoy the absurdity of the conversation.

"That's it, ma'am."

"Therefore I will call you Earnest," she proclaimed.

"Earnest, eh? I like it!" He took some hard brown bread out of a sack and broke it in two. "Sorry there's not better fare. They did have a nice bit of cheese, though, and some pheasant. As I see it, 'tis better to grab at a humble morsel than to starve waiting for better to come along."

"As I see it, Earnest, you should untie my hands so that I can feed myself."

Yet he hesitated to untie her.

"You can keep my middle tied to the tree if that would make you feel better. But as a grown woman, I'd much prefer to feed myself."

Earnest looked at her for several seconds, deciding. "All right, girlie. Here you go, then," he said as he freed her hands and quickly dodged away lest she try and get a handful of his thick black hair. The Lord only knew how many hairs he had lost in the line of duty.

As they shared the small meal together, Jane felt a small bit of hope. Perhaps she could talk Earnest out of this. But even if she couldn't, she knew a time would come when he would let down his guard. No man was on top of things all hours of the day.

She would bide her time and try to make her captor garner as much trust in her as possible.

❧ ❧ ❧

"Nicholas!"

Patrick's voice reverberated along the wooden rafters of the great hall.

He spun around from where he and Skeets were taking stock of the gold and silver plate. Patrick's urgent tone brought on an immediate expression of concern. "Yes, doctor?"

"When was the last time you saw your mother?"

"Before I retired last night."

"She wasn't in your room when you awoke this morning?"

"No, but that's not unusual. She's an early riser. Why?"

"I don't wish to alarm you, but we have reason to believe she never came back last night after she was called away to a patient."

"Then we must go look for her!" Nicholas shoved down a rising panic. "She could be hurt out in the woods somewhere."

"Do you know the way to Agnes's home?"

"Yes. Is that where she was going?"

"Yes. Unfortunately, Agnes said they never called for her. We don't know who the urchin was who came for her. But it's all we have to go on. I fear she may be in danger. We'll start off in that direction. By your leave, Skeets?" he asked the old man for permission to borrow his assistant.

"Of course. Jane has been a friend to us all. I'll come with you to the stables."

He did just that, and within minutes they were walking into the straw-strewn outbuilding.

"Richard!" Skeets called. "Saddle up Bedivere for the good doctor!"

"Sir?"

"You heard me. You'll need the two fastest horses we've got."

"I'll take Jasper," Nicholas said in a rather lordly manner.

Richard bowed and was off barking orders to the grooms.

"Don't leave until I get back," Skeets said mysteriously and hurried into the keep.

"Have you broken your fast, Nicholas?" Patrick asked.

"No. But I don't think I could eat anything."

"Be that as it may, why don't you go into the kitchens and have Agnes prepare us a sack of food. We have no idea how long this will take."

Nicholas was off, and Skeets was coming down the steps of the keep as fast as he could, which wasn't very quickly. Two swords, tucked into their scabbards, were held in each hand. "I thought you might need these. One never knows what might turn up in such an event. I shall pray, however, that the blades won't see the light of day on your search."

"Thank you, Skeets. I left mine back at my house. I don't normally need it on my rounds. Although," he jested, "there have been times where I wished it had been by my side!"

"I'm sure you have. Here comes Nicholas." He held one of the swords out to the cook's boy. "For you. Just in case."

"But isn't this my—"

"Yes. Say no more."

Patrick was confused and began to open his mouth to ask a question but was cut off by the sound of Richard bringing the horses out into the courtyard. Nicholas handed him a bag of food.

"That was quick," Patrick remarked.

"Word has already made it to the kitchen. They were getting the sack together before I walked in."

Lady Alison came out of the keep as they mounted their horses. "What is going on here?" she demanded.

Patrick turned to face her. "Jane Lightfoot is missing."

Alison calculated the hours and suddenly became magnanimous. Her man had at least a seven-hour head start. They would never catch up to him now. "Richard!" she called to the retreating stablemaster. "Saddle up another horse for another man. I really think you should take another armed man along with you, Patrick. From the garrison."

Patrick could hardly believe his ears. He became immediately suspicious, but he wouldn't turn down another hand. "Thank you, Alison. Nicholas, ride across the bailey and get Geoffrey."

"Yes, sir!"

Stephen came running out of the kitchen, his hair made dull by flour dust, his face sharpened by concern. Mattie and Gregory were on his heels. "You'll find her, won't you, doctor?" Stephen uttered, his voice shaky and nervous. "We don't know what we'd do without her," Mattie said.

"Cheer up, good folk," Gregory tried to be optimistic. "Perhaps she was gathering some herbs and lost her way. Those woods are awfully big."

Everyone nodded, glad to hold onto any bit of hope. But they all realized that Jane knew the forest as well as anyone. And she was cautious, besides.

The sun was well over the horizon by the time the three horsemen were clear of the gate house and galloping over the meadow toward the forest. Lady Alison watched them from her tower room, and when they disappeared into the dense woods she turned to Percy, who lounged upon her bed.

"Thank you for delivering that message, my boy. I think you should reward yourself by going to London today."

"May I see the tailor?"

"If you wish to go to an old shoppe instead of having him come here."

"I do, Mother."

"All right, then," she nodded agreeably as she pulled some coins out of the small purse which hung from a silken cord which rested on her hips. "Here you go, then."

Now all she had to do was wait and see how the drama twisted and turned. But in the end would be death.

She smiled.

༺ ༺ ༺

The messenger arrived at the palace while the king was hearing Mass. He waited patiently in the corridor, glad it was good news he was to give to his liege.

Soon the door opened and the king's personal priest exited. He was announced and presently stood before the royal presence.

"You've returned already from Marchemont. Good. What news have you for us, then?" Henry asked.

"According to his physician, Doctor MacBeth, the infection seems to be subsiding, your majesty, but it's too soon to tell whether or not it is permanent or just a temporary stay. But the earl's condition has indeed improved since last night. The doctor bade me tell the king, if he so desires, a messenger will be sent this evening to report to him of the earl's progress."

"Thank you, you may go."

The messenger bowed and left.

King Henry summoned Sir Ronald to his presence. "The earl's condition improves."

"Praise God." Ronald crossed himself.

"Yes. I feel that my good friend Alexander de la Marche will survive this assassination attempt. He's always seemed a healthy soul. You have an arrest to make at Marchemont. Do it discreetly," the king declared. For one so young, he could garner much authority into his voice.

"As you wish, my liege." Sir Ronald bowed and was gone. Toward Marchemont he, Sir Justin, and Sir Niles rode in all haste.

"Women are the worst to arrest," Niles grumbled to Justin. "All that hair-pulling and scratching."

"I heartily agree. They say that Lady Alison is not possessed of a strong constitution. Perhaps she has little fight left in her."

"If there's a woman on this earth with little fight left in her, I'd like to see her!" Sir Ronald joined in the conversation. "But as far as I've seen, they're all little she-cats just waiting for someone to scratch!"

The three knights laughed and rode at a sensible pace toward Marchemont.

THIRTY

Well, I must say, 'tis a much more pleasant journey now that you've got that scarf from round your mouth."

"True words you speak, Earnest," Jane replied from her seat in front of him on the saddle.

The sun was nearing its zenith, and Jane automatically experienced a fleeting doubt that she hadn't prepared enough food for the castle's dinner. But she hastily put the thought aside and continued the conversation, her eyes always seeking a way of escape. But so far, only woods lay before and behind them. And she knew if she jumped down and started to run, Earnest would have no trouble scooping her back up and onto his horse with him. The fact that he chose to employ himself in such a dubious manner led her to trust little in his genial demeanor. He would probably turn on her quickly and keep his guard up permanently from that point onward.

"So where are you taking me? I've been wanting to ask you that all morning, but you insisted on telling me about your nieces and nephews. And I must say they sound like wonderful children. Especially Isabel."

"Aye, she's my favorite. We're traveling west. To Berkeley, in Gloucestershire. We're heading to the Severn River, actually. Not far from Berkeley Castle."

"So you'll throw me in, I suppose, and then there will be no body around Lord Alexander's estates to draw attention. I will have mysteriously disappeared."

Earnest blushed behind Jane. " 'Tis the plan. But let's talk of something more cheerful. 'Tis quite unusual for me to be discussing with the victim her own demise. As I see it, in this line of work, the less that's said about it, the better 'tis for all involved."

"I don't see it that way at all! I like to prepare myself. There's a little more dignity in it, don't you think?"

He cocked his head thoughtfully. "There is that, I suppose. And to be perfectly honest with you, I've never taken anyone quite this far away to commit the deed. This is a new experience. I probably should have kept you gagged, and then I wouldn't be getting to know you like this. It's going to be hard to do what I have to do now that we've talked for all these hours."

"A little pleasant conversation lightens any task, I've always found."

Earnest laughed. "It's a good thing all my commissions aren't the likes of you, Jane! Or I'd have to find something else to do!"

"A wonderful idea! Why not start right now?" Jane shot back.

"Ah, ah, ah, I can see what you're trying to do. And it won't work. I've already been paid, and I'll keep my word. Even men such as me have a code of honor we live by. As I see it, that code separates the villains from the lunatics."

"Does that mean we have to be quiet from now on?"

"Do you want to be?"

"Not really. I'd rather my last hours be pleasant ones. And you do keep up good on your end of a conversation."

"Thank you. This kind of employment gets lonely at times. It's actually quite nice to have someone to talk to."

The ludicrousness of the conversation was not lost on Jane, but she found it humorous, nonetheless. "So, tell me about

Berkeley Castle. Marchemont is so magnificent—living there has given me only a slight interest in other residences. Who holds the estates?"

"The FitzHardings. It was originally founded by William FitzOsbern, the steward of Normandy soon after the invasion."

"Are you Saxon or Norman?"

"Saxon. You?"

"My last name is Lightfoot."

"Descended from Martin Lightfoot, the companion of Hereward the Wake?"

"That's it exactly. I believe he was an uncle somewhere way back when."

"Well, isn't that wonderful? As I see it, heroism descends down through birth. You must have a little of that in you still."

"I'd like to think so. I certainly would have been part of the resistance had I lived back then."

"As would I. And now King Henry is more continental than ever. It makes me wonder when we're all going to turn into Frenchmen!"

"Heaven forbid that should ever happen to us, eh, Earnest?"

"Truly, Jane. Truly."

"So continue on about the castle," she invited.

"The FitzHardings were given it under Henry II, and they put in a stone keep and began the construction of the curtain walls. It's not completed yet, but it will be magnificent when it's finished."

"It sounds as if you know a lot about this place."

"Well, if you must know, I grew up in Gloucestershire, not far from the castle."

"I see. You're taking advantage of the nature of the job, and going home to see your family."

"Yes, you've found me out."

"Shame on you, Earnest! Using my plight to further your own happiness. Well, never mind. At least some good will come out of this trip. I'm sure your sister and her children will be happy to see you."

"I've got a few gifts from London for them in my saddlebag."

They continued talking, and as they did, Jane felt the peace of God upon her, reassuring her that all would be well. Earnest rode along in utter confusion at the way this commission was turning out. He was promising himself that Jane's end would be quick and easy, not the method that Lady Alison had paid him for.

In the end she'll be just as dead, he thought, *and that so-called lady will be none the wiser.*

❧ ❧ ❧

It was easy to find the spot where Jane had been taken.

Not long after they stepped on the forest path leading to Agnes's house, they found a bit of shawl stuck to a fallen tree trunk. And several feet away Jane's medicine basket lay over-turned on the ground. There were signs of struggle in the broken branches, and narrow, muddy slivers in the earth left by Jane's heels as she was dragged to the horse.

The three men looked at each other.

"She was taken away on a horse," Geoffrey declared.

"How can you tell?" Nicholas asked.

" 'Tis easy. I can track almost anything. Did a lot of poaching in my youth, and never got caught. Believe me, I've tracked animals a lot smaller than a horse."

They went further along, and Geoffrey still looked at the ground. "He wasn't going very fast at this point. It was dark when he took her."

"When did she leave the gate house?"

"Looked near to midnight," Geoffrey answered Patrick.

"They've had quite a head start, then."

"Yes. But there's only one horse for two people. That will slow them down a bit. Even with the eight or so hours they've got ahead of us, I think we can catch up with them."

Provided her captor doesn't kill her beforehand, Patrick thought, not wishing to frighten Nicholas. "Let's hurry then." He decided to pick up on Geoffrey's optimism. "They will probably stop to rest when daylight is in full.

"'Tis what I would do," Geoffrey agreed.

"Who would wish to do this to her?" Nicholas asked later on, unable to find the answer in his own mind.

"I'm not sure. But I think this may have something to do with Lady Alison."

"How so? She offered to have Geoffrey come along, didn't she, doctor?"

"That's what makes me suspicious of her. Alison's never done anything nice in her entire life. At least not since I've known her. She was trying to throw suspicion off herself."

Geoffrey nodded. "She's got a dark temper, that one. You can see it in her eyes."

They all agreed, Patrick praying silently to God the entire while.

❧ ❧ ❧

Lady Alison regarded Sir Ronald with an icy calm. An imperious frown. "How so?"

"We caught up with your man's squire, Lady Alison. He was only too willing to tell all."

"You can't prove anything."

"I don't have to. I'm here on the wishes of King Henry."

Alison knew that as king, Henry had the right to arrest anyone that he chose. It was useless to fight. She nodded angrily, however. "I see. And I presume you are taking me to the Tower?"

271

"Yes, my lady. I would prefer a quiet, dignified exit from Marchemont."

"As would I. May I be permitted to bring a maid and a few luxuries?"

"Of course."

"So you're one of Henry's henchmen, then? It amazes me that one with so little comeliness of body or face should rise so in the ranks," she said with acid tones.

Sir Ronald said nothing.

And so it was arranged. Quietly Lady Alison Hastings was arrested under the order of the king for the attempted murder of his friend Lord Alexander de la Marche, the Earl of Lambeth. She left without a physical fight, much to the relief of the three knights. But she cursed them violently and foully under her breath whenever their ears were close enough to catch the words.

⚜ ⚜ ⚜

Meanwhile, Percy was enjoying himself at his tailor's establishment. Bolts of fine material were laid out in profusion, and the colors were rich, ripe with visual pleasure.

"I'm just not sure." Percy paced before the displayed fabric. "I love these colors, Jacques, but I always seem to go back to black when it comes to my supertunic."

"Feel this wool, m'lord." The tailor held forth an offering. "So soft you could butter bread with it."

"I agree. Yes, that will do. A new pair of embroidered gauntlets to go with it will be necessary and, while I'm here, I believe a new tunic is in order, as well. That red-and-yellow striped material there, let me see it."

The tailor eagerly complied. Sir Percival Hastings was one of his best customers. "I envision this with hanging oversleeves and split skirt panels, as opposed to a dagged hemline."

"Ah, yes. And a new undertunic, too, should just about settle my needs for today, Jacques."

"Thank you, m'lord," Jacques bowed. "Shall I bring them to the castle for the fitting?"

"Naturally."

And Percy was gone. His barge was actually beneath the Tower Bridge as the knights' horses with Lady Alison's litter dangling between two of them began to cross the great expanse. Their expressions were as those standing too close to a hornet's nest.

Someday, Percy thought, *I shall be one of the most powerful men in the kingdom, as well as the best-dressed.* He laughed. But the thought caused him to stare at the reflection of himself in the mirror of his mind, and the man who stared back in honesty bespoke the fact that he was hardly ready to be the Earl of Lambeth. He was hardly an introspective man, so when such foreign activity crept up on him, it made a heavy impact.

It was then that Percy realized he wanted his uncle to recover completely.

꙳ ꙳ ꙳

The kitchens were quiet for the rest of the morning. The only people to prepare dinner for were the servants and the soldiers. So the delicacies were spared, the pomp was saved for another day, and the great hall was quiet. All that could be heard was the sound of knives slicing, and the occasional dog barking for a bit more. Conversation was severely limited, as was everyone's hunger.

It was a good day for the dogs. By the end of the meal, they were so full they practically crawled on their bellies toward the fire, where they promptly fell asleep for the rest of the afternoon.

❦ THIRTY-ONE ❦

Earnest and Jane traded yawn for yawn for the better part of the morning. And now the sun began to glow the particular shallow gold of early afternoon, and they were still hours away from their destination.

"This is taking longer than I thought," Earnest said, stifling another yawn.

"How much longer?"

"About six hours."

"Oh." Jane couldn't keep the disappointment away from her voice. "Having never been further than London, I had no idea how long it would take us to get to the western coast."

"We're not going all the way to the coast."

"That's right, Berkeley Castle is near the Severn."

"Yes. As I figured it, we'd do about ten miles every hour with two of us on horseback. We should be there before dark."

"You've been yawning for the past hour, Earnest. Why don't we stop for a bit of rest? I know I'd like to sleep for a little while."

"It's tempting, but I don't know. You may escape."

"That's true. But no matter how tightly you tied me up, Earnest, I could sleep like a babe. I'm that tired."

"Well, I agree with you. Do you think someone will be pursuing you?"

"Yes, I imagine so."

"Who?"

"Patrick MacBeth. He's a physician from London."

Earnest steered the steed over to a denser grove of trees. "You've talked me into it. But only for an hour. As much as I respect physicians, as I see it, they're more adept at thinking than fighting. Just a little rest won't do us any harm."

Jane decided not to enlighten Earnest regarding Patrick's second nature. Instead, she let her strange friend lift her down, tighten the bonds on her wrists, and tie her ankles together. His last effort at securing her was to tie a length of slim rope from her wrists to his own wrist.

"If you try to move, I'll awaken immediately, Jane," he warned.

Jane nodded. She understood perfectly. Inwardly she sighed. The time for escape would most probably not be yet. She gave herself up to a delicious nap, too tired to feel the tight but not cruel ropes which bound her. And amid everything, the peace of God reigned supreme. She had been through worse.

Earnest, leaning up on his elbow, looked over at her as she slept. Her sweet face, the pointed chin, the wide mouth...he hadn't had much chance to see them as she had been in front of him on the saddle. *She is a beautiful woman*, he thought, but pushed his admiration aside. If he was going to get some rest, he had better do so quickly.

⛬ ⛬ ⛬

Patrick was growing impatient. The tracks seemed to be an endless succession, never ceasing, always forward. And with each hour that flowed by them, his resolve grew stronger to find Jane. The air was tense, strangely invigorating as he periodically felt for his sword, mentally preparing himself for the fight he soon hoped to find himself in.

"He's not that worried about covering up his tracks," Geoffrey called behind his shoulder. The riders had settled into a triangle.

"He's keeping off the main road," Patrick remarked, "which means she's probably bound up."

"Yes, but he's careless; he is doing nothing to cover up his tracks. Then again, he probably knows he has quite a lead."

Patrick spoke, his agitation making his voice sound harsh. "What could he possibly want with Jane?" *Could this have anything to do with Nicholas and the earl's plans?* he thought.

"Let's hope we find that out sooner than later."

"And when we do, I'm going to make him regret the day he so much as looked at her."

"I'll be right beside you, doctor. Right beside you."

Nicholas still remained silent through it all. He suddenly felt very young. But there was a valiant spark in the lad's soul, and he silently vowed his sword arm, weak as it was, to his mother as well.

Patrick retreated to his thoughts, wanting in the practical, scientific side of himself to prepare for the worst. But the other half of him, the passionate warrior, was ready to fight whoever it was who had abducted his lovely Jane. That half refused to let the other overpower his mind. And hope that he would find her overshadowed all else. He clung to that hope as a child clings to its mother when she lowers him down to the water to be bathed.

Promises were made as he rode.

Promises to God, promises to Jane. *If I ever get her back, I'll marry her straightaway. No more waiting for Nicholas to be proclaimed as heir. I need her in my life, Father,* he opened his heart up in prayer. *I need her now.*

It was all over for Patrick MacBeth. He was utterly and entirely Jane's from that moment on. They spurred their mounts on faster, watching the sky above the trees, checking the position of the sun. The great orb of light seemed to be passing over its course even faster than usual.

❧ ❧ ❧

Gregory yelled above the din. "Work harder! We want this kitchen to be sparkling like marble when Jane gets back! Come now! Up your pace!"

Everyone groaned a bit, but they applied more muscle to their task than before. Gregory knew that it would do no good to any of them to sit around and stare at each other while they waited for news. So he gave them a mission.

"Jane certainly will be surprised, won't she, Mattie?" Agnes said as she helped the older woman scrub down the work surface of one of the tables.

"That she will, lass. I can't wait to see her face when she sees how beautiful the kitchen looks. And how fast we accomplished it."

"I just can't wait to see her face," Agnes said sadly. "You don't think—"

"Hush now. Don't even think such things."

"How do you know what I was going to say, Mattie?"

"Because, girl, I'm thinking it myself."

They worked harder than ever, as Gregory pulled Stephen aside and into his clerk's closet. "It's been hours since they left," the clerk reported. "Do you think someone else should be sent out?"

"That's not for us to say, sir."

"Well, maybe I should talk to Skeets about it. Do you ever remember anything like this happening before?"

"No, sir. Fortunately not. Listen, Mister Gregory, some of the others of us were talking out there, and we were wondering if we could set up some kind of vigil, you know, after the work is done for the night."

"What do you mean?"

"Well, just one of us staying up in the kitchen all night. I'll go first, until midnight. Then Mattie. And then Agnes will come in extra early and take up the post. You know, just in case word comes. We'll all want to know right away."

Gregory nodded, overcome by their love for Jane. "That is up to you. As long as your performance doesn't slip tomorrow because of it."

"Of course not, sir."

And so Jane's friends began their wait, their eyes snapping toward the door each time the post was darkened by a shadow.

❧ ❧ ❧

The white tower was easily viewed from Tower Bridge. The keep of the ever-expanding fortress called the Tower of London was begun by William the Conqueror himself in 1076. It was a daunting, whitewashed square, with massive stone walls and a turret on each corner. The arched windows were of the rounded, Romanesque style so prevalent in architecture at the time of its construction. It looked strong enough to last a thousand years.

Perhaps it would.

The fortress was a source of pride to English kings and a cause for fear to those who found themselves within its walls by force. With little excitement, Alison was installed on the second floor of the great keep in a room that was once a part of the apartments of the royal family before other residences became more fashionable. In between the keep and the river a new building was to be constructed, another of King Henry's pet projects: a new residential tower.

Alison trod into her room, her anger multiplied tenfold since she had left Marchemont. *How dare they?* she thought. *Don't they know the power I hold? Don't they realize I have the power not only to lay down my life but to take it back up again?*

The room was not empty. Waiting patiently for her arrival was an emissary of the king. "Lady Alison Hastings?" he said respectfully.

"Do you really not know who I am, or are you trying to make yourself an even bigger fool than you look," she said disdainfully.

"I have a message from your king, and it is this. As punishment for conspiring to murder your brother, the Earl of Lambeth, you will be taken to Tower Hill at sundown tomorrow night—"

Alison smirked. "—and there my head shall be stricken from my body? Is that it?"

The emissary looked extremely uncomfortable. "Yes, my lady."

"Is that all?"

"Yes, my lady."

"How did the king learn of my supposed little plot?"

Sir Ronald Rey stepped into the room, dismissing the grateful emissary and answering Alison's question. "The squire of the Condottieri was found by myself and two other knights. It was easy enough to get the information from him."

"What did you promise him? A manor? A comely wench?"

"We promised him an easy death. He was hung only an hour ago."

"Ha! You speak of death as easy?"

"Yes, and so do you, Lady Alison. The death of your own brother."

"Alexander will have something to say about this!"

Sir Ronald nodded. "Yes, he most probably will. But, you see, King Henry is the one who will decide, not Lord Alexander. You and I both know he is far too merciful to those who supposedly love him."

"He is a fool! And so are you. You think me cruel, but how much more cruel will your king be tomorrow when you lead me to Tower Hill on his orders!"

"If we are cruel, then it is because of the nature of the crime, Lady Alison. Fratricide is serious in the eyes of your king and in the eyes of God. Anything less than the death you are to be given would be unjust!"

"What do you know of justice? There is no justice but that which men and women carve out for themselves." Her words were bitter.

"We've said enough." Sir Ronald turned and walked toward the door. "Make sure the room is guarded at all times," he said to the soldier outside as he allowed Alison's maid to slip into the room.

The king's most trusted knight calmly shut the door behind him.

❧ ❧ ❧

Skeets would almost rather have walked across a large brazier than carry out the task he was assigned by the king's messenger who had arrived from the Tower several minutes previously.

He sighed, muttering to himself as he climbed the stairs to the earl's solar. "Well, at least the king had the courtesy to write the ill tidings himself."

Still, he didn't want to leave his lordship while he read the message, and he had no idea what his reaction might be. It wouldn't be violent—there was no fear of that. But Skeets was never one to deal well with emotional tirades of any variety.

He stiffened his shoulders, drew back his head, and knocked upon the door.

"Come." The earl's voice sounded much stronger than it had that morning.

" 'Tis I, my lord."

"Skeets! Good. Come in, please."

The earl was sitting up in bed, with the bloom of life slowly restoring itself to his complexion.

"You're looking much better, your grace."

"Thank you, Skeets. I feel as if I've crossed over the threshold. What have you there in your hand?"

"It's a message for you, my lord. From the king."

Lord Alexander held out his hand. "The king? Bring it here. That reminds me, I'd like a messenger sent to tell his majesty that I am on the rise."

"He knows that already, sir. The doctor had a message sent before he left this morning."

"Left this morning?"

"To find Jane Lightfoot. She disappeared last night. Mysteriously so."

The earl's brows drew together in true concern.

Skeets continued. "I hate to add more bad news to the day of your recovery, but Nicholas went with him to find her."

"What!" The earl winced as he rose higher on his pillows.

" 'Tis true. I didn't try to talk him out of it."

"He's too much like me to be talked out of anything. How long have they been gone?"

"Since before the servants' breakfast."

Lord Alexander thought about that for several seconds, then remembered the skill with which Patrick had fought on the lists during the Grand Melee. "He will be safe enough with Doctor MacBeth."

Skeets held out the message once more. "Here, my lord. I feel I must prepare you. What you will read is not going to cheer you."

"All right, then. I'd rather read it by myself, Skeets."

Skeets bowed, and felt a wave of relief wash over him. "As you wish, your grace."

He was out the door before the earl had even broken the seal.

❦ ❦ ❦

A beetle landed heavily on her face, and Jane was pulled from her deep sleep with a jerk. Earnest immediately opened his eyes from the movement beside him. "What?" he mumbled sleepily, then he jolted to his feet.

Jane laughed at his bleary eyes and studied him closely. "Why, Earnest, you really are a handsome fellow! I haven't seen hair that black on a man in years! And your eyes are bluer than a lake."

"I'm also a stupid fellow. Look at the sun. We've slept for at least three hours."

"Well, then, you must have needed it!"

"Spoken like a true mother."

"Why, of course, since I *am* a mother."

"How many?"

"One son," she explained while he easily lifted her and set her astride his horse. "His name is Nicholas, and he's 15."

Well, 15 isn't so bad an age to lose your mother, Earnest thought with relief. "We've got to hurry now. We should make it there just as it's getting dark." He swung up behind Jane.

"And you so wanted to have supper with your family." Jane filled her voice with disappointment.

"Ah well, 'tis the way of it. Do you mind if I ask you about this Doctor MacBeth who's following you?"

"No. After all, if I'm to die at your hand and soon, there's no reason to have any secrets between us, I should think."

He knew the best thing to do right now would be to end this conversation, to put Jane back to where she belonged in his mind: as a job, a source of income. But he couldn't. The feel of her narrow back against his chest, and the way his arm went around her small waist so comfortably as they rode along. He had to know more. Through no machination of himself, he wanted to know all about her.

Jane proceeded to tell him her tale, and he admired her ability not only to survive amid hardships, but to thrive. An hour went by, and she told him every detail she could remember of Nicholas's childhood, and then the fateful day she met the doctor at the abbey.

"I love the abbey, don't you?" she asked Earnest.

"Never been inside."

"Never? Not even for Mass?"

"No. I get jobs in London, and I don't make it over to Westminster much."

"Well, you must go sometime. They're building a new Lady Chapel, and I heard that King Henry will be rebuilding the entire monastery in honor of Saint Edward."

"I heard tell he revered the saint," Earnest remarked.

"Oh yes."

"How do you hear about all this?"

"It's all part of working for an earl, I suppose. Funny, though, oftentimes I've felt as cloistered at Marchemont as I imagine the monks do at the abbey. I think I would have made a good monk had I been born a man."

"Do you? Not me! I love the freedom of the wind and a good horse under me, and the ability to go everywhere or nowhere. As I see it, a man's as free as he allows himself to be."

"But you must admit, you're forced to ride off the main road, and your freedom comes at a high expense to others."

"I guess so. But they can afford it."

Jane's words were soft but heavy with impact. "I can't."

Earnest quickly put her back on topic. "So what happened with you and this MacBeth after you met that day at the abbey?"

So Jane complied, praying that somehow she could convince him to let her live. She told him of the budding relationship, the love she felt in her heart. "The first love I've ever felt, ever known, Earnest. Imagine that, at the age of 32!"

"Was he going to marry you?"

"He never formally proposed marriage to me, but you know us women—we have a sense about these things. I believe we will end up together . . . or, would have ended up together. But—"

"I know. I know."

Jane offered no more conversation for the present, and Earnest ceased his questioning. They rode west in silence, each deep in thought. Earnest wondered how in heaven he was going to carry this out, and Jane wondered how in heaven she could be at such peace. It was as if an angel was whispering into her ear, "It's all going to be all right, Jane. You're in the Father's care."

e've got to water and feed these horses soon," Geoffrey said, wiping his arm across his forehead. The day had turned somewhat warm, and their pace did little to cool them down.

"Let's find an inn if we can. You must be hungry, too—eh, Nicholas?"

"I don't think I could eat anything right now." They were among the only words Nicholas had spoken since they found Jane's basket.

"I suggest you take a bit of nourishment while the horses eat. We don't know how long the journey ahead of us may take."

An hour later they came to a road which dissected the woods and led out into sloping fields. A tendril of smoke wound its way up into the sky from below the hill.

"Turn here," Patrick ordered. "That doesn't look too far away. Even if it's only a farm, I'm sure they will give us some meat and ale and feed for our horses."

As providence would have it, the source of the smoke was neither from an inn nor a simple farm, but from a manor house. The men hurried their horses forward and were relieved to find that a charitable, friendly baron abided therein. After they hurriedly explained their plight, their needs and orders were hastily barked by the ancient gentleman who sat in a chair before the fire. His teeth were all but missing, as was his hair and eyesight. But something deep inside—some love of life, God, and family—sparked up to the surface, and he entertained them with an amusing tale of the time his sister was abducted by a notorious libertine who had taken a fancy to her from a nearby manor. The searchers were eager to be on their way, but since the horses were being taken care of, they felt the need to be polite to their host.

"Aye," the lord chuckled, drawing in on a clay pipe, rubbing the soles of his pointy shoes together as he recalled what had happened so long ago. "Lord Rufus took her in the middle of the night, right from under our noses! But we got her back, and with her maidenhood intact, I might add."

"Did you have to search for her long?" Nicholas asked, oblivious to the hungry eyes of a curly-haired, buxom serving woman who placed the food on the great wooden table. Her raven eyes looked upon him with longing, for he was growing most fair, and manly, too.

"We searched for a few days. It turned out that though he sought to take advantage of her, she ended up driving him almost mad. You see, in the forest where his horse was tethered was a patch of poison oak that poor Edith was terribly reactive to. She was itching and scratching so much, and Rufus, being of sensitive skin himself, was eventually beside himself with the constant sound of her nails against her skin. When we found them in a large Welsh cave, he begged us to take her from him!"

Geoffrey couldn't help but laugh.

Patrick stayed stonefaced; nevertheless, the story lent a small bit of hope that life was certainly unpredictable. It gave him a new thought. "Do you think that's what it could be?" he turned to Nicholas. "Could your mother have been taken by an admirer?"

Nicholas thumbed rudely at Geoffrey. "The only person I know who would be besotted enough to do something like *that* would be Geoffrey, here."

Geoffrey laughed. He was the only one in a fine mood, his natural disposition being bent toward adventure. "You'd be surprised, Nicholas, of the talk at the garrison. It's not conversation we'd have around her son, but rest assured, your mother's beauty and grace is well-esteemed."

"At her age?" Nicholas asked just like a son.

"Because of it! Jane works hard and is independent-minded. To many men that is quite alluring."

"It is to me," Patrick agreed.

The old baron nodded. "The women in my family were always known for their strength, which leads me to the end of my story. After we got back home, Edith decided that during those three days she was gone she liked the smell of Rufus. She was always particular about smells. And, after a year of pursuing him, she finally led him to the church door!"

"A happy ending!" said Geoffrey, putting the last morsel of grouse into his mouth.

"Yes." The man held aside his pipe. His blind eyes looked in Patrick's general direction in earnest. "I will pray, my son. I will that. When you get to be my age, you find that prayer is the most strenuous activity your body and mind will afford itself."

They were made aware that the horses were ready, and again they set out on the trail that Earnest and Jane had made earlier that day. The rest had done both man and beast well, and each rode with an even greater sense of purpose, and a stronger, more hopeful state of mind.

❧ ❧ ❧

Jane knew the time had come. There had been no chance of escape as she had hoped. Though friendly, Earnest had been well on his guard the entire time.

She was ready to plead for her life.

There was a time to hold her head up high, to remember how she had taken her own life and made of it what she could. But now was not that time. Now she realized that the only thing which came between her and Earnest and a certain death was God Himself. She didn't want to leave Nicholas yet, just as he was becoming a man. And love was so new. How could she let pride possibly stand in the way of life with a loving man, a tender man who loved her back?

Without a word, Earnest dismounted and lifted her down from the horse. He untied her ankles and guided her forward. "Let's look at the Severn," he suggested, gathering the reins of the horse to lead it to drink.

"Obviously, we've come to the end of our travels, Earnest. Obviously, I have also come to the end of my time here on earth."

"Don't worry, Jane," he reassured her, "I won't kill you here. I just want to have a last bit of conversation as we watch the sun go down."

He helped her down a path on the steep riverbank to a small cove. The tide was out and the water was shallow. Some rocks were exposed along the shoreline, and there they sat. From above she could hear the horse whinnying, munching at grass. Had it been under more pleasant circumstances, Jane would have relished this quiet scene of a waning day. And what a day it had turned out to be!

They sat on the damp rocks.

"I try to watch the sunset almost every night from the castle walls. It is a beautiful sight, the waters of the Thames all gold and lovely."

"She wants me to tie you here, Jane. To leave you to the mercies of the tide. I am to make sure you have a lot of time to think about what will happen as you lie here. I am to watch from above the bank to make sure your body is gone when the tide goes out."

The time had come. "Earnest, please—in the name of God—"

"Don't say anything, Jane. For you must know that if I could lay a hand against you, it would be quick and benevolent. But—" He stared long into the pink of the autumn sky.

"But?" Jane prompted.

Earnest grabbed the small dagger from its sheath. Jane gasped, beginning to pull away from his grasp. "But I could no more kill you than I could my own sister." He cut the bonds off her wrists. "You are free, Jane. As I see it, we have nothing more to do than to wait for your doctor to come and save you. I figure that he should be here within three hours."

"How do you know he will find me?"

"I started leaving obvious tracks a long way back, Jane. After our first conversation."

"You knew even then."

"Yes, but I had to get further away, for my own sake. After this, I shall never be welcomed in London again. I shall have to seek employment elsewhere. Perhaps even in another country."

Impulsively, Jane reached forward and hugged Earnest. "Thank you, my good friend Earnest. Thank you!" She kissed his weathered cheek and he blushed, but it could not be seen in the rosy glow of the sun. "My name is Edward."

"Edward," Jane echoed. " 'Twas my father's name."

❧ ❧ ❧

"Are you having any trouble now that it's getting darker?" Patrick called up to Geoffrey.

"No, my lantern is showing me the tracks just fine. But I would almost swear upon my honor that whoever has her wants us to follow him."

"How so?"

"He started dragging something from his horse. A sack of some sort, I believe."

Nicholas and Patrick were both alarmed. "You don't think—"

"No, no. It's not heavy enough to be a body. Believe me, when a person is dragged behind a horse, the tracks are peculiar and unmistakable!"

"There's still hope," Patrick said for Nicholas's benefit as much as his own.

"There's always hope when the tracks keep going. It's when they stop that you have to start worrying," Geoffrey assured them. "But I think we're gaining on them. Will you be ready to fight?"

Patrick nodded. "Yes. Always. My sword has shone sharp under the Saracen sun. An English night will not dull its blade. A fight is a fight."

"There is only one of him and three of us," Geoffrey said optimistically.

"That's not necessarily true. He could be planning something. And I don't trust him."

"Even a merchant's only son could find the way with these tracks."

"We need to prepare ourselves for a real fight."

Nicholas was still failing to join in much on the conversations. As far as he knew, his father might die, and his mother had mysteriously disappeared. It was the darkest day of his life. Suddenly, becoming the next earl didn't seem to be the greatest turn of events ever to come upon him. He merely wanted to be a son. Every man was a son at some point in his life. He didn't want it to end just yet. Yet, still he couldn't bring himself to pray, although he occasionally looked up at the stars between the trees as the forest was now growing more sparse. He knew God was there. He knew God was watching him and his mother and his father. And somehow it seemed right, though the thought brought him little hope, and even less peace.

"So you fought in the Crusades?" The conversation was continuing between Patrick and Geoffrey.

"Yes."

"I've often thought I'd like to do that. Make a name for myself. Perhaps even garner a knighthood out of the experience. Like yourself." Geoffrey had heard about the Red Knight. "Or do I wrongly assume you got your knighthood over there?"

"You assume correctly. But war on such a scale isn't an experience I'd like to repeat again. It isn't as easy as you think to kill a man."

"I always thought it would get easier as time went by."

"It doesn't."

"Still, I don't want to be in the earl's garrison forever."

"When does your time of service at the castle end? Shouldn't you be going back to your father's farm soon?"

"Aye, should be. But I'm finding I like the life of a soldier, and I have lots of brothers to help run the farm. I'm going to see if I can stay on, rise up in the ranks a bit. Who knows, maybe I'll become a knight that way. Especially with the tournaments coming back into fashion. I've been heartily enjoying the training exercises."

"Well then, you've found the life for you. Many men endure a rocky journey to find a life. Let us pray the journey is a much easier one for you."

Geoffrey cocked his head thoughtfully and turned back to look at Patrick. "There's something to be said for an easy path." He raised his lantern high and forward and continued following the tracks before him.

❦ ❦ ❦

Alison's now-pinched face visibly relaxed as Percy was let into the room. "You came!"

"Mother!" He ran forward and took her hands. "What have they done to you?"

She held up her palms pitifully. "It is as you see. I am a prisoner."

293

"I don't understand."

"No. You wouldn't. I've been charged with attempting to murder my brother."

"Uncle Alexander? Surely not!" His eyes flickered momentarily with doubt that it just might be so, then, "It's absurd!"

"Yes, my lamb, it is."

"How did this come about?"

"On the orders of the king, Sir Ronald Rey and some others pursued and captured the squire of the Black Knight. He pointed the finger in my direction."

"I still don't understand, Mother."

She put her arms around him and held his cheek next to hers, still a mother for all her faults. "Oh my dear Percy, I don't wish to talk about this anymore. It tires me so."

He had learned long ago better than to argue. "What can I do for you? Are there any needs to which I can attend?"

"I was hoping you'd ask just that, my darling."

She walked away from him, distancing herself for this request. She looked out the arched window over the city of London. "They didn't afford me a river view here. Imagine that."

Percy said nothing. He was numb with shock and dismay. He of all people knew how his mother had always taken her life and his into her own hands. The doubt of her innocence was already larger than a mere thought. Still, he sought to squelch the voice and waited patiently for her to speak again.

"Do you remember where Tatty-Nan lives?"

"Of course. And if I don't, I'll rely on the rhyme the children sing."

"I made that rhyme up when I was only six years old. It was the first time I came into contact with Tatty-Nan. I've learned many a trick from Tatty-Nan. All quite harmless," she rushed to assure him, although it was far from true. "I need you to go to her cairn and ask her to make me a decoction of dog's mercury. If she asks any questions, tell her I shall be with her soon. Tell her I'm counting on her."

"Dog's mercury? What is that for?"

"I'm not feeling well again as of late, and I know Patrick MacBeth won't be visiting me here! I need to take care of my own ills."

"I heard that the cook has disappeared. Terrible thing."

"Is it?"

Percy looked shocked. "How can you say that, Mother? What is she to you?"

"Nothing, Percy. You're right. I should say no such thing. It's just that son of hers, so proud and vain. You'd think he was preparing himself to be the next earl!"

"Nicholas is the least of our worries, Mother. But now, I shall do as you ask. I'll be back as quickly as I can."

"Try to come back tonight, my darling. Please."

"But it's past sunset."

"It matters not. I fare not well. This decoction will make all the difference. Promise me, son. Promise me you'll do this for your mother."

He walked to the window and tenderly kissed her mouth. "I promise, Mother."

Percy left his mother with a mysterious smile on her face. And, of course, she was looking out the window.

꿎 꿎 꿎

The central hearth of the kitchen glowed red. All of the lamps had been extinguished except for a couple of candles on the main table. Supper was finished, the kitchen cleaned and swept, and Jane's friends sat around the table, sipping some of the wine which Skeets had brought down.

"I remember when she first came," Skeets said with a sigh. "Do you, Mattie?"

"Surely I do. She looked so frightened and unsure of herself. And Nicholas. Oh, he was a wee thing. But sweet."

Stephen agreed. "I remember feeling so sorry for them. But within two weeks, she started to fit right in."

" 'Twas no surprise to me," Mattie quipped, "when she became the head cook. In fact, I even predicted it, didn't I, Stephen?"

The baker nodded.

"Well, I've only known her for a short time," Gregory joined in from his seat next to Agnes, "but even in such a span I've certainly come to appreciate her hard work and her cheerful attitude."

Agnes piped up. "Oh yes! Jane can make kitchen work such fun sometimes!"

"Well, all is done for the evening." Gregory took the last little bit of his wine. "Why don't the rest of you get some sleep? I'll sit here until midnight."

"And you'll send us word if you get any news?" Mattie asked.

"I certainly will. You can be sure of it."

"Why don't you stay here and keep him company, Agnes?" Mattie suggested.

Agnes looked shyly at the clerk. "Well, I do have several tasks I need to do some catching up on. If you don't mind, sir, I'd just as soon do them now as in the morning."

Gregory nodded. "I'll go get my account books."

Soon the large room was empty except for the two of them. Not much was said, but after an hour Agnes had to admit that the way he held his head as he pored over his books was quite endearing. And Gregory realized that he had never seen such graceful movements on a kitchen maid.

But words were not spoken. They were both much too worried about Jane.

❧ THIRTY-THREE ❧

The sky was a dome of star-speckled blue. The river was a hushed sigh in the darkness. The breeze was chilly. Earnest gave Jane his cape.

"I have my hauberk on beneath my tunic. I'm quite warm. Besides, as I see it, a man's true warmth comes from his chivalry!"

"Thank you, good sir." Jane gladly allowed him to place the garment around her shoulders. "But I have a difference in opinion as to your chivalry, being abducted by you!" She laughed.

He let out an almost imperceptible sigh. "That is in the past. I do believe my days of crime are quickly coming to a close."

"How so?"

This time the sigh was bigger. "Oh, Jane, I'm getting too old for all of this. It's time I settled down, had a family of my own to keep me on the straight path. The Lord knows I don't need the money anymore."

"Have you saved yourself a small fortune, then?"

"Yes. I suppose I always knew this day would come. I had planned it to go on for at least five more years, though."

"Why the change, then?" Not that she was trying to talk him out of it!

"You. That lady who hired me. It didn't occur to me that by my services I allowed people to rule others' lives, to take away others' freedoms. I've always valued my freedom, Jane."

"Yes. You said so earlier."

He nodded thoughtfully. "And so, after your doctor friend comes to get you, I'll be on my way. Back home to the farm to take up where my parents left off when they died. We have two hides of land that my sister has been renting out to villeins. I've been paying taxes to the lord for years on it."

"Can you leave your past behind so easily?" Jane couldn't believe it.

"Certainly."

"Just like that?"

"We're not all of a self-flagellatory nature, Jane."

She laughed. "I know. I just expect everyone to be like myself. I like to think I'm terribly average, you know!"

"You're anything but that. You've changed my life. With your peace, your sense of rest. Fear has always fueled my hardness of heart. When I looked into the eyes of my victims and saw they feared death, it hastened me to the task. But you, Jane, you fear not death because you fear God. But you fear Him in a different way than I do. You fear because you love. I fear because I know of the judgment that awaits me. Your peace has given face to my fear. I never really saw it before now. Or at least I never allowed myself to."

"But having once truly realized that God is watching," Jane said, "that one day He will judge, a man can never be the same."

"No. And because of that, I know that I'll leave this riverbank a different man."

"Different forever, though?"

"I don't know. I hope so. But one can never be sure about such things."

Jane shook her head. "I think you're wrong about that. How long has it been since you've stepped in a church or even prayed?"

298

"I can't remember the last time I was in church, and I stopped praying the day my father died and my mother went mad."

Sadness overtook Jane, and she took his gloved hand in hers. "I'm sorry, Edward."

"I was, too. Until I heard your tale, Jane, and I realized that everyone has his own story to tell, and they're not all pleasant."

"Is your mother still alive then?"

"No. She followed him to the cemetery not long after he made the trip himself. After that I left home."

"Well, perhaps in some strange, divine manner, He actually caused this trip to happen. If it brings you to God, my friend, I will find it worth every mile of discomfort."

"Jane, will you pray for me?"

"Yes, Edward, I will. I shall pray for you every day from this day on."

"You promise me this?"

She took his other hand and looked deeply into his eyes. "I promise. Now go. Find your family. And don't look back, but always press forward, forgetting that which is behind!"

"But . . . you'll be alone—"

"Nonsense! I'm perfectly capable of finding my way back. As you said, you left quite a trail. I'll probably meet up with Patrick along the way. Just give me a few coins and your mantle, and I'll be fine. Please, Edward, I want you to start on your new journey before you have second thoughts. Go now!"

"I don't want to leave you."

Her smile was gentle at this contradiction of a man, so childlike yet so worldly. "I know, but you'll always know where to find me. And I'll always welcome you to my table, Edward."

He leaned forward, placed some coins into her hand, and kissed her cheek. "Thank you, Jane."

"Good-bye, Edward. Godspeed."

He went to the steed, pulled down the bag of food and a skin of wine, and left it in the grass. Soon he was galloping toward the northeast, a purple silhouette along a ribbon of moonlight.

Jane wasn't sure whether this change of heart would really last in Edward, but she knew that she would keep him in the center of her prayers for many years to come.

She prayed for several minutes, not only petitioning for Edward's soul, but thanking God profusely for her deliverance. After that, she stood to her feet, grabbed the sack, hung the wineskin on her shoulder, tightened the mantle about her, and began the long walk home.

꙾ ꙾ ꙾

The moon continued to rise over the Tower of London. Alison began to get agitated. The potion glistened like a midnight gem as she held the vial up to the moonlight. She remembered, as those who soon will die do, what it was like to be a child. Mother had been so beautiful in her swirling silks and fluttering headpieces. Every day she came to the nursery. But she was never there for long. Alison was left in the care of a gruff old nurse who was a lazy thing, letting the responsibility for Alexander fall on the young girl's shoulders. She would cling to her mother's skirts, begging the woman to stay. But always there was something else to do.

But there's no use blaming Mother now, she realized. *I chose my path the day I found Tatty-Nan and claimed her as my own.*

Tatty-Nan had taken her down a darker trail—one she had never regretted, even now. It had given her a sense of freedom, of control. She gloated over Jane's sure demise even then. And Percy would be the earl soon. For certainly, Tatty-Nan would take up her cause. That was the old woman's way. Inasmuch as she was Alison's teacher, she was also her servant.

And yet, in some ways, Lady Alison was tired. She would not go to the block. She would not die at the whims of a boy sovereign who cared only for interior decorating, she thought.

"Well, my little king," her whisper fell on the quiet streets of London, "you shall not imprison me. And you shall not tell me when I am to die. I leave that up to me."

She tipped the vial of dog's mercury into her mouth. When her maid awakened early the next morning, Lady Alison Hastings was dead.

ক্ষ ক্ষ ক্ষ

She was a lone figure on the grassy plain, still not far from the river. But Patrick would have recognized that outline anywhere.

He cupped his hands to his mouth. "Jane!"

"Mother!" Nicholas joined in.

The three riders galloped forward, Patrick dismounting before Bedivere had even come to a halt. He pulled Jane Lightfoot roughly into his arms, relief unlike any other he had known pouring through every portion of him like a gushing cataract. "You're all right!"

Nicholas wasn't far behind. "Oh, Mother, you're safe!"

Jane pulled away from Patrick and quickly hugged her son. "Yes, son, I'm fine. I'm just fine!"

Patrick pulled her back into his arms, his chest welling with emotion he couldn't begin to let out. They held each other for several minutes, Patrick's embrace many times more frantic than Jane's.

"What happened, Mother?" Nicholas said.

"Who took you?" Geoffrey added.

"It was all due to Lady Alison, but I shall tell you more of the details later. Right now, all I want is a warm fire and a full belly."

So Geoffrey and Nicholas searched for firewood along the banks of the river and, having found several armfuls, prepared to build a most comely blaze. Jane was so overcome by the warmth of the fire and the eyes of those she loved that her urge

301

to start cooking whenever she smelled a fire kindling was stifled. She merely watched the three men as they went about their tasks. The mere fact that she was in their presence was not being taken for granted.

Geoffrey led the horses down to drink from the river. Patrick coaxed the fire to a state of utter glory, and Nicholas assembled a meal atop the sack which had held Jane's victuals. The kitchen staff had provided some wonderful items as well.

"There!" he said proudly, standing back to admire his handiwork. "I still haven't lost my ability to arrange a proper spread!"

Jane clapped her hands. "Such paltry fare looks like a king's banquet at the touch of your hands, my son. I'm quite hungry."

They all were. And passing around the wineskin left by Edward, they heartily enjoyed what they were eating. "As I see it," Jane joked, remembering her abductor, "an empty belly turns the most simple of fare into dainties worthy of a thousand nobles."

"Here, here!" Geoffrey said and lifted the wineskin to his mouth.

It was a small but happy gathering. The great tasks set before them were met. God's peace had kept Jane alive, and the men had found her safe and sound. Much to everyone's delight, Geoffrey took a small pipe out of his pouch and began to play a merry tune. His grateful audience clapped in time to the music. And Nicholas eventually found two sticks, beating an accompanying rhythm to the delightful melody.

The fire danced in the autumn breeze, and the smoke circled up to the benevolent Creator, who, though in their midst, still watched from above. Patrick, lyrical by nature, could stand it no longer. He jumped to his feet and pulled Jane to hers. Hands clasped with one another, they danced around in great circles, laughing at their clumsy motions most heartily. When the nature of the tune changed to a less rollicking one, Patrick taught Jane some simple steps from his native land. An hour went by until finally Geoffrey, sheepishly exhausted, placed his pipe back in his pouch.

All the energy was gone.

Nicholas and Geoffrey rolled themselves up in their cloaks and promptly fell asleep. Jane sought to do the same, but a hand on her arm detained her.

"Jane?"

"What is it, Patrick?"

He was on his haunches beside her, his expression grave, though his cheeks were still flushed from the small celebration. "Can we talk?"

She didn't ask questions or say she was tired. For certainly she would rather be with him than sleep. "All right. What is it?"

He sat down beside her and put his great arm around her narrow shoulders. "We've told each other of our love. But as we were riding to find you, I realized that I needed us to make a more permanent arrangement. Jane, I don't want to wait until Nicholas is proclaimed the heir. I want you soon. I want to be your husband."

Jane looked at him frankly. "Patrick, do you really think it will work? You are a knight and a physician. I am a humble woman. A cook and nothing more."

"It matters not to me, my love. I had no doubts about it before you were taken, and I should certainly have none now. The ride here was torture. Always going forward, hoping and dreading at the same time, wondering what I should find at the end of my journey. And all I wanted to find was you, Jane, safe and alive. Jane, I love you."

"I love you, Patrick. You know I do. If you're asking me to marry you, I suppose I'll just have to say yes, for I don't believe you'll accept any other answer!"

He pulled her into a hard embrace, but when she sought his mouth with her own, he avoided it.

"What is it, Patrick?"

"Jane, before I ask you to marry me, there are some things you must know. You don't know everything about me, and it's only fair before you agree to spend the rest of your life with me, that you know just who it is you're getting."

Jane was a bit startled by that comment, but she remembered the first time she had met him, the calm reserve he had shown, the way he had seemed thinly veiled from the rest of the world. "If you think it matters, then go on, Patrick. After all, if you can accept my past, then I can certainly accept yours."

"That remains to be seen. But I didn't want another minute to go by before I told you the reason I left Ireland—no, *fled* Ireland. You see, my darling Jane, I am a murderer."

◆ THIRTY-FOUR ◆

Ireland, a.d. 1201

Young Patrick MacBeth ran in from the driving rain on a chilly March evening. He was splattered with the mud of the fields, the day having held a full load of heavy toil. His mother cast a worried eye in his direction as she handed him a bucket of warm water and a rag.

"Take yourself out back and clean off. I want you to hurry up and come back for your broth and bread. Then to sleep. Your father's gone out again."

The 14-year-old lad, growing quickly upward but not outward, drew in his breath. "Is he . . . ?"

"Drunk? Yes. Now quickly, lad! Do as I say! The lord's men were by today asking for the taxes. 'Tis a good thing you were working the fields. I told them we'd have it tomorrow. We *will* have the necessary payment. Won't we, Patrick?" Her voice was stern, but her eyes were sad and sorry.

"Yes."

"How?"

"I'll give him Lily."

"You can't! You've raised that horse from a colt! Oh, lad, she's your only joy in the miserable life your father's created for us."

"Don't argue with me, Mother. We've got to keep this place. There's only one way to see that we do. For you and Kathleen."

She sighed painfully. "I wish your brothers were here to help us."

Patrick should have been angry at his older brothers for leaving soon after their father started drinking to drunkenness each night, but he wasn't. He wished he had the boldness to do the same. "They did the smartest thing by leaving. And we would too, Mother. William's been begging us to come to Dublin. He's doing well there."

"I won't leave my husband. He needs me."

"He needs ale!" Patrick became angry.

"It doesn't matter. I'm not leaving him."

"Then I'm not leaving you. But I'll tell you this, Mother, if he ever sets his hand to Kathleen as he has to you and me, I'll kill him."

"Don't say such things, Patrick! I forbid you to speak like that!"

They seemed to have the same conversation in many variations night after night. When he was on his pallet and Father returned, he heard the sounds of violence. He had tried to interfere once on his mother's behalf. But she had turned on him viciously, slapping his face and telling him to leave the room, to let her handle her own problems. And then Father had dragged him out the door and beaten him until he lay unconscious in the mud beside the hut.

Mother did nothing.

Still, he couldn't hate her for it. She had been a wonderful mother back when Father was a successful physician in the city of Dublin. Then, for reasons Patrick never knew, the drinking had started, and his treatment began to harm instead of heal. He left the city in shame and took to farming instead. Well, he took to Patrick's farming. Patrick's oldest brother, William, started out with them. And James, the next oldest, rightly seeing the situation for a horror, joined a monastery.

Coupled with the hope that one day this dark dream would all be over, misery was Patrick's helpmeet. Perhaps they would be healthy, prosperous, rich once again.

A bitter hate for the man whose seed had spawned him grew inside.

Three months later, everything changed.

Patrick had heard it said that heat can addle a man's head. It was a warm July. The fields were swelling with oats, and he worked outside each day until it was too dark to see. Better that than abide in that hellish hut with his father.

The walk back home was a long one. Part of their meager lands was separated from the rest, and Patrick had to journey three miles each way to get there. Now that Lily was no longer there to carry him on her back, it lengthened the day that much more.

He was hungry. The bread and nuts Mother had sent with him did little to stem the gnawing hollowness down in his gut. But he doubted if there would be anything better to eat upon his arrival. Mother seemed to be retreating further and further into a place where he couldn't reach her. Kathleen sought to keep the house as best as she could, knowing Mother would be beaten if some food wasn't on the table when Father got home from his daily wanderings.

The simple act of walking through the door changed his world forever. And the boy that was Patrick fled away to the safest place he knew: the innermost caverns of his heart that were quickly being mortared over by a new Patrick. A stronger Patrick. A Patrick with veiled eyes and a pleasant smile.

However, that smile would not evidence itself for a few more years. For just then, Mother lay dead, and Kathleen, prostrate over her mother's body, looked up at him. The normally cherubic lips were split open, bleeding down onto her chin and onto the front of her torn gown. Her left eye was swollen shut, the puffed lids discolored, dark, and sore.

She sat up. "Paddy?" The words were a plea. *Help me. What's happening?* "Is she dead?"

Patrick, pushing down the rage that sought to overpower him, knelt down next to his mother. Her skin was cold. "How long ago did he leave?"

"I don't know. It was still light for some time after." Tears fell from her eyes. She was so sore.

Patrick stood to his feet and went to find the once-esteemed Doctor Duncan MacBeth.

❧ ❧ ❧

Jane was pulled from the tale when Nicholas stirred, throwing the blanket off himself.

Jane looked at Patrick. "Let me cover him up."

She arose from her spot of ground and gently tucked the mantle back around the heavily-sleeping Nicholas.

"I'll continue then," Patrick said as he set his chin firmly. Jane nodded and sat down, awaiting the next portion with dread in her heart—not for herself, but for him.

"I desired to seek him out straightaway, but I turned back. Kathleen needed me more just then than I needed revenge. The death of my mother wasn't completely real yet, which is strange, because inwardly she had died weeks before, her spirit having left us all to fend for ourselves."

Patrick's soft accent increased in its intensity as he returned to that wicked day.

"I cleaned up Kathleen and washed Mother's body to prepare it for burial. Already I knew what I would do. A public hanging was a fate altogether too easy for my father, and the fact that we had no one to take us in made my next actions seem to be the right thing. I meted out justice upon my father as soon as he walked through the door. He cried like a baby over the body of Mother, whom he had destroyed. I won't tell you, Jane, how I killed him, but I did. I called his name so that he would stand up and look me in the eye. Not much later he was dead."

He paused, flexing his hands into fists. Unflexing. Flexing.

"Go on, Patrick. You need never speak of this again." She laid a soft hand upon the fist.

"I buried the bodies not far from the hut, in a dense copse of trees. I sought to camouflage the burial spot with leaves and branches, and I still remember working there in the dark summer heat, crying with each spadeful of dirt which fell upon their bodies. Looking back now, I realize that every monstrous cir-cumstance which has ever befallen me has been because of the abuse of wine or ale."

"What?"

"Never mind that now. I need to go on, just as you said. I want to reveal to you the truth you deserved to know from the beginning."

Even as Jane's heart became heavy with the tragic tale, she couldn't help but feel better. Surely, the tale couldn't get any worse. And surely she understood, somehow, his plight.

"I packed a few meager provisions in a knapsack, and Kath-leen and I were on our way toward Dublin. William wept when he heard of Mother, but no tears were shed for my father, as you might well have guessed. Because of the murder, William sent me off to a monastery near Paris for an education. I was eager to go, for in leaving Ireland, I felt as though the spirits of my miserable childhood would be left behind.

"I was wrong.

"I worked hard—learning has always come easily to me. At the age of 17, I ran away from the monastery to answer the call of the Crusade. After all, what man could resist the thought of never having to endure purgatory, as the pope promised, if we took the cross?" His words sounded sarcastic, and Jane looked at him sharply, but said nothing. "Armed with a cheap sword, I went eastward with a group gathered by a French nobleman.

It was there that I learned how to fight. I had to, or I would die. It was that simple. And fight I did.

"Jane, I killed and killed. And in each face that died before my blade, I saw my father. Inasmuch as I sought to escape him, the Crusades that I involved myself in, that first one in 1204 and the other 15 years later, gave me the opportunity to kill him a hundred more times.

"In between the Third Crusade and the Fourth Crusade, I studied medicine in Paris. I also gained much knowledge in the Holy Lands from the Eastern physicians. After my last crusade, I sought to finally expunge the demon by helping to heal instead of kill. And for almost ten years, having come to London and set up practice, I thought I was doing just that. But I wasn't. The promise of freedom from purgatory was ill-kept, for I lived in a type of hell for many years.

"Finally, several years ago, I returned to Ireland to the grave of my parents. I saw my brothers, who assured me they carried no hate in their hearts toward me. I went to the sheriff and told him all that had happened those many years ago."

"What did he say?"

"He said he remembered a little boy who worked away his childhood for a drunken man. He said he remembered a woman full of bruises and a little girl with frightened, hollow eyes. He said he took the land for himself and became richer because of it. He said he bore me no ill, and that obviously, having come back so many years later, I had been paying with guilt for my crime for much too long."

"So you were free?"

"Yes. And no. I live with my deed every day, Jane. It's not something a man can simply put behind him and forget about. But I have learned that I am able to go on."

"Obviously, you were willing to pay for your crime."

"Oh yes, that and more. All he required of me was to bury my parents in a proper grave near the local priory. That alone cost a great deal of money. In his words, 'a benevolent fine,' which I gladly paid."

"Some of us are given an extra measure of grace to put the past behind us . . . to not look back at the demons which lurk in the darkness. But I suppose you and I aren't that kind of people, Patrick. I'm glad we'll have each other to lean on, whatever the future may hold."

"Does that mean you'll still marry me, Jane?"

"Of course, my darling. How could I ever judge you?"

"That's exactly how I've always felt about you, Jane. We were unquestionably created for one another."

"Yes, I believe that, too. All these years, all the pain and the sorrow we've borne served only to prepare us for each other, only prepared us to love. God is truly merciful."

"He is." Patrick put his arms around her and held her close against his chest. "You're my first love, Jane. My only true love."

"And you're mine. Patrick, I do love you so."

The matter was settled. As soon as possible, Jane and Patrick would become man and wife. They settled back upon the ground, Jane's head on Patrick's shoulder, and fell into the first utterly peaceful sleep either had experienced since they were innocent children.

❧ ❧ ❧

Sir Ronald arrived at Marchemont at first light. Normally, a messenger would have brought the news from the Tower, but King Henry wanted Lord Alexander to receive the news of Alison's death in a more personal manner.

He was shown into the great hall, and Skeets was called. After the explanation that the message was from the king, he hurried up to the earl's solar and woke Lord Alexander.

The earl was still quite stiff from his wound, but he had passed a good night of sound sleep. Dressing as quickly as possible, it wasn't altogether very long before he joined Sir Ronald by the central hearth of the hall. A servant had been fetched to build the fire back up, and now its flames were raised high and hot. It was a cool morning.

Sir Ronald broke the news as quickly as he could. "Your grace, your sister, the Lady Alison, was found dead in her room at the Tower this morning."

Lord Alexander's face registered no surprise. "How did she die?"

"Poison, my lord. We believe she drank the stuff herself."

The earl nodded. "I would like to request of the king that her body be brought back to Marchemont for an honorable burial."

"He suspected as much, my lord. And it is already being prepared for transport on his orders."

Lord Alexander bowed his head, controlling his emotions, but not wanting the other man to be privy to the expressions in his eyes. "Thank you, Sir Ronald. You serve your king with honor and loyalty."

"Thank you, my lord. I'm sorry that events turned out like they have. King Henry sent me to find the squire of the Black Knight. Naturally, I had no idea your sister would be the one we sought in the end. I'm sorry."

"You did what you had to do, sir knight."

After only several more exchanges, Sir Ronald took his leave. But the earl continued to look into the fire.

"So it is over," he whispered to himself. "It is finally over for Alison."

He knew Alison's suicide proved her guilt. She would never have done such a thing had she been innocent. No, Alison was too calculating for that. She had believed in her own self, and when she was violated even to the smallest degree, she would let you know.

"She died at her own hand," he said to no one. "It is the only way she would have wanted it."

Life was never simple, was it?

An hour later he called Percy to him, who sat numb with shock when the news was imparted. That large part of him that was Alison seemed to fade down to nothing, leaving him wanting and fragile.

"She will be buried here in the chapel, Percy. Honorably, I assure you. I have no desire that in her death she should be painted anything other than a de la Marche."

The young man nodded, his hand fondling automatically the hilt of his sword. He couldn't say anything for a long time.

"She'll be buried at sundown this evening."

Percy nodded in acknowledgment and started to leave the room. He turned back to his uncle. "She had me bring the poison to her, Uncle. I thought it was merely a remedy for one of her many ills. Had I known—"

Lord Alexander held up a hand. "It's all right, Percy. You've always been a good son to her. No one could ever fault you there."

Percy's eyes cleared and became very frank. "It wasn't always easy, you know."

"I know, nephew, I know."

The young man disappeared from the doorway.

Several minutes later he could be seen in the courtyard with his trainer, fighting most handsomely and with an even greater ferocity than any had ever seen him exhibit before. The man that was Percy was already filling the great gap left behind in the boy by his mother's absence.

☙ ☙ ☙

Agnes had arrived back at the kitchens at four that morning. Stephen and Mattie found her asleep with her head on her arms when they came in to start up the oven.

Stephen started to rouse her, but Mattie held up a hand. "Let the child sleep, Stephen. She deserves it."

"I'll just carry her into Jane's room."

Mattie sighed. "No news, I suppose."

"I suppose not."

The day was promising to be a dreary one.

�⋇ ⋇ ⋇

Skeets came into the earl's solar an hour later. "My lord?"

"What is it, Skeets?"

"I have some terrible news for you."

"More? How many ill tidings can one man take in a day?"

Skeets bowed. "I'm sorry, your grace."

"That's all right, my friend, go on. Tell me the news, and let us then pray that tomorrow yields a kinder harvest."

✥ THIRTY-FIVE ✥

Geoffrey had been the first to awaken, and before the sun had risen above the horizon, they were on their way back to Marchemont. Now having the luxury of keeping to the roads, the journey back was much quicker than when they had been traveling in the opposite direction.

Jane rode with Patrick. They made each other laugh with embarrassing stories of their childhoods, and of course, Jane told him all about her journey with Earnest. And the times when the conversation slipped into a comfortable lull, Patrick would hum soothingly in his tenor, and Jane thought she had never heard anything so wonderful.

"You always looked to me like someone who could sing," she smiled back at him. "You don't do it often enough."

He laughed. "I'd hardly say our moments together up until now afforded me the luxury. But if you like my singing, my love, then you shall hear it often enough. I love to sing. When I'm traveling alone, I always seem to fill up the empty miles with song."

"I'm sure you learned many from your travels."

"Oh yes. From many different countries."

"Have you ever heard Marchemont's bard?" she asked.

"Naturally. A wonderful musician he is, as well. His lyre playing is extraordinary."

315

"Yes. When I was younger I used to go up and listen to him in the evenings after my work in the kitchens was done. His voice always made me cry, though, and I soon found that it just wasn't worth it."

Patrick knew what she meant. "I do believe there is a stage in the process of dealing with our past that relishes the sadness. But as we get older, we seek only to forget."

"And when we can't do that, we find someone who'll just be by our side through the journey. If we're so blessed, that is."

Patrick looked optimistically at the sky and squeezed her gently around her waist. "I don't know, Jane. I think in time you and I may look at each other and not be able to significantly remember a time when the other wasn't around to bring us joy."

"I hope you're right, Patrick. Indeed, I do. But you know what I found so amusing about my journey with Earnest?"

"No. But I'm sure you'll tell me!"

"It was his ability to just walk away from his past. He made it sound so simple saying, 'Well, Jane, we're all not self-flagellatory in nature.'"

Patrick laughed. "I suppose he's right. It's so true: Once the deed is done, it's done. Why go back and revisit it time and again?"

"Because it makes us feel more holy if we continue to hate ourselves, if we continue to brood on what we did. But in truth, I think the opposite should be true. If a sin continues to come between us and God, then it is doing a double damage. If God's forgiven us our sins, there's really no reason to clutch them to our breast, other than wanting to torture ourselves."

"We humans are good at that sort of thing, Jane. Don't you think?"

"Much too good for our own good!"

"Then let us go forward from today. What do you say? God has forgiven us; we know He loves us still. Nicholas loves you. My family still loves me. And we love each other. What fascination can the past possibly have for us, when the present and the future is so wonderful to behold? It's a decision we can make, Jane. I truly believe it."

Jane turned in the saddle, a difficult task, and put her arms around his neck. "Oh, Patrick, you really are so good for me. Do you know that?"

He kissed her quickly. "Know that? I'm counting on it!"

She laughed, and he stifled the sound with another kiss, this one lengthier and holding all of love's eternal promises.

From behind, Nicholas made a loud kissing sound as any self-respecting teenager would have done. Inside, he couldn't have been more pleased.

⋟ ⋟ ⋟

"There it is!" Geoffrey cried. "I see Marchemont!"

The group let out a little cheer. It was good to be back. Though gone less than two days, Jane felt that she had been away half her lifetime. Certainly it was a different, happier Jane who rode with Patrick through the gate house and into the bailey. They all were loud and happy, but their joy was soon stifled at the deathly pall that hung over them suddenly.

The chapel bell was tolling. The singular knell of death.

Nicholas went white. "No!" he shouted, jumping off his horse and running toward the keep.

Patrick was alarmed and quickly dismounted, lifting Jane down and setting her on her feet. "I would have sworn he was coming out of it when I left."

He followed Nicholas and caught up with him at the bottom of the keep steps. No sooner were they about to enter the massive building when Lord Alexander de la Marche appeared at the door, the coffin of his sister behind him.

"Father!" Nicholas couldn't help what he yelled, his joy so overwhelming. "You're alive."

Percy, behind the earl, went white. Lord Alexander took no notice, but gladly gathered his son into his arms. "You're safe, my son. You came back safely. And what of your mother?" He looked up and saw for himself, as Jane walked toward the kitchens. "So you saved her, then?"

"Mother didn't need our help, m'lord. She talked her abductor out of it herself."

"She can be most persuasive. But enough now, Nicholas. It is for Lady Alison that this bell tolls. Let us forget all that has happened up until now."

Understanding perfectly, Nicholas bowed his head, stepped aside, and let the funeral procession pass by. It was a short service, and Lady Alison's coffin was lowered into the small crypt beneath the chapel.

That night a small figure made its way from the woods, through the tunnel, and into the compound of Marchemont. No one ever knew that Tatty-Nan had come, and that Alison's body rested no more within the walls of Marchemont Castle.

ঌ৵ ঌ৵ ঌ৵

Supper was quiet, despite the fact that Mattie, Stephen, and the others had given Jane a royal welcome just after her arrival. She ate with Nicholas down in the kitchen, where she heard the other devastating piece of news from Gregory. Patrick heard it from the earl himself as they ate their supper in the great hall.

"When did it happen?" Patrick said, his brows knit together, his heart heavy for his friend.

"Sometime during the night. They found my lady this morning." He turned to Patrick and laid a hand on his arm. "Why didn't you tell me Marie was so sick, my friend?"

"I couldn't, my lord. She made me promise to keep her secret. She didn't wish to worry you."

Lord Alexander nodded. "That would be just like her."

"What will you do now?" Patrick inquired.

The earl shrugged. "I don't know. I don't wish to marry again. That is certain. Now that Marie is dead, I suppose there are many roads down which I can travel. But just now, all of them seem dark."

"I suppose so," Patrick said sympathetically, thinking how odd that this had turned out to be the happiest day of his life. Alison was dead, and as much as he regretted the turn of events which put her in the grave, he would be less than human if he was not the least bit relieved that any knowledge of their secret liaison, other than his own, had died as well. Jane had agreed to marry him, and his favorite patient had lived, and as they had talked about before, God was a forgiving God. Patrick had repented many times since for his actions.

"She will be buried tomorrow morning," the earl sighed.

"Here at the chapel?"

He shook his head. "No, in the abbey. Richard of Barking has been here much of the day for comfort. He would have stayed tonight, but some pressing state matters stole his attention from Marchemont. We'll take her body over by barge soon after first light. Will you come, Patrick?"

"Yes, my lord. It would be an honor."

And so, once again, Patrick found himself in Westminster Abbey, watching as the gentle woman's frail body was lowered beneath the great stone floor and into the crypt.

Jane and Nicholas stood away from the crowd. She wept for the woman who had given her life for the poor, at the expense of her health and the well-being of her husband. But she felt the most pity for Lord Alexander, who looked down into the grave, helpless and completely unsure. The castle cook nudged her noble son forward. "Go to him, Nicholas. He needs you now."

Nicholas's expression wanted to question the wisdom of such an action, but Jane knew a parent's heart. "Go now. It will be all right. I promise."

Down the long nave of Westminster Abbey, Nicholas trod toward his father. It was a simple process to claim him as his own. He merely took his father's arm and led him down the aisle and out the great arched doorway. Jane had been right. The earl uttered no protest but leaned on his son for the support that Nicholas was only too willing and completely capable of giving.

Just then, two small figures, hands clasped tightly together, entered the abbey. Patrick lifted his eyes heavenward in thanks. He would have forgotten the promise he made less than a week ago to a little girl begging on the street. Little Mary.

Not even a week ago?

He could hardly believe so much could happen in such a short space of time. After speaking briefly with Jane, Patrick led the street children away and began caring for their needs.

THIRTY-SIX

The time had come to tell Percy. Several days after the countess's funeral, Alexander de la Marche realized that the moment had arrived.

"Skeets, have Percy brought to the hall."

"Do you wish to have the room empty, my lord?"

"Yes, empty it out."

"He'll be here presently. I'll find him myself."

"Thank you, Skeets. And make sure Percy leaves his sword behind. I want him unarmed when he comes to me."

Twenty minutes later the two were seated before the great hall fire.

"Percy," the earl began, "I've always believed a man should face his life straight on, see it for what it is, and go forward. Would you agree?"

"Yes, sir." Percy nodded. He was in a very calm way this morning, having never foreseen what freedom his mother's death would bring. Yes, he mourned her deeply, but he couldn't deny that her death delivered a share of relief. It wouldn't have occurred to Percy to feel any sense of guilt concerning the latter.

"You are, of course, aware that the countess and I never had any children. But I am not without a child."

Percy looked at him hard. "A bastard."

"Yes," the earl nodded.

"I believe I know where this conversation is leading, Uncle. I always knew that the earldom of Lambeth would never be mine."

"I'm sorry. But in honor of my sister's memory and all that she did for me as a child, I'm prepared to give you my estates in Normandy, Percy. I realize it's not what you have been expecting for the last ten years, but I don't wish to leave you with nothing."

"It's Nicholas."

"Yes."

"I heard him call you 'Father' before Mother's funeral."

"Yes. It is Nicholas."

Percy appeared emotionally blank, but then the true state of his mind revealed itself to him, and he felt as though relieved of a dire responsibility. His brow cleared as once more he looked in the mirror of his mind at himself and found an entirely different Percy staring back at him. The portrait his mother had painted of him there was gone. Only Percy remained. And he knew what he wanted.

His tone was breezy, confident. "Uncle, truth be told, life at Marchemont was becoming difficult for me. My life has consisted of Mother, swordplay, and the occasional dalliance. I'm 22 years old now. I've never been north of York or east of Paris."

"So you'll take my offer?"

"Thank you, Uncle, yes. But not for a few years, if it's all the same to you. Mother left me quite well off, you know. I'm ready to be my own man now. I'd like to travel. See Spain, Italy. I've always wished to view the Alps. And then, who knows, perhaps I shall start competing in more tournaments."

"Will you ever settle down? Get married?"

Percy shook his head. "No. I've learned much here at Marchemont—how to fight, how to joust—and I do believe I shall make a name for myself in Germany and France. Perhaps elsewhere. I'll enjoy earning my spurs."

"It's a hard life on the circuit. But a good one. Especially if you become proficient at winning."

Percy smiled disarmingly. "I have every intention of winning."

"And I believe you will do just that, Percy."

"And now, may I beg your leave, Uncle? I leave at first light, and there is much to do to prepare."

"Certainly, nephew. You know," he said, a tinge of regret in his voice, "it's sad that it took your mother's death to bring us to a better understanding of one another."

Percy shrugged off the comment. "Mother had a way of coming between people. It made her happy." He sniffed.

"Don't be a stranger to Marchemont, Percy. Promise me that."

"Nay, Uncle. I cannot. Sometimes the past can be overcome and forgotten, but sometimes a man must simply go on." He bowed in a courtly manner and turned around.

Percy's footsteps echoed in the great room as he made his way across the hall.

"Well, my son," the earl said to Nicholas later that day, "I stand before you now as your father, and life awaits us. The first venture we will undertake together is falconing."

Nicholas's eyes lit up. "Really, Father?"

"Absolutely. In fact, let's get started right away. It's a beautiful, clear day, and I know Esmeralda will be anxious to fly in such weather."

"Esmeralda?"

"My favorite. You'll find that I am unquestionably a man of favorites. And once I make up my mind that something means so much to me, I never change it."

Nicholas knew what he was saying, but his eyes twinkled. "So that means you won't be giving me Bedivere in the near future?"

"Exactly, my son. But fret not, for soon we shall go to the horse market in London ourselves, and you shall pick out the finest horse in southern England. Now, let us be off. The day is yet young, and we have much to do, the chief of which is telling the world that we belong to one another."

"No more secrets?"

"Never again." Lord Alexander was thankful that God had sent Nicholas. It made these trying days so much easier to bear.

ക്കു ക്കു ക്കു

The nave of Westminster Abbey was far from quiet. Richard of Barking had ordered the workmen building the Lady Chapel to silence their hammers and chisels, to lay down their saws and picks. Just for a little while. But Patrick would have none of it.

"Keep them working, Richard," he smiled. "What more joyful din could there be in which to wed than the building of a church that will glorify God?"

Richard beamed. "All right, Patrick. As you wish."

And so the din continued, the loud chink of stone being hewn and chipped, hammers pounding, their roars echoing all the way down the nave. Men called to each other and had no idea a wedding was about to take place. They were too involved in their craft.

A small crowd gathered before the screen. Richard smiled at them all, bidding them welcome in his church with a wink of his eye. He smiled at them as Jane hurried into the church's west entrance, worried she was late for her own wedding. Unfortunately, one of the servants at Marchemont had cut herself while chopping up some sage, and "I couldn't very well leave her there to suffer until I got back," she had explained to Nicholas, who rushed her off to Westminster in the Earl of Lambeth's barge.

But here she was.

And there he was. Up the aisle, talking to Geoffrey, the once-soldier now clad in the robes of a knight as a reward for finding the mother of the heir of Alexander de la Marche.

Patrick.

Her heart leaped within. And a smile erupted on her lips. A week had passed since they had returned from the west country, and in that time both realized their love was an uncanny thing. So pure and . . . easy. Their love was a haven, bestowed on them by God Himself, and they wanted nothing to disrupt the peace they both fought so hard to gain.

"Jane."

She joined him in the silence, saying nothing, but speaking all with her expressive brown eyes.

He took her hand.

Richard, Nicholas, Geoffrey, and Skeets smiled unceasingly as Jane and Patrick became one in the eyes of God, the eyes of the church, and the eyes of England. And Stephen, Mattie, Agnes, and Gregory did their best not to cry. Each one knew that this couple, above all others, deserved the happiness they found in each other.

A wedding feast was prepared at Marchemont. The great hall rang with shouts of congratulations as most of the servants celebrated their Jane's nuptials. Mattie solemnly refused to stop crying now that they were away from the church, even when Stephen dragged her into the middle of the dance. Agnes and Gregory sat together in quiet confidence, the joy of the day infusing into the space just around them.

"Think of it, all these years," Mattie sobbed to Agnes a bit later, "she was hiding her sorrow and bringing so much joy to us all. God bless our Jane!" she said, crying harder, and Stephen, hearing the comment, picked up his cup of ale and raised it high, his great voice echoing above the din.

"God bless our Jane!"

The hall echoed the cry. "God bless our Jane! And the good doctor, too!"

Jane stood up from her seat on the dais, her face flushed with emotion, her eyes misty as she pulled Patrick to his feet. Lord Alexander de la Marche stood up as well, holding high his goblet of wine.

"Long may they live! And even longer may they love!"

"Huzzah! Huzzah!" Those gathered lifted their voice with a mighty cry. "Long live Jane and Patrick!"

Patrick turned to Jane, swept her into his arms, and gave her a joyful kiss, much to the delight of everyone.

The roar soon hushed as Patrick motioned to speak. "Thank you, friends, one and all, for sharing this day with us. Your loss is most certainly my greatest gain. And now, I beg your permission to take Jane home. She looks in need of some proper kissing!"

The crowd cheered again as the newly married couple walked out of the hall, Jane hugging many of them, Patrick thanking them. The procession followed them to the coach.

Jane laid a hand on Patrick's arm. "Wait, there's someone I must attend to."

Nicholas stood at the edge of the crowd. Jane wove through the well-wishers and pulled him into her arms. With a motherly kiss and a caress on his cheek, she looked at him tenderly. "Thank you, my son."

"But, Mother, I didn't—"

"Hush. You did. As long as there was you, I had hope. And now, all my hopes and dreams have come true."

"I love you, Mother."

"I love you, too, Nicholas."

Nicholas looked behind her and waved to Patrick. "But now, I think there's someone there who's waiting for his bride."

Jane smiled. "Yes. A bride. That's what I am, isn't it?"

"And the most beautiful one who's ever been at Marchemont. Go now—you don't want to keep the bridegroom waiting!"

Jane turned around and hurried to the coach, where a new life would begin. New. Untarnished. New.

"Where are we going, Patrick?"

"As I told you, it's just a little trip."

Later that day, as the sun set, Patrick and Jane sat upon the banks of the Thames. Much to Jane's surprise and delight,

Patrick had purchased an old manor right on the river, not far from Marchemont. The splendid stone house once belonging to a knight of the abbey, Sir Griffin Eadricson, was being re-built for their life together, but the workmen had already left for the day. He had named the small manor "Goldfields."

"Welcome home," he said, as she laid her head against his shoulder. Patrick, putting his arms around her, held her close to him. In the distance, the bells of the abbey pealed, calling the monks to vespers. No matter how men lived and died around the venerable building, it stood there reminding them that a greater Presence lived. And though changing outwardly under the workmen's skilled hands, it was still present, made of stone, a monument to God who created every man.

Patrick smiled down at his bride. "Well, wife, what will you do to occupy your time now that you won't be cooking all day?"

Jane looked thoughtful, and then decisive. "I'm going to walk in the mornings and in the afternoons. I'm going to learn to embroider! That's what I'll do. Do you remember the dress you saw me in for the first time at the abbey?"

"How could I forget what you looked like then in your fine blue garment!"

She laughed. "It was gold, you knave! But nevertheless, I've always worn a simple girdle with it. Naturally, not being a woman of means, I couldn't afford a finely embroidered one. So...that is what I shall do. Make a beautiful girdle for that dress."

Patrick kissed her temple. "I can afford to buy you one, you know. It would make me happy to do that for you."

"No, no! I want to do it myself. I've always had an eye for color, you know. And I don't know what I shall do all day if I haven't anything to do with my hands. My hands are used to being busy."

"Then I shall buy you the finest linen and embroidery silks in London!"

Her eyes twinkled. "And *I* shall let you!"

They became quiet for several minutes, enjoying the peace after the celebration, soaking up the autumn breeze. Both could hardly believe they were sitting there . . . married . . . at peace . . . their hearts ransomed by love. Not merely by the love they felt for each other, but ultimately by God's love, for it was He who planted the seed of love in their hearts. It was He whom they praised silently, He whom they thanked for taking on a debt they could never begin to repay.

Patrick looked out over the water. "Nicholas told me that everything of import that has ever happened to you has happened by the Thames."

"Yes, that was true once."

He kissed her temple. "But not now?"

She was silent for a moment. "Did you just hear the bells of the abbey?"

"Aye. I'm glad we can hear them down this far."

"Yes. I am, too. They remind me of two most auspicious occasions. Meeting you . . . and marrying you. So . . . I'd have to say that the Thames is a pale shadow of the abbey when it comes to moments of significance in my life."

Patrick pretended to be dismayed. "So, I can see that our first kiss wasn't that special, eh?"

She shrugged. "You'll just have to keep working on it. And I, for one, am very willing to let you practice all you want!"

"Shall we start now?"

" 'Tis a good idea, Patrick."

And so they did.

When the sun lights up the Thames of a summer's eve, it makes the waters a field of gold.

The words were still true, and just then the river was a glorious, molten sheet, glistening with the gold of heaven. And Jane and Patrick, tried by the Refiner's fire and joyful now because of it, resigned themselves wholeheartedly to a life of love.

About the Author

Lisa Samson has always taken a keen interest in history. During a time of study at Oxford University, she fell in love with British history. Out of that love grew *The Highlander and His Lady* and subsequent novels including *The Legend of Robin Brodie*, *the Temptation of Aaron Campbell*, and the first book of this series, *Conquered Heart*. A graduate of Liberty University with a degree in telecommunications, Lisa lives in Virginia with her husband, Will, daughter, Tyler, and son, Jake.

Other books
by
Lisa Samson

❧ ❧ ❧

THE ABBEY
Conquered Heart

THE HIGHLANDERS
The Highlander and His Lady
The Legend of Robin Brodie
The Temptation of Aaron Campbell

HARVEST HOUSE PUBLISHERS

For the Best in Inspirational Fiction

Lori Wick

A PLACE CALLED HOME
A Place Called Home
A Song for Silas
The Long Road Home
A Gathering of Memories

THE CALIFORNIANS
Whatever Tomorrow Brings
As Time Goes By
Sean Donovan
Donovan's Daughter

THE KENSINGTON CHRONICLES
The Hawk and the Jewel
Wings of the Morning
Who Brings Forth the Wind
The Knight and the Dove

ROCKY MOUNTAIN MEMORIES
Where the Wild Rose Blooms
Whispers of Moonlight

CONTEMPORARY FICTION
Sophie's Heart

MaryAnn Minatra

THE ALCOTT LEGACY
The Tapestry
The Masterpiece
The Heirloom

LEGACY OF HONOR
Before Night Falls

Ellen Gunderson Traylor

BIBLICAL NOVELS
Esther
Joseph

Joshua
Moses
Samson
Jerusalem—the City of God

Virginia Gaffney

THE RICHMOND CHRONICLES
Under the Southern Moon
Carry Me Home

Dear Reader:

We would appreciate hearing from you regarding this Harvest House fiction book. It will enable us to continue to give you the best in Christian publishing.

1. What most influenced you to purchase *Love's Ransom?*
   - ❑ Author
   - ❑ Subject matter
   - ❑ Backcover copy
   - ❑ Recommendations
   - ❑ Cover/Title
   - ❑ Other

2. Where did you purchase this book?
   - ❑ Christian bookstore
   - ❑ General bookstore
   - ❑ Department store
   - ❑ Grocery store
   - ❑ Other

3. Your overall rating of this book:

   ❑ Excellent   ❑ Very good   ❑ Good   ❑ Fair   ❑ Poor

4. How likely would you be to purchase other books by this author?

   ❑ Very likely   ❑ Somewhat likely   ❑ Not very likely   ❑ Not at all

5. What types of books most interest you? (Check all that apply.)
   - ❑ Women's Books
   - ❑ Marriage Books
   - ❑ Current Issues
   - ❑ Christian Living
   - ❑ Bible Studies
   - ❑ Fiction
   - ❑ Biographies
   - ❑ Children's Books
   - ❑ Youth Books
   - ❑ Other

6. Please check the box next to your age group.

   ❑ Under 18   ❑ 18-24   ❑ 25-34   ❑ 35-44   ❑ 45-54   ❑ 55 and over

Mail to:
Editorial Director
Harvest House Publishers
1075 Arrowsmith
Eugene, OR 97402

Name _____

Address_____

State _____ Zip _____

Thank you for helping us to help you in future publications!